THE
GRACE OF DAY

By the same author

Daughter of Darkness
Pandora's Girl
Angelina
From This Day Forth
Against The Tide

THE
GRACE OF DAY

JANET WOODS

ROBERT HALE · LONDON

ISBN 0 7090 7432 8

Robert Hale Limited
Clerkenwell House
Clerkenwell Green
London EC1R 0HT

2 4 6 8 10 9 7 5 3 1

Typeset in 10/13 Garamond
Derek Doyle & Associates, Liverpool.
Printed in Great Britain by
St Edmundsbury Press, Bury St Edmunds, Suffolk.
Bound by Woolnough Bookbinding Limited.

For my grandaughters
Cherie Jane and Jamie Louise Gallagher
with love

CHAPTER ONE

Noel Dearborn didn't look like a killer – he looked like a victim.

'Ben was two years old,' Betony told him.

Her gaze, as smoky and purple as dusk, followed him when he moved to the window and gazed over the rooftops. The winter sun sent a gleam of lemon-tinted light through the grey clouds. It touched the dome of St Paul's, illuminating its perfection for a second or two before it was extinguished.

'You'd been drinking.'

'They were in the middle of the lane when I came around the bend.' Two fingers pressed against his forehead, his voice was a bone-weary whisper – as if he'd relived the incident, time and time again. 'There was ice on the road, the car went into a skid. Your husband didn't react. He just stood there.'

Betony squashed the flicker of pity that touched her heart. 'You were drunk, and you got away with a fine.'

'No, not drunk. I'd had a couple of drinks, that's all, Mrs Nichols. I was well within the limit. The court decided I was capable of driving.' The incongruity of the statement hung in the air for one quivering moment, then he gave an imperceptible shrug. 'I'm so sorry. You have my cheque. If there's anything further I can do to help . . . .'

Did he really think he'd get off that easily? Did he think a cheque and an abject apology would put things right? Her sister had given her good advice when she'd forwarded his letter on.

'Meet him face to face, Betony,' Rose had said. 'Get rid of your anger by telling him exactly what you think of him. Remember, an eye for an eye.'

She'd never been aggressive, she'd never had to be. Her two half-sisters had always fought her battles for her.

An eye for an eye.

The quote had festered in her head like a boil until it had reached bursting point. It seemed a fitting punishment for a man who'd killed her husband and son.

It had taken all of her courage to come here and confront him. Now they were face to face, the irrationality of the act was achingly apparent. She shrugged off the creeping doubt before she changed her mind, and choked out the reason for her being in his office on this depressing Friday afternoon in February.

'There is something you can do for me. You can give me a son to replace the one you killed.'

Looking confused, he turned towards her. 'I have no sons—' Incredulity dawned in his eyes. 'Are you suggesting . . . ?'

She nodded.

'You must be mad.'

She *was* mad, mad with grief. It would have been Ben's third birthday today. Her arms were empty without him – her life was empty. She wanted him back. She *needed* him.

She swallowed the impulse to give in to hysterical laughter as she ripped the cheque he'd sent her in half. She must keep on top of the situation. 'Did you imagine I'd allow you to salve your conscience with money, Mister Dearborn? You owe me my son. You don't strike me as the type of man who'd find the act of endowment too distasteful.'

A darkly speculative glance wandered over her slim-fitting dress and the long, exposed length of her calves. She resisted the urge to tug at the hemline. He wouldn't find her unattractive, men never did.

For a moment, desire battled the conflict in his face. His eyes met hers for the first time – and she glimpsed his torment. A rueful grin plucked one corner of his mouth awry. 'It's out of the question.'

'Is it?' Throwing her coat around her shoulders, she set a business card on his desk.

'Think about it. Call me later in the week and let me know your decision.'

'You do realize that I'm married, Mrs Nichols?'

'I'm not asking you to divorce your wife.' She turned when she reached the door, her smile a grimace. 'An eye for an eye. You're an accountant. Think of this as debt recovery and it will make sense to you.'

When his office door closed behind her, Betony sucked in a deep, trembling breath. Feeling nauseated, she had to stand still for a moment to recover her equilibrium.

'Is everything all right, Mrs Nichols?'

She managed a polite smile for his secretary. 'Fine, thank you.' But her stom-

THE GRACE OF DAY

ach began to churn as the elevator conveyed her to the ground floor. Heading for the ladies' toilet, she locked the door behind her. A few moments later she rinsed her mouth, then shook a tablet into her hand and swallowed it.

A critical glance in the mirror revealed an image of someone who appeared rational, but what the hell had she done? Ben's blue eyes gazed back at her through the violet haze of her own. She wanted him back – she needed him to bring her fragments together. Her arms formed a cradle and she rocked back and forth. She closed her eyes and for a few precious moments she captured his essence, his warmth against her body and his breath gentle against her cheek.

Simon's child. But Simon was gone too. Strange how she missed the son but not the faithless husband.

Someone came in behind her. Emptiness crowded in on her when she opened her eyes.

Noel watched her emerge from the building into the dusk, a woman in blue on the busy pavement, three floors below. He wondered what had taken her so long to get there.

She glanced around her, then waved. A cab did a U-turn in a gap in the traffic before pulling up at the kerb. He didn't bother to conceal himself when she gazed up at his window. Their eyes met for the space of a heartbeat, then she stooped into the cab and was gone.

He turned her card over and over in his fingers. Betony Nichols had guts. She'd almost convinced him her request was perfectly reasonable. He appreciated the irony of her thinking, but how could he make love to a woman whose husband and child he'd killed?

He'd never be able to forget that split second between life and death, the horrified expression dawning on the face of the man, the smile still on the child's face as he was tossed against the low stone wall. He'd had a yellow teddy bear clutched against his chest.

He shuddered. He'd lived with the accident for the past year and had to put it behind him. But what of her? She must have been through much more.

An eye for an eye. There was a certain justice in the thought, but the woman needed help. She was grieving, and probably suffering from depression.

He stared guiltily at the card. If he hadn't lost his way that day, he wouldn't have taken that road. He shook his head. Hindsight wouldn't bring the child and his father back. Nothing would.

He hesitated, then flicked the card into the waste-paper basket. Damn Betony Nichols, why couldn't she have let sleeping dogs lie? But then, she might have if he hadn't sought to salve his conscience by sending her a cheque. It had been a stupid and insensitive move on his part.

He shouldn't have allowed Sylvia to talk him out of seeking counselling, but his wife had been embarrassed by the whole idea. 'People will think you're crazy.' His conscience twinged. He'd been neglecting her lately. Perhaps he should take her away for the weekend.

Lifting the receiver he dialled home, frowning when the connection rang out. Then he remembered she was visiting her mother in Bournemouth. He stabbed in his mother-in-law's number. 'Put Sylvia on, would you please, Dorothy,' he said after exchanging the usual pleasantries.

'Oh, she's not here, Noel. She knows I'm going to the country to stay with my brother this weekend.' Noel could almost hear her mind ticking over. 'If I recall, she said something about going to Cornwall with a friend of hers. Anne, something or the other.'

'Sullivan?'

'That's right.'

Cornwall? Noel frowned. It was an odd time of year to visit the Sullivans' holiday cottage.

'Oh, yes, I'd forgotten.'

Dorothy rattled on about inconsequential things whilst he mulled it over. He'd seen Anne and Jeff the previous evening at a dinner party. Cornwall hadn't rated a mention.

When he got rid of his mother-in-law, he rang the Sullivans' house, expecting the live-in nanny to answer. It was Anne. 'Do you know where Sylvia is?'

'Wasn't she going to her mother's for the weekend?'

'Ah, is that where she's got too.' What the hell was Sylvia playing at? 'Is Jeff there?'

' 'fraid not. He's gone to a seminar in Newcastle. I can't imagine what dentists find to talk about for a whole weekend, can you?'

He forced out a laugh, quashing the ludicrous thought forming in his brain. Sylvia was far too inhibited to have an affair.

He fished Betony's card from the waste-paper basket, staring thoughtfully at it.

'Look, if you're at a loose end why don't you come over for dinner tomorrow? The kids would love to see you.'

'Thanks, Anne, but no thanks. I'm staying in town. I just thought I'd let Sylvia know.'

'I'll tell her if she calls. Bye, Noel, be good.'

He gave a wry grin. For the first time in eight years of marriage, the offer to be otherwise had been served up to him on a plate.

Betony Nichols, teacher of piano. There was a grand piano printed on one corner of the card. The phone number had been blacked out, a substitute scrawled underneath. He leaned back in his chair, picturing her body hugged by the blue dress, her long, supple legs. Her eyes were hauntingly beautiful, and vulnerable. She couldn't be more than twenty-five, but she had class. What had it cost her to come and confront him?

For the first time since the accident, he felt like a drink! His secretary came through with some letters for him to sign. Joyce was one of the old school, verging on middle age and conscientious. Sylvia referred to her as the poor relation and her condescension towards Joyce annoyed him. 'Auntie Joyce is a stupid old trout,' she always said, an analogy so totally unfair it was ludicrous. Joyce had a degree in business management.

Sylvia's management skills resolved around himself and the home. She'd arranged everything in his life. She'd leased his office for him, lined the walls with expensive wood panelling, furnished it with leather club-style chairs. He'd learned it was easier not to argue.

'It's discreet, and will inspire confidence in your clients,' she'd said.

He'd never felt comfortable in it.

Sylvia had bought his suits, selected his ties and had found them a suitable house in Essex at the right price. Her mother's money had paid for it, but his own expertise had recouped every penny over the past few years, then doubled and redoubled it.

He was about to expand into the vacant suite of offices across the hall, take on a partner and relax a bit. The move hadn't been discussed with Sylvia. The new suite would be decorated to his own taste, and furnished with modern furniture that took up half the space. He smiled. He was a big boy now, he'd earned his independence.

'Any more appointments today, Joyce?'

'No. Mrs Evans cancelled. I've rescheduled her for Monday afternoon after the partnership interviews.'

'Why don't you bring me a cup of tea, then take the rest of the afternoon off.' He held the card to his nose, detecting a trace of the faint, provocative perfume Betony Nichols had been wearing.

When Joyce left he plucked the receiver from its rest. He'd never had an extra-marital affair, and wasn't about to. Besides which, he doubted his ability to father a child. He needed to talk to the woman though, to make her understand that the accident wasn't his fault. He might even be able to convince her to get some help. God knows, she needed it. He'd heard many crazy ideas in his time, but this . . . ?

The answerphone cut in, her voice creaming against his ear with a delightful huskiness, to make the hairs at the nape of his neck stand on end. He hung up without speaking, aware of a faint sense of disappointment.

He shrugged. What the hell! He'd promised Sylvia he'd wallpaper the bedroom this weekend, anyway. Flicking the card at the bin he uncoiled from his chair and stretched. He was strangely reluctant to go home.

Joyce brought his tea through, then stooped to pick Betony's card from the floor and place it on his desk. The damned thing refused to go away so he slipped it in his jacket pocket.

'Is there anything else you want me to do?'

'Thank you, no. Enjoy your weekend.'

It was bitterly cold when he finally left the office, the pavements almost deserted. A thin film of slush swished under the vehicle tyres and flicked up dirty water. Flakes of snow drifted against his shoulders. He pulled his collar up round his ears. He disliked weekends, they were so boringly predictable.

He also disliked the over-furnished house he lived in with Sylvia. 'Sod the wallpaper, I'll stay in town and take in a show,' he muttered, and headed at a brisk walk towards the two-roomed bachelor flat he'd once lived in, and now kept for emergencies.

The card slid from his pocket when he threw his jacket on to the bed. He stared at it, common sense telling him he should ignore it. The internal argument was short-lived.

'Betony Nichols,' she purred against his ear ten seconds later.

As he loosened his tie he was beset by a strange sense of not being in control of his future. Odd, when he'd never subscribed to the notion that destiny was anything more than what one made it.

'We need to talk, Mrs Nichols. What you proposed this afternoon is totally out of the question, of course.'

Betony stared at the phone for a long time after he'd called, her heart thumping against her ribs. The anger in his voice had been unexpected, but it was controlled, and seemed to be directed inward. His unexpected sensitivity had unnerved her.

She hadn't been out for months. She hadn't done anything except sit in the house, think, weep, and fend off phone calls from her sisters.

Rose and Cecily wanted her to go back to Little Abbot. She couldn't go home. She couldn't face seeing the place where Ben had died. She was barely holding herself together as it was. Her glance went to her bag. She'd already taken the prescribed dose today. Damn it, she needed one to get through the evening. Swallowing the pill with half a glass of milk, she made her way upstairs, opened the wardrobe and pulled out a silk jersey dress.

Betony Nichols lived in a quiet mews in Chelsea.

Noel sucked in a deep breath when she answered the door. The earth seemed to shake beneath him. Absolutely stunning in a slim-fitting black dress, her hair was upswept and secured with a pearl slide.

There was a tenseness about her mouth, and she didn't smile. 'Would you like a drink before we leave?'

'I have a cab waiting.'

She nodded. 'I'll only be a minute.' She returned in less, a three-quarter-length cape draped over her shoulders and an evening bag clutched in her hand. Closing the door behind her she said, 'It's snowing.' As if the event was something alien to mid-February.

'I'm surprised you hadn't noticed before.' He regretted the ironic remark when the spark of excitement in her eyes died.

'I feel the need to apologize to you, Mister Dearborn.'

He slid her a glance. She seemed calm, but her breathless voice revealed her inner tension and her hand had a faint tremble to it. He felt pity for her when he handed her into the cab.

'There's no need to apologize. Shall we forget about your visit to my office and try to enjoy the evening?'

'I made a fool of myself, didn't I?'

'No more than I did. It was insensitive of me to offer you money under the circumstances. I did so with the best intentions. I didn't know how you were situated without . . . a husband's support.'

The wry grimace she gave was unexpected. 'Actually, you were very kind, Mister Dearborn.'

A hint of dryness crept into his voice. 'Could you force yourself to call me Noel? I know I'm a few years older than you, but I'm not exactly decrepit.'

Her soft chuckle seemed to startle her. Her hand flew to her mouth and the sound died away.

His hand covered hers. 'It's OK to laugh.'

'I haven't laughed for a long time. It sounded sort of . . . oh, I don't know. Odd, I suppose.'

'It will get easier.'

'When did it get easier for you?'

'It hasn't, not yet.'

An awkward silence grew between them as the taxi conveyed them through the streets. When they drew up outside the theatre restaurant she gently squeezed his hand. 'Perhaps we'll prove to be good karma for each other.'

There was something touchingly naive about the remark, for if fate had brought them together it had chosen a diabolical way of doing so. In view of his earlier feeling, unease rippled through him.

He conceded it was possible they could help each other. He felt drawn to her. Her vulnerability made him ache, and God knew, he needed to be needed. An affair was out of the question of course. It would be wrong to take advantage of her.

Yet, later that night, when she unexpectedly touched his cheek with her finger, it was an effort to turn and walk away.

CHAPTER TWO

Sylvia Dearborn emerged from the bath, dried herself and gazed critically at herself in the mirror. Pinching the skin on her hips, thighs and waist, she gave a sigh of satisfaction. Not a sign of cellulite – and she'd dropped a dress size.

The weekend at the clinic had been gruelling and expensive, but the results well worth it, she thought, heading into the bedroom to dress.

Perfumed and perfectly made-up, she slid into a pair of size eight, pleated pants, and a baby blue cashmere sweater that matched her eyes.

As she set the dining room table, she hoped Noel wouldn't be late home, not tonight. She hummed as she polished the silver and crystal glasses, running a critical eye over the flower arrangement. Placing a small wrapped box by her husband's plate, she hurried through to the kitchen to check on the dinner.

Chelmsford railway station was a five-minute walk from Noel's house. Icy needles of sleet slanted against his body but he didn't notice. His mind was on his new partner. He'd taken to Daniel Jacobs straight away.

Dark-haired, dark-eyed, and self-assured, the man had displayed a sardonic sense of humour when he'd stated he couldn't add up without a computer. A handful of experienced men had wanted the partnership, older men who'd retired early with superannuation to invest. Daniel Jacobs was newly qualified, and had only half the capital needed.

'Family savings,' he'd grunted. 'My parents are investing in my future. I can pay the rest off from my salary, and I'll bring new clients to the firm.' His grin had been wide and self-effacing. 'My extended family are shopkeepers. They'll trust me to handle their accounts.'

Dearborn and Jacobs had a certain ring to it. The contracts would be signed at the end of the week. Now he had to break the news to Sylvia.

He cast a jaundiced eye over the high hedge surrounding the house. He'd wanted to replace it with a wall, but Sylvia wouldn't agree. As a consequence, he spent many summer evenings clipping it. The house behind it was a red brick, mock Tudor, with diamond shaped, lead light windows. The oak door was set with a wrought iron grilled window, and adorned with iron studs and fancy hinges. It would have looked perfectly at home in a prison, or a *Ye olde English beef and Yorkshire pud* restaurant.

He cursed as he caught his thumb in the flap guarding the keyhole. Shaped like a curled tongue, it caught him every time. One day he'd wrench the bloody thing off the door and throw it into the hedge.

The smell of roasting wafted over him when he opened the door. His stomach rumbled. If nothing else, Sylvia was a damned good cook.

'Don't forget to change into your slippers, Noel,' she called out. 'Leave your shoes on the newspaper. I don't want filthy water tramped on to the carpet.'

Did she think he was a moron? There was a moment of mutiny in him, then he obeyed out of habit. The Prime Minister's face oozed disapproval as it soaked up the slush from his shoes. He grinned. 'Don't worry, I didn't tread in anything nasty.'

'Who are you talking to, Noel?'

'The Prime Minister.'

'Oh, my goodness!' Sylvia was already untying her apron when she appeared around the corner. She tied it up again, her expression as disapproving as that of her idol when he grinned, said, 'My apron came undone.'

There was something different about her, but he couldn't think what. He eyed her fluffy blonde hairstyle. 'Have you had your hair permed?'

She sighed in exasperation.

'Really, Noel. It's been like this for several weeks.'

He shrugged out of his overcoat and followed her into the lounge, depositing himself in an overstuffed, green brocade armchair. He aimed the remote at the television to catch the end of the news. An instant expert was pontificating about the perils of the euro.

'You forgot to redecorate the back bedroom at the weekend.'

'I stayed in town.' He didn't have to see her to know her lips were pursed. 'I'll do it next weekend.'

'Just make sure you do. The new curtains will be ready to hang the Monday after, and I want the room to be ready.'

A terrorist bomb had killed several people, and Sylvia was worrying about curtains. He pressed the off button. 'Ready for whom?'

'Well, you never know, we might have guests drop in. I want it to look nice.'

'Uhuh.' He went into the usual ritual. 'How was your weekend?'

'Fine.'

Had there been a slight hesitation in her voice? 'How was Dorothy?'

'Much better, she's recovered from her cold without any ill effects. How was your weekend?'

Had she always lied so easily? 'So-so.' He decided to wait until after dinner before telling her about his new partner. 'I tried to phone you at your mother's on Friday evening.'

Straightening a cushion she stared critically at it for a few moments. 'Really, what for?'

'To tell you I wouldn't be home at the weekend. Dorothy answered.'

'What did she say?'

'She said she was going to visit her brother.'

He could almost hear her mind ticking over. 'Yes, she was. Such a nuisance. I'd forgotten. I got a flat tyre on the way down so I had to call out the service people. Mumsy had already left when I arrived. It seemed stupid to turn around and come all the way back.'

'I guess it was.'

'I've been thinking, Noel. Perhaps we should invite my mother to live with us. We've got plenty of room.'

So that's why she was going to so much trouble over the back bedroom. He'd be nagged out of existence. 'I don't consider it to be a good idea.'

'But, Noel—'

He didn't raise his voice. 'Definitely not. Dorothy's perfectly capable of looking after herself.'

'You're being unreasonable.' Sliding on to the arm on his chair in a cloud of Chanel, she kissed the top of his head. 'You get on with her, don't you?'

'Only because we live apart.' He stood up and stretched. 'She's welcome to visit, but she's not moving in. Is that understood?'

Her eyes narrowed. 'Do I have to remind you that my mother's money provided the loan for this house.'

'You don't have to, but now you have, *I'll* remind *you* it's been paid back with interest.' Annoyed, he strode past her towards his study. 'Call me when dinner's ready.'

His study was freezing. Turning on the radiator, he threw himself into a leather chair and stared at the silver tantalus with its three crystal decanters. It had belonged to Sylvia's father. The hunting pictures on the wall had belonged to him too, and the desk and chair with its red, studded seat.

There was a photograph of Judge Throsby on the mantelpiece, dressed in wig and gown. He'd been slightly fleshy, but handsome, and looked smugly self-satisfied, as if he'd just enjoyed an afternoon of good sex. Not with Dorothy, he'd bet. She was too much like Sylvia.

Next to the photograph was a bronze stallion rearing over a mare, a gift from his colleagues on his appointment to the bench. Perhaps they'd known something Dorothy hadn't.

Judge Throsby had died before Noel had met Sylvia, but he knew he'd never be able to measure up to him in her eyes. His study was a shrine to the man. He was bored with the whole damned set-up.

'Noel, I'm sorry.' Her little girl voice put his teeth on edge. 'I didn't mean to upset you on our special day. Dinner's ready.'

He remembered Joyce slipping a small wrapped parcel into his pocket as she reminded him it was their anniversary. Good old Joyce!

He managed a smile. 'It's not that I don't like your mother. It's just . . . .' No, he wouldn't give in. It was time he took a stand. Still, he wished the back bedroom would develop an acute case of dry rot to help him out.

'You don't want to share me with anyone, do you?' She rushed across the room and threw her arms around his neck. 'You're so jealous sometimes, darling, but there's no need to hide it under a brusque manner. My mother wouldn't intrude, but if you really don't want her here I won't argue with you about it.'

He kissed her, more in relief than anything else. She was slight in his arms, her small perfect breasts, hard nubs against his shirt. He slid his tongue into her mouth, his hands under her buttocks.

She acted predictably, giving a breathy giggle and wriggling away from him like a virgin bent on preserving her bargaining power. She dabbed at her mouth with the edge of her frilly apron. 'Not now. Dinner's ready.'

'Later, then.'

An arch look was thrown his way before she trotted pertly off to the kitchen. 'We'll see.'

He wouldn't hold his breath. Sylvia had a set repertoire of excuses. A headache, her period, or just *sorry, terribly tired, darling.* When his need was urgent he'd coax her into it, but he wondered if the release was worth the trouble. Since she made it clear that the act was distasteful to her, it left him feeling as if he'd committed an act of rape.

Later, when they were in bed, Betony's face drifted into his mind. He bet she wouldn't lie passively on the bed, looking like a meringue in cutsie, fifties-style baby doll pyjamas. It was impossible to grope more than an inch under the elasticised legs of the frilly drawers. 'For once, I'd like to make love to you naked.'

'It's cold.'

Anger thrust at him. How prissy could a woman get? 'For pity's sake, Sylvia, can't you forget your inhibitions for once. We *are* married.'

'Very well, Noel . . . as it's our anniversary.' The martyred voice did nothing for him. There was a slither of nylon when she removed her drawers. 'There, go ahead. I knew you'd want something in exchange for those awful earrings. Trust an accountant to come up with something like that. I shall have to take them back and change them.'

He grinned savagely into the darkness. The earrings had been dangling gold coated halfpennies. He wondered if Joyce had decided to pay Sylvia back for past slights.

The cuff-links he'd received from Sylvia was the eighth pair, and one of the many sets that had belonged to her father. If he stayed married to her long enough he'd probably end up with one pair for every week of the year.

Fifty-two years of Sylvia was a sobering thought. He couldn't remember ever seeing her naked, it was always a frigid grope in the dark. Feeling bloody minded, he flicked the bedside light on.

'Turn that light off.'

'Why?'

She gave an exasperated sigh.

'You know I don't like doing it with the light on.'

'I do.'

'I didn't realize you were a pervert.'

He went limp. A pervert, for Christ's sake? If that was supposed to warn him off, she could think again. He turned off the light and reached out for her.

Her body was rigid. What was the matter with her? In the eight years they'd been married she'd never been able to relax during lovemaking, or experienced an orgasm as far as he could tell.

He wondered if Betony Nichols would enjoy making love? He imagined her slender body writhing under his, her long legs wrapped around his waist. His sudden hard-on surprised him. It would be a shame to waste it. He thrust himself into his unresponsive partner, his mind filled with a vision of Betony.

A disgusted little sigh quivered in his ears when he finally rolled off her. The air twitched with tension. Feeling guilty, he turned on to his side.

Sylvia rose from the bed and padded silently towards the bathroom. The door shut behind her, leaving an oblong of light in the wall. Water gurgled into the sink.

Five minutes later she got back into bed, smelling of soap and personal deodorant. She pecked him chastely on the cheek. 'Good-night, Noel. You will reconsider about mother, won't you?'

Over his dead body! About to drop off to sleep, he realized he hadn't told her about Daniel Jacobs.

Noel left her a note the next morning, advising her of his change in status. When he walked into his office the phone was already ringing.

'How dare you take in a partner without telling me?' she whipped him with.

'I didn't see the need. I'm sure you'll like Daniel.'

Remembering the halfpenny earrings, he gave Joyce a wide smile when she placed his early morning cup of tea on his desk and said, 'The new office furniture has just arrived, Mister Dearborn.'

'What new furniture?' Sylvia shrieked. 'What have you done with the furniture I bought you?'

'It's been sold to the lawyer who's taking over my present office. I've signed the lease of a suite of offices across the hall. Must dash. Joyce and I have got a lot to sort out.'

'Noel, what's going on? How dare you move offices without consulting me.'

'I'm perfectly capable of running my business without your help,' he said as pleasantly as possible. 'And as I'll be working late, I will stay in town tonight.'

Met by an affronted silence from the other end of the line, he took the opportunity to replace the receiver.

By the end of the day he was worn out, and so was Joyce. They gazed around the new offices, smiling at each other.

'We'll need nameplates, and another secretary.'

Her smile faded. 'I'm sure I'm capable of managing alone.'

He realized she was worried about her future. 'We'll hire a receptionist, then. There's a secretarial college round the corner. They offer a placement service for their graduates.'

'There's really no need to go to extra expense.'

'Yes there is. I can't have you run off your feet. She can answer the phone, make the coffee, and do any extra typing that might be needed.'

When her face assumed a frosty expression, he grinned. 'I'll leave the hiring to you, Joyce. I'm promoting you to office manager.' Grin still in place, he engaged her eyes. 'Award yourself a rise in salary to go with the position. A couple of halfpennies, perhaps?'

Her mouth twitched. 'I'm sorry if they proved to be unsuitable, Mister Dearborn.'

'I thought they were eminently suitable.'

The twitch became a small smile.

'Thanks for putting in the extra work today. Raid the petty cash tin and take a taxi home.'

'May I say something before I go, Mister Dearborn?'

'As long as you're not about to resign. I couldn't manage without you.'

Her face turned pink. 'As if I would. I wanted to tell you that you have my absolute loyalty. I know Mrs Dearborn persuaded you to offer me this job, and sometimes she contacts me at home and, well, you know, asks about things.'

'I've never doubted your loyalty for one moment,' he said, which wasn't exactly true. He cursed Sylvia for placing Joyce in such an awkward position.

'Oh, and before I forget. Mrs Nichols rang a few moments ago when you popped outside. She wants you to call her when you've got a minute.'

He reached for the phone as soon as the door closed.

'I just wanted to thank you for Friday night. I enjoyed your company.'

'We'll have to do it again, some time.'

'Perhaps the next time you're staying in town?'

Her husky voice conjured up a vision of long legs, long hair, violet eyes, and the way she chewed on her bottom lip when she was anxious.

He sent a smile down the line. 'I'll be staying in town tonight. I've been moving my office.'

She hesitated for a mere couple of seconds. 'Could I cook you dinner, or something? It will have to be something simple. I haven't got much in.'

'There's a good Italian restaurant just round the corner from where you live—'

'I know the one you mean.' The enthusiasm in her voice stroked his ego. It needed stroking after a weekend spent with Sylvia, who had perfected ball-breaking to a fine art.

'Half past seven. I'll meet you there.'

Nerves attacked Betony's stomach when she deserted the bath for the bedroom. She'd never deliberately pursued a man before.

Noel hadn't struck her as the type to cheat on his wife. He seemed a bit staid, his profession suited him. A wry smile touched her lips. She must beware of stereotyping him too easily. There was something charismatic about him, a quiet charm that was all his own.

Her glance fell on the framed photo of her late husband. Simon had been self-assured, handsome, vain, and a good, but sometimes a selfish lover. He'd also been unfaithful many times over. Men, it seemed, thought nothing of extra-marital sex.

She shrugged, shoving the photo into a drawer. Noel seemed genuine somehow. She gave a bitter laugh as she slid into her jeans and a white, roll-necked
sweater. His wife probably thought so too. Tying her hair at the nape of her neck
with a purple scarf, she pulled on a navy jacket and headed for the door. She
cursed when the phone rang, experiencing an acute sense of disappointment.
Was he going to cancel?

'Hello, Betony, it's Rose. I've just finished drawing up your chart. Your life is
about to change.'

The very last person she wanted to speak to. 'I'm just going out, Rose. Can it wait?'

'Oh no, the change is imminent.' Her sister's voice deepened into the mysti-
cal tones she used for her sessions. 'Finally, you're going to meet your soulmate.
Happiness is within your grasp, if you don't push him away.'

Rose sounded exactly like the horoscope she wrote for a woman's magazine,
but Betony didn't laugh. Her sister's predictions often contained an element of
truth. Besides, Rose believed in her powers, and she wouldn't hurt her for the
world.

'I'm as happy as I'll ever be, right at this moment.' Glancing at her watch, she
sighed. 'Look, I must go, I have an appointment.'

Rose's voice adopted a chatty tone. 'Someone nice?'

'My accountant.'

'Ooh, business.' She sounded disappointed. 'Look, dear, just be careful. Your
long-term chart shows divided paths. Only one will lead to lasting happiness, but
you might not recognize it as such.'

'I'll be careful. How's Cecily?' she asked, just to change the subject.

'As jumpy as a flea on a dog. Daddy wrote and asked me to send more
money.'

'Sell some of the junk from from the house.'

'There's not much left to sell. Father will be furious when he discovers how
much is gone.'

'Why should he be, it doesn't belong to him?' Though Betony had to admit,
over the years he'd received most of the benefits from the sales of the smaller
antiques.

Their father was a constant drain on her resources, and almost a stranger to
her. He'd taken off when her mother had died, putting in an appearance only
when it occurred to him he had a family. She'd been five when he'd left, her
upbringing left to her sisters.

She remembered him as a tall, forceful man, of whom they'd all been in awe.
No, it hadn't been awe on her part. Sensing his dislike of her, she'd been frightened of him.

She sighed. 'Don't worry about it. I'll post him off a cheque. Is he still in Egypt?'

'Mexico. He's found a dig site that hasn't been fully explored, but the university won't fund it. Make the cheque out to me and pop it in the post, dear. I have access to his bank account.'

Whilst she scribbled out the cheque, Rose rambled on. 'Cecily was saying the other day, it would be nice to see you. Why don't you come down for the weekend? We miss you so.'

Betony pulled an envelope from a drawer, addressed it and shoved the cheque inside. Her tongue slid along the flap. She could buy a stamp at the corner deli. 'Not yet. It's too near to the anniversary.'

'I placed some flowers on Ben's grave from you, dear. Cecily and I go to the cemetery every week and keep his little bed tidy. There will be daffodils in the spring. Golden trumpets for our little man.'

A lump rose in Betony's throat and tears filled her eyes. 'Thank you Rose. I appreciate it. Give my love to Cecily. Bye.'

She strode into the bathroom for a tissue and gazed accusingly at her reflection. 'You traitor,' she hissed. 'You're going to meet the man who killed him. How could you?' She needed him, she told herself, pushing back her guilt and willing herself not to cry. She was doing it for Ben.

Hands shaking, she unscrewed the top from a pill bottle and slid a couple of tranquillizers into her palm. For a moment she stared at them, wondering when she'd taken the last dose. She shrugged. The pills had become a friend to lean on over the past year, a friend who made no demands on her. Tossing them into her mouth, she swallowed them down and headed for the door.

At first she didn't recognite Noel. Gone was the stuffy business suit. He looked arresting, and rather dramatic in casual black pants and roll-necked sweater. A black leather jacket hung on the back of the chair. Lean and enigmatically sexy, his looks hit her in the diaphragm with the force of a sledgehammer.

He rose when he spotted her, his face breaking into a smile of welcome.

Shaken by the desire shafting through her body, her words exploded in shivery little jerks. 'So sorry I'm late . . . the phone . . . have you been waiting long?'

'Hello, Betony.' He smiled and, helping her out of her coat, pulled out her chair.

She shivered when his arm brushed against her hair. This man had killed her baby. How could this be happening to her? Taking a grip on herself, she returned his smile. 'Hello, Noel.'

He held her gaze for longer than was comfortable, his dark eyes a thread drawing her straight into his soul. You're going to meet your soul mate, Rose had said. Surely not Noel? With conscious effort she broke the contact and gathered her scattered wits together.

Rose was the eccentric half of her twin half-sisters, and wasn't to be taken seriously. She did quite well for herself, though. Apart from the magazine column, she made a steady income from charting horoscopes, holding seances and personal tarot card consultations.

The statuesque Cecily, on the other hand, considered herself a natural healer. If anyone had told her that her meditation, her aromatherapy, and her herbal cures were a variation of what Rose was doing, only applied to the physical body, she would have scoffed. Her sisters were as different in looks and personality as two people could get, yet they complemented each other perfectly.

'A penny for them,' Noel said softly.

Her eyes drifted to his. The pills were kicking in. Beginning to feel warm and relaxed she gave her companion a wide smile and her full attention. 'You look different tonight.'

'Different from whom?'

'From the accountant I met the other day.'

His mouth twitched in wry amusement. 'I've left him at the office tonight.'

'Are you good at your profession?'

'Fairly successful,' he said, without a trace of pride in his voice. 'Are you good at teaching the piano?'

'I haven't taught recently.' She considered for a while, whilst Noel ordered dinner for them. 'I don't suppose I was bad.'

'I've never met a pianist before. Where did you train?'

'London conservatory. I'd set my sights on a career as a soloist.'

'So, what happened?'

'I married Simon.' She picked up the fork and traced a pattern on the table-cloth. Noel was a good listener. 'I was pregnant when I married Simon. After Ben was born music didn't seem to matter. You don't mind me talking about them, do you?'

His hand covered hers. 'You might regard me as an adding machine on legs, but I'm not.'

'You're not a psychologist either.'

Their eyes met and he laughed. 'Transparent as glass, huh!'

'In a nice way. I have to come to terms with what happened in my own way, Noel.'

'And I. So why are we seeing each other?'

She withdrew her hand. 'At first I needed to keep my anger alive. It was all I

24

had left. I didn't count on liking you.'

'And that hare-brained scheme you cooked up?'

A tiny, shamed grin lifted the corners of her mouth. 'It was rather, wasn't it?'

'You would have been disappointed anyway. Eight years of marriage hasn't produced a child. I just want you to know that.'

'In case I proposition you again?'

A self-deprecating smile touched his lips, his voice was soft. 'Not exactly. In case we run into each other again and I'm foolish enough to proposition you.'

CHAPTER THREE

The village of Abbotsford was built in the early 1930s when inheritance taxes forced the Honourable Julia Dubeney to sell most of the estate surrounding Little Abbot.

The land was bought by a property developer, who built solid brick homes designed to discreetly display the wealth of the intended buyers. Abbotsford maintained its comfortable exclusivity by the simple device of pricing itself above the common herd.

Little Abbot itself was situated on a gently wooded hill above the village. Distance added a certain aloofness to the hamstone and lime façade. The profusion of narrow windows gave the house an enigmatic and slightly disdainful air. Up close, it looked tired and grey, like an aristocrat who was reaching the end of a long life.

None of the ladies attending the meeting of the village betterment committee had ever been inside the old manor, though Fiona Bunnings was fond of telling people her father had built the village, and she'd been a close friend of the Honourable Julia.

Blue-rinsed, and wearing a tweed trouser suit smelling faintly of horse dung, she placed her teacup in its rose-patterned saucer, and brought the meeting to order with a cough. 'Ladies, we shall conclude the meeting with general business. What are we going to do about Little Abbot? It's rumoured that Rose and Cecily Gifford are going to open the gardens to the public for money.'

There was a collective gasp from five of the six women present. None of them approved of the Gifford twins. Rose had been involved with the vicar's predecessor when in her teens, it was rumoured, and a bronzed, nude likeness of Cecily stood on a pedestal in the council chambers for all the world to see.

'Little Abbot does have lovely grounds,' Judy Cross said. 'Cecily Gifford certainly has a green thumb.'

'She also has a gardener,' Fiona pointed out, and quelled Judy with a look. 'The village will be inundated with coach loads of holiday makers during the summer. They'll picnic on the green and throw wrapping paper and empty drink cans into the stream.'

'And where will they go?'

'Go? To Little Abbot, of course. I just said so.'

Judy turned pink. 'I mean, *go*. We haven't any public conveniences.'

They fell silent for a few moments, contemplating the horror of tourists urinating against the trees in full view on the village green. Abbotsford had won the prettiest village in the county award, for three consecutive years.

'There's the village hall?'

'I doubt if the septic system would cope,' the wife of the borough engineer said loftily.

'The village is connected to the mains.'

Several frowns were aimed at Daphne Harrington, a newcomer to the village, and the youngest member of the committee at the age of twenty-five. She wouldn't be on it at all if her husband hadn't happened to be a private secretary to a cabinet minister.

Daphne smiled. 'We could open the hall to the public at weekends, do cream teas and such. It would bring in some money for the restoration of the church.'

There was a disapproving silence until Judy offered, 'It's worth considering. After all, I don't think we can stop Little Abbot being opened to the public.'

'It would give us more control over things, I suppose.' Fiona, wishing she'd thought of it first, hoped Judy would keep further opinions to herself and stop undermining her position as president. 'Perhaps we should write to the Giffords and ask them to confirm what we've heard, then take it from there.'

'Wouldn't a phone call be easier?'

'A letter is more official. It will show them we mean business. I'll write to Mrs Nichols. It's her house. Poor soul. I can't imagine why her mother married a man so beneath her, especially one with two wayward teenage daughters to support. If Julia hadn't died, things would have been very much different for her daughter now.'

'Richard Gifford is an Oxford Don. He was knighted a few years ago for his contribution to archaeology, or something,' Daphne murmured.

Cups clinked on saucers as everyone stared at her with a new interest.

Fiona shrugged. 'They dish *those* knighthoods out to anybody, these days. Whatever he is, he shouldn't have left that child so soon after her mother's death. An indifferent upbringing takes its toll. It must have been a happy release for the girl when that awful husband of hers died.'

'Her baby died too, Fiona. That would be a dreadful cross for any woman to bear.'

'My heart went out to her, of course. The girl had to be supported by her sisters at the funeral.' Fiona sniffed.

Neither of them had the decency to wear black.'

Daphne's fingernails drummed on the table. 'Let's get back to business, shall we? I happen to know Betony has lived in London for the past year. Do you have her address?'

Hiding her irritation as best she could, Fiona wondered at the familiarity with which Daphne had used Betony's name. 'I'll send the letter care of Little Abbot.'

Daphne rose, checking her skirt for dog hairs before picking up her handbag. 'I could deliver it to her personally. We attended school together, and I'll be lunching with her next week.'

'How wonderful!' Judy cried. 'Do give her my kindest regards.'

Fiona's eyes narrowed. 'Perhaps it *would* be better if I wrote to her directly. If you'll kindly let me have her address—'

'I'm sorry, a confidence and all that. But do feel free to drop the letter off when you've written it, Fiona. I can get it to her much sooner.'

Judy rose to her feet, a self-conscious, but determined look on her face. 'This, of course, allows the committee the perfect opportunity to introduce the matter personally, with Daphne acting as our representative.'

Fiona bristled. 'I don't consider Mrs Harrington has been on the committee long enough to undertake such a responsibility. Besides, it has to be voted on.' She threw Daphne a pointed look. 'In private.'

Daphne was laughing when she left the meeting and a chirrup of assent reached her ears.

It wasn't true. She didn't have Betony's address, but she'd run into her in Harrods the previous week. They'd arranged a lunch meeting, albeit reluctantly on Betony's part. Betony had been buying undergarments, the nature of which would shock most of the Abbotsford wives.

Also true, they'd attended the same school. In her final year Daphne had been caught in the process of losing her virginity to the gardener's assistant in the tool shed.

Her memory of Betony was a shy, introspective girl whose spare time was devoted to practising the piano instead of pursuing a sexual education. She'd been talented, and had grown up to be a stunner, despite her slightly haunted appearance.

Daphne grinned when she saw Rose Gifford coming towards her, a long black coat flapping in the wind. The woman's rusty hair was secured by a brightly coloured rag around her forehead, and it flowed over her shoulders in a cascade of wiry crinkles. Slightly overweight, she was being towed along by two panting labradors.

'Good morning, Miss Gifford,' she said when they drew abreast.

Rose appeared somewhat startled at being directly addressed. A pair of hazel eyes gave her a perfunctory once-over. Her head bobbed up and down. 'Mrs Harrington?'

'I ran into Betony the other day in town,' she said as the other was about to hurry past.

'Did you ... did you indeed?' One of the dogs yelped when she jerked to a halt. 'Sorry, Josephine.' She patted the bitch on the head and dropped the leashes. 'Sit and stay, Napoleon, you unruly bugger!'

This time her scrutiny was more prolonged, and uncomfortably astute. Her mouth screwed into an ironic pucker of a smile. 'Ah, yes, I remember you from the nativity play. You were the Virgin Mary, I believe. A case of serious miscasting on someone's part. You left school in rather a hurry, if I recall.'

The bitch! Daphne, who'd never blushed in her life, ripened to the colour of summer tomatoes under her knowing scrutiny.

Rose nodded slightly and her eyes hooded over. 'Don't be embarrassed, dear. The state of grace has always conflicted with moralistic values set down by men for women.' She snorted. 'The male of the species have yet to learn they exist to serve women, not the other way around.'

'Does that include vicars,' Daphne retorted before she could stop herself.

Rose wagged a finger at her. 'I do believe I'm going to like you. Sex is always scandalous to some, but ah ... how they like to be titillated by the private acts of others. I could tell you a thing or two about the hypocrites in this village, my dear.'

'I can't wait.'

The knowing glance Rose gave made her chuckle. Rose's smile widened to show her teeth. She was really quite an attractive woman, if slightly offbeat.

'See how compatible our vibes are. Come up to the house and have your tarot read, sometime. I usually charge, but I'll read you for nothing. Give my love to Betony. She's like her mother, needs someone to lean on. Now, where's that dratted dog off to? Come back, Napoleon.'

Napoleon ignored her to squat comfortably on the manicured grass verge outside Fiona Bunnings' house.

'A perfect place to crap,' Rose murmured as she walked towards him.

*

Cecily was filling a small gauze bag with seeds when Rose arrived home. Inserting a sprig of lavender into the top, she secured it with a bow of purple ribbon, then added the bag to a cardboard box labelled 'pot-pourri'.

Crushing a sprig of lavender between her fingers, Rose allowed the heat of her palms to warm the oils, then placed them over her nose and took a few deep breaths. 'Lovely,' she sighed. 'So calming.'

'Your editor rang. She wants to know if you'll do the column on previous lives.' Without standing up, Cecily shoved the kettle on to the hob with her foot. 'She said the first batch of photographs are in the post. The usual bunch of bored, middle-aged housewives, I suppose.'

'Now, now, Ces. Bored middle-aged housewives provide our bread and butter.'

'And teenagers. The shop is crowded with them. I have to watch them like a hawk. One of them slid an incense stick down the crack of his bum the other day.'

'You should have lit the end as he walked out.'

Cecily gave a deep, throaty laugh. 'Miss Hardwick made another appointment.'

Rose groaned. 'She's seventy-six. How much future does she think she's got left.'

'Charge her more. I'll make up a notice informing the customers that consultations over the half-hour will incur an extra charge.'

'*Clients*, Ces. Shops have customers. Oh, that reminds me. Daphne Harrington will drop in sometime. I've offered her a free reading.'

She raised an eyebrow. 'Is that wise? Clive Harrington's awfully possessive of her. He might object.'

'I doubt it. It's only a tarot reading.'

'She belongs to the village do-gooders committee, doesn't she?'

'Only to keep her finger on the pulse for Clive.' The kettle began to steam. Rose filled two mugs with water and absently jiggled tea bags up and down. 'She's seeing Betony.'

'That's nice. Betony needs a friend, especially since you sent that letter from Noel Dearborn on to her. Why couldn't he have just let things lie?'

'Fate works in strange ways, Ces. If I play it right, Daphne might be able to persuade Betony to return before it's too late.'

Her dark eyes engaged those of her sister. 'Too late for what, Rose?'

'For us to finish what we started when we were children.'

'Don't be ridiculous. That was just fun. We agreed Betony isn't the one.'

But Rose was staring into some inner space, her eyes curiously blank. The tea bags dangled from her fingers, swaying gently back and forth above the cups.

'*There's another in the shadows. Betony will deliver her to us.*'

Cecily suddenly shivered. Surely Rose wasn't going to start her nonsense all over again. Her hand swiped across her sister's cheek. 'Stop it, Rose.'

Rose's eyes flew open and the tea bags dropped to the floor. 'What did I say?'

'Nothing of importance, nothing at all.' Relieved she'd remained unaware, Cecily drained her cup, then rose and pulled on an old raincoat hanging behind the door. 'I'm going to take a turn around the garden before it gets too dark.'

'If you visit the garden shed, tell Alex about Daphne's visit, hmmm. He'll be *most* interested.'

Rose's sly smile faded when the door thudded with some force into its frame. Cecily was setting herself up for heartbreak again, but she wouldn't be told.

Hurrying into her den, she removed a leather-bound journal from a wooden chest. She turned carefully to the page she wanted and began to read, her eyes glittering with avid interest.

Isabella Dubeney. 15th day of February 1798

> *My brother, Sebastian Dubeney is the devil's messenger, a sadistic man who prac-tises the rites of darkness.*
>
> *Katherine, my infant daughter is dead, snatched from my breast and sacrificed on the altar of Mamon.*
>
> *Deep beneath the house is a secret chamber of evil. There, I was forced to watch Katherine perish. Her cry seeped into the stones with her dying breath and trembled like a soul in torment. I have never known such agony. Dearly beloved innocent, I swear I will not leave this place until I avenge you.*
>
> *That night, when he was in his cups, I crept from the house and buried Katherine in the south corner of Abbot's field.*
>
> *She has a stone for a marker, and beneath it lies the cross I wore about my neck.*

Picking at her salad, Betony wondered if the time was ripe to ring Noel again. She wasn't much good at reading men's motives, but he *had* seemed interested.

'Have you contacted your sisters about what we discussed,' Daphne said. 'Fiona Bunnings is on my back.'

She tore her mind away from Noel. 'If she wants to know their business, she can go and ask them.'

When Daphne gave a gurgle of laughter, she smiled. This was the second time she'd lunched with her, and it had brought some normality back into her life. She'd warmed to Daphne, despite her initial misgivings. 'I can't imagine you as the type to join the village committee.'

Daphne flicked a curve of silky, hennaed hair back from her cheek. 'Clive thinks it's a perfect way to keep abreast of the gossip. Working the crowd is second nature to him.'

'I'd imagine most of the gossip centres around Little Abbot. Rose and Cecily have been stirring it up for years.'

'It crops up on a regular basis, I must admit.' Daphne's green eyes caught hers, and they were full of laughter. 'I don't know what the village would do without them. Tell me, is there really a nude statue of Cecily in the council chambers?'

'Yes, she was briefly married to the Italian sculptor, Fiorenzo, when she was in her twenties.'

'What was he like?'

'Italian effusive, but objectionable when Cecily and Rose were absent. He lived in Rome for part of the year, but when he came to Little Abbot he used to rant and rave when I practised the piano. He said it disturbed his creativity. I was rather scared of him.'

'Bloody cheek, when it was your house he was living in.'

She shrugged. 'He thought it belonged to Cecily and Rose and they didn't enlighten him.' She recalled something that struck her as odd now. 'Fiorenzo used to play them off, one against the other. There were always arguments between them when he was around.'

'I would have chucked the oily prick out on his arse.'

'At the age of ten?' Betony raised an eyebrow. 'Then again, I wouldn't have put it past you. You were never the type to buckle under. I always admired you for that.'

'Admired me!'

'I was too timid to say boo to a goose. You seemed so free spirited.'

'All that got me was expulsion,' Daphne said wryly. 'Still, that had its compensations. You should have seen Miss Martin's face when she caught us. It was green with envy.'

Betony's throaty giggle drew glances from the other diners. Noel had told her that laughter would get easier, and it had. But what would it take to make him laugh? 'I'd never have had the guts to do what you did. I was still a virgin when I met Simon.' She shrugged when she received an unbelieving look. 'Simon didn't believe me either, until afterwards.'

'Was he good in bed?'

In other circumstances, the turn in the conversation would have struck her as odd. With Daphne it just came about naturally, and Betony responded to it. 'I guess I never had anyone to compare him with.'

'Be thankful you didn't try out the gardener's assistant, then.'

'Was . . . he good?'

'Balls like a stallion and an appetite to match. We shacked up together for a few days. When I ran out of money he took off. My father was flaming mad when he had to foot the hotel bill, but he didn't tell my mother.' Her grin was irrepressible. 'I reminded him of the weekend he took his secretary to the same hotel.'

'Does your husband know about Alex?'

'Of course. Clive insists I detail every moment of every man I've had. It's a real turn on for him.'

Daphne's candour shocked her. 'Have you had many lovers?'

'Enough to pepper a best seller with. Clive adores hearing about them.'

Betony picked her words carefully. 'It doesn't sound a very . . . loving relationship.'

Daphne's eyebrows arched in surprise. 'I'm surprised you still believe in the myth of romantic love?'

'You don't seem to believe in love at all.'

'Of course I do. Show me a great wallet and I'm in love.'

'That's lust.'

'Don't knock lust, it provides great memories for when you're past it. Clive loves me in his fashion, otherwise we wouldn't be married. As long as I keep him satisfied, and it's expedient, we'll remain married. Now, enough about me. Have you got a man in *your* life?'

'I don't know. No, I guess not.'

Daphne tapped an elegant fingernail on the edge of her plate. 'Either you have, or you haven't.'

Crooking her finger at the waiter for the bill, Betony sighed. 'I've met someone I like, but it's too soon to even think about a serious relationship.'

'I'm talking about a lover, not a husband. Sex is a great reliever of tension, and your nerves seem to be stretched as tight as they can get without breaking.'

Which reminded her. Drawing an engraved snuff box from her pocket Betony shook a pill into her palm and swallowed it down with the remains of her wine.

Her companion raised an eyebrow.

'Prescribed. They help me through the day.'

34

'Uhuh!' Daphne took the bill from the waiter and said nothing more until they were standing on the pavement outside. 'Tranquillizers are not the answer, Betony.'

'You've never lost a child.'

For a moment, Daphne looked pensive. 'I can't have children however much I'd like one, so I can only guess what you've been through.'

'Thanks,' she murmured. 'I'm sorry if I touched a nerve.'

'I've reconciled myself to the fact.' Fingers lightly brushed her cheek and their eyes met. 'You can't bring Ben back, Betony. You've got to start living again. If I were you I'd give *"guess not"* a call. You didn't buy that sexy lingerie for nothing.'

They arranged to meet the following week. Watching Daphne's trim figure moving off down the street, she experienced a stab of envy. She was so confident, so matter of fact. But she couldn't ring Noel after all this time, and expect him to come running, could she?

By the time she got home her confidence was running high again. She rang Noel's office and asked the receptionist to put her through to him.

'Mister Dearborn has a client with him at the moment. Shall I ask him to return your call when he's free, Mrs Nichols?'

'Thank you.'

It was an hour before he called, an hour in which she paced up and down suffering an agony of indecision. Pursuing a man was so cold-blooded. He'd be pursuing her if he was interested. Of course he wouldn't ring back. He was married, for God's sake.

Every nerve in her body twitched when the phone rang. She stared at it, listening to it ring. It could be Rose or Cecily. Her fingers stretched towards it, closed around it.

'Betony?'

Every particle in her seemed to recharge itself until she was buzzing. 'How are you, Noel? I was wondering, are you free for dinner?'

There was silence for a few moments, then he cut to the essence of what the relationship would amount to. 'Are you sure this is what you want?'

Was it? She'd never been sure of anything. 'About half past seven?' she suggested before her courage fled, then insuring herself against disappointment. 'I'll understand if you're too busy and can't make it.'

'I'm not too busy. How have you been?'

He sounded genuinely interested. 'Fine. I've lunched with an old school friend of mine a couple of times. It was fun.'

'That's good. Where would you like to go?'

'My place. I'd really like you to see it.'

'Half past seven, then.'

She dropped the receiver back on its rest and, hands trembling, poured herself a glass of white wine. She gulped it down in one hit then flung open the refrigerator door. What the hell was she going to give him to eat?

Panicking, she slammed the door shut, then rushed upstairs and gazed at the home-made patchwork quilt adorning the single bed in her virginal, white-painted bedroom. Someone should write a book of etiquette for conducting affairs. Would he expect her to be ready and waiting in a lacy, black corset complete with garters and fishnet stockings? Would he expect anything? Of course he would. He'd more or less laid it on the line just by accepting the invitation to come here.

She grabbed up a sweater and folded it. What the hell was she doing? She couldn't bring him to this room. It was the only one in the house she considered truly hers. The grieving woman who slept here didn't have casual affairs.

Closing the door, she entered the bedroom on the other side of the small landing, grimacing as she slowly gazed around it. The initial distaste she experienced was replaced by a slowly growing amusement.

'Thank you, Simon,' she whispered, beginning to laugh. 'This will be just perfect.'

CHAPTER FOUR

The interior of Betony's house surprised Noel.

The chairs, sculpted cubes of red and blue vinyl-covered foam, stood on black and white chequered tiles. The impression was of pawns on a chessboard. Tables were glass on chrome. Black plastic shelves supported red and blue objet d'art glass. Blue Venetian blinds painted stripes of light over it all, courtesy of the street lamp outside.

The place seemed to have been furnished for effect alone, the effect being a visual nightmare. He experienced a gnawing sense of disappointment in her taste as he stared at what he thought might be the focal point – a painting hanging over the fireplace.

It was an abstract, notable only for its obscenity. The man was huge, red-slashed and grotesque; the woman had lascivious black, slanting eyes.

Betony joined him in his examination of it. 'What do you think?'

'Hmmm . . . .'

'It is, isn't it?' she said lightly. 'What you *really* think?'

Slanting her a glance, he shrugged. 'It stinks. I can't relate the style to you, I guess.'

Her mouth tightened. 'My husband used to entertain his girlfriends here.'

He didn't quite know what to say, but it didn't matter. As he'd expected when she'd phoned him, she was in the mood to dump her problems in his lap.

'I didn't know it existed until he died. It's odd how one can be married to someone, and not know *them*.' She gave him a bright, twisted smile. 'The main bedroom is worse. I don't sleep there.'

He spread his hands. 'I'm sorry. I didn't know about—'

'Of course you didn't know.' She sucked in a deep, ragged breath. 'I've had some Chinese food delivered. It's keeping warm in the oven.'

The sudden change of subject threw him. It seemed she was as reluctant to discuss Simon Nichols as he was, but for a different reason.

Head to one side, she gazed up at him. Her eyelashes were long and curving, darker than her hair. A flute of white wine rested against her cheek, the bubbles fizzing upward like tiny pearls. 'I'm a bit tipsy, would you like to join me in this happy state?'

'I haven't drunk alcohol since . . . that day.'

'That was the day I started.' Her hand fluttered to her hair when he flinched. 'I'm sorry, Noel. This isn't as easy as I thought it would be. I don't know how to initiate an affair.'

The perfume she wore was subtle, working with her pulse to release notes of fragrant sensuality. She knew, all right, but at a purely instinctive level. She just wasn't the type to take a lover in cold blood. Neither was he, come to that, so what was he doing here?

He took the glass from her fingers and set it on the table. 'You don't have to initiate anything. Relax, let's just eat and enjoy each other's company.'

She seemed pleased to have something to do as she busied herself readying the table, throwing on dark blue place mats, plain white china and stainless steel cutlery.

He couldn't keep his eyes off her. Dressed in a pair of dark blue silky pants with matching top, her hair coiled into a loose topknot and threaded with a wispy matching scarf, she looked all variations of sexy.

Her glance danced over the table as she added a silver lantern studded with coloured glass stars – not critically, as Sylvia would have, checking each item was laid out with absolute precision – but with a certain amount of pleasure in her eyes.

'That's pretty,' he said when she set a match to the candle in the lantern.

'It was a present from one of my sisters. The candle is perfumed with sandal-wood.' Her eyes slowly came up to his. 'Are you sure you wouldn't like a drink?'

'Water will be fine.'

Her smile was apologetic when she removed the foil-topped cardboard cartons from the oven and transferred the contents to small white bowls. 'I'm not a very good cook.' She shrugged. 'Can you use chopsticks?'

He took the seat she indicated. 'I've never tried.'

Her laughter was a jittery, nerve-edged giggle. 'Neither have I. You first.'

By the end of the meal they were no more chopstick proficient than at the start, and the table was scattered with grains of rice and noodles. At least the tension had eased.

'Tell me about your new partnership,' she said, when they looked as though they might be in danger of running out of small talk. She was skirting round the personal and he was happy to let her. The tentative relationship they'd formed was fraught with peril, but he had no intention of pushing it to a premature conclusion.

'It's working out well.' An understatement. Daniel Jacobs seemed to have a hundred relatives needing their services. 'We might have to hire a clerk if business keeps increasing.'

'Oh, I see.' She stared into her glass. 'I thought you might be able to advise me about my financial affairs. As a client of course.'

A smile edged across his face. Mixing business with pleasure, if that's what this was, could be risky. 'What is it, an income tax return?'

She gazed blankly at him.

'You must get your income from somewhere?'

Her face cleared. 'Money is paid into my cheque account every six months from investments. I don't know much about them, or anything about tax returns. Simon used to take care of all that.'

'Do you have a file?'

'It's in the cupboard in the bedroom. I'll get it.'

She was gone for ten minutes. When she returned, she appeared more relaxed. Her eyes were deep, huge and lovely. 'I think everything is there.'

The bulging concertina file she carried surprised him. 'Would you mind if I handed it over to my partner? I'm snowed under at the moment. Once he's sorted through it we'll make you an appointment and he can explain it all to you.'

'I'm relieved. I don't understand a word of it.' She laughed, her eyes tangling with his in a way that made him breathless. 'You're a cautious man, Noel.'

He managed a tiny smile. 'I'd be lying if I didn't tell you I'm being guided by instinct at the moment.' And his instinct told him to give her a chance to bail out.

Reluctantly, he rose to his feet. 'It's getting late, I'd better go or I'll miss my train.'

'Catch another,' she whispered, coming to stand in front of him. 'Your instincts are right.'

There was an inevitability about the moment. Her perfume reached out to him, drawing his senses into the realms of the carnal. *God, how he wanted her!*

Her mouth was quivering now, her bottom lip seductively soft and full. 'I'd rather like you to stay.'

Cupping her face with his hands he forced her to look at him. 'I'd be lying if I said I didn't want to, but a relationship with me could destroy you.'

'I want to be destroyed.'

'*Betony.* 'He tasted her name on his tongue as he savagely crushed her against him. 'I have to live with my own pain. If this doesn't work, you'll never forgive me and I'll never forgive myself. We might learn to like each other too much. What then?'

Her voice took on a touch of bitterness. 'Do you imagine I could ever learn to love a man who—'

He shoved her to arm's length. 'Don't say it. I don't need constantly reminding.'

Tears flooded her eyes, separating her eyelashes into spikes. 'Why did you come here, to make a fool of me?'

He was more brutal than he needed to be. 'You invited me.' He felt her quiver as he kissed the salty tears from her eyes. 'You wanted me to give you a son, remember? Now you know that's unlikely you've decided you want me in your bed. What's on your agenda, Betony? Revenge?'

She slipped inside his arms with a, crooked, heart-tugging smile. 'Making love was inevitable from the moment I walked into your office. Admit it. It was on your mind then, as it has been all night. Is it so hard to accept the fact that there's no ulterior motive, that I just feel attracted to you?'

'I admit my ego finds that notion agreeable.'

'I don't take hostages. If you want me, there will be no strings attached.' Her body edged closer until every curve nestled against him. 'Let's go to bed before one of us says something we might regret. If it's a mistake we'll know it?'

'It might be a good idea.' It was a *wonderful* idea!

Her hair fell down her back in a glossy sable torrent as he loosened the scarf from her hair. Her mouth tasted like sweet, crushed grapes under his. Desire churned like a volcano in the pit of his stomach, and the niggle of doubt he'd been experiencing was scorched into ashes.

'Not here,' she whispered when he began to fumble with her buttons. She pulled him up the stairs and pushed open a door.

The room was in darkness. He stopped for a second, trying to get his bearings. Whilst she wrestled with his zip, his hands found her top and ripped it apart. He needed no light to find the soft, satin-covered peaks of her breasts. Surprisingly full, the hard nutty nipples were an invitation to bite.

She giggled nervously when he gently tongued them. She was still fumbling with his zip. 'I can't get this undone, and it's getting harder by the minute.'

He gave a soft chuckle, and stilling her hands before she did him a mischief, stripped them both naked. Winding her arms around him she took a step backwards. They tumbled into the middle of something soft and satiny. Her perfume rose to meet him, one breast swelled against his tongue and a tiny sigh escaped from her mouth. 'It's been a long time.'

'For pity's sake,' he groaned when her hand closed around him. 'I won't last five seconds if you do that. I just wish I could see you.'

'Afterwards,' she whispered against his ear. 'Let's make this trial run quick, so we won't be so damned awkward with each other.' She guided his hand to the hot, moist centre between her thighs. 'I'm nearly ready, and so are you.'

Within thirty seconds she achieved her first orgasm, and he was inside her, anchored to her body by two slim legs entwined around his thighs. His breath came in harsh, urgent gasps as she arched against him.

Her fingers wriggled down between them, circling him, keeping him hard and punishing until he thought he'd scream from frustration as he thrust in and out of her. Then her muscles tightened around him in a vice-like grip and her fingers released the constriction. Her hands came up and curved around his buttocks. She was trembling.

He thought she'd never stop shuddering as he quickened inside her. Everything was blotted out by wave after wave of pleasure. Through the blood pounding in his ears came her voice, urging him on. There was a final satisfying burst, when they shared a triumphant cry of release.

Her body felt as though it belonged there as she snuggled herself into him. She gave a low, husky laugh. 'You're really something, Mister Dearborn.'

He grinned into the darkness, ashamed of his eagerness. 'It was too fast.'

Her hand covered the centre of his chest. 'As an hors d'oeuvre it was satisfying. Next time, we'll take things slowly.'

His eager penis nudged gently against her thigh. He chuckled. 'I wouldn't count on it.'

Something clicked above them and a soft light glowed. 'Look above you.'

'*Bloody hell!*'

Reflected in the mirrored ceiling, and captured in a circle of light, were two pale bodies curled together on a black satin bed. The bed was the only furniture visible in the room. One wall was curtained off.

'What's behind the curtain?'

'A screen. There's a space for a video camera in the ceiling.'

Alarm sent the blood pounding through his ears, and he tensed.

'Relax,' she said with a laugh. 'I got rid of it. Simon used to make films. This bed was the equivalent of the record producer's casting couch.'

Anger spurted through him. 'You used me to get revenge on him, didn't you?'

'If I'd wanted revenge I'd have picked up a hundred men and brought them here.' She smiled, tracing his lips with her finger. 'Except for Simon, you're the only man I've ever made love with. It just sort of evened things up for me.'

He could understand her need.

She reached for a switch and flooded the room with harsh light. 'Have a look at the rest of the room.'

Eyes adjusting to the glare he gazed around him. Red paintwork. The walls were papered in black and gold with scenes from the Karma Sutra. Several of the females had heads pasted on them, cut from photographs.

'Simon's conquests. It doesn't leave much to the imagination, does it?'

He propped himself up on one elbow. Gazing down at her, a woman all soft and flushed from lovemaking. He wondered if he was any better than Simon. He'd just cheated on his wife, and intended to do so again.

'What would you have done if you'd known about this?'

'I don't really know. Divorced him, probably. We weren't all that happy together.'

Would Sylvia divorce him if she found out about Betony? Would he care? Probably not. He experienced a twinge of guilt. 'Switch the damned light off. I've seen enough.'

'Didn't you want to see me?' She rolled over on to her back.

He turned the main light off, leaving them in the soft glow of the spotlight as he knelt above her.

He sucked in a deep breath. She was as stunning as he'd imagined, her body one fluid curve from top to toe. The apex of her thighs sported a silky little pelt. He experienced a sudden urge to kiss her there and dipped his head.

'Son of a bitch!' she gasped a few moments later.

The next fifteen minutes were a sensuous blur of excitement, until, giving a grunt, he collapsed on top of her, all the stuffing knocked out of him.

Her laugh was one of pure joy. 'What a fantastic bonk!'

He gathered her into his arms, rolled her on top of him and began to laugh with her. They were slicked with sweat, and sticky. Her hair was a mass of tangles, her eyes alight with mischief as she threw her head back and gazed up at the mirrors.

'I'm going to redecorate this bedroom, make it more us.'

His hands cupped her breasts. 'What style is us?'

Her hair tickled his chest and the prize in his palms grew heavier as her face came down to his. 'Comfortable and uninhibited. I'm going to change the whole damned place.'

The fact that she was thinking long term made him slightly uneasy. 'Uh, is that wise?'

In a couple of seconds the enthusiasm in her eyes was replaced by mockery. 'We've already set the ground rules, Noel. You've still got time to catch the last train home.'

Although it was deserved, being slapped back into line smarted. He tried to imagine Sylvia straddling him like this, moist and throbbing against his stomach. He couldn't. Betony had been an accident waiting to happen. Her smell wrapped around him like exotic, spiced honey. Her smile told him she had him, and she knew it. He could think of worse places to be.

He smiled, the ball of his thumb grazing her nipples into arousal. 'I rather like the mirrors and spotlight.'

'It is a bit of a turn on, I guess.' Her hair fell about him in a perfumed mist when she leaned forward to kiss him again.

He forgot all about the last train.

Sylvia was careful not to let her fury show in front of Anne and Jeff.

'Noel's probably worked late and is spending the night at the flat. He often does.' Damn him, why hadn't he called her? He knew the Sullivans were coming to dinner.

She smiled brightly at Jeff as she started to clear the table of dishes. 'Help yourself to a drink. You know where it is.'

As soon as she reached the kitchen she snatched up the receiver and dialled the number of the flat. Her fingers drummed impatiently on the Oregon pine counter when it rang out. His office delivered the same result. His mobile was turned off. About to phone Joyce, she dropped the receiver to its rest when Anne joined her.

'I shouldn't worry about Noel. He's probably on the last train.'

'Oh, I'm not worrying. He's often late these days. I'm sure his new partner can't be pulling his weight.'

Anne pushed her hair back from her eyes and gave her a pitying look. 'Who are you trying to kid? I know you from way back. You hardly ate anything for dinner and you're losing weight.'

Which was more than could be said for Anne. Her stomach and thighs were beginning to bulge. Sylvia sugared her smile. 'You're not pregnant again, are you, dear?'

Anne flushed and sucked in her stomach. 'Jeff and I decided three were enough.'

'I suppose having all those children is a drain on the finances. It doesn't leave much time to care for one's own needs.'

'We happen to think it's worth it.' Anne's smile had a wintry edge. 'Perhaps you should try it sometime. It might take some of the bitchiness out of you.'

Trust Anne to throw that at her. If she ever *did* have a baby, it wouldn't be anything like Anne's noisy and ill-mannered offspring, she'd make sure of that.

She sighed as she began to stack the dishwasher. 'If you must know, I *am* worried about Noel. He hasn't been the same since the accident. He won't talk about it, as if he's trying to pretend it didn't happen. On the surface our life seems the same, but sometimes he's so distant we're almost like strangers.'

'Perhaps a little bit of tender loving care might help.'

'It's me who needs that. I look after his house, cook his meals, keep myself nice. What more does he need? He doesn't even seem to notice.'

'What's your sex life like?'

'I beg your pardon?'

'Your sex life. Is Noel still interested?'

A blush suffused her face. 'It's not nice to discuss the intimacies of the bedroom.'

'We used to when we were single,' Anne said bluntly.

Her lips pursed. 'We're not single now.'

'It was all lies, wasn't it? You didn't have any lovers.'

'What if it was? I was only trying to keep up with you. I was brought up to regard promiscuity as a sin. My mother told me my body was a temple, and only the man who truly loved me should touch me.' She suddenly bit down on her lip. 'To be quite honest, I've never really enjoyed it.'

'Am I to take that to mean there isn't any intimacy?'

'Of course there is. Noel's absolutely insatiable in that department.' She shrugged. 'I put up with it, like most women do. One has to.'

'You don't enjoy making love? Oh Sylvia, that's terrible. You should see a doctor, get some therapy or something.'

'See a therapist?' She bristled with outrage. 'It would be *too* embarrassing. Why should I? As long as Noel gets what he needs he's happy. Actually, it does-n't bother me that much. It's just a bit messy. I'm beginning to dread Saturday nights. He makes me feel like a tart instead of his wife.'

Anne gave her a pitying look. 'Saturdays, huh?'

The irony was lost on Sylvia. 'A man should treat his wife with respect. Daddy always used to. He and my mother occupied separate bedrooms, and look how long they were married. A woman shouldn't make herself too available if she wants to keep a man interested, my mother said.'

'You don't happen to be your mother, and Noel's not your bloody father. The way you talk about your old man sometimes makes me think you're trying to mould Noel into his image.'

'What a horrible thing to say.' She busied herself placing coffee cups on a tray. 'Besides, it just isn't true.'

'Isn't it? Every time Noel tries to do something it's always, "Daddy wouldn't have done it like that". Sometimes you belittle him in company by saying, "Of course, daddy wouldn't have agreed with your opinion".'

Resentment filled her. Anne had no right to run down her father. 'I can't see what's wrong with that. Noel needs things pointing out to him. He doesn't mind.'

'Have you ever asked him if he minds?'

'There's no need. Allow me to know my own husband better than you.'

She'd never known Anne to be so disagreeable. 'What's got into you? You're quite spoiling the evening.'

Anne gave her a level stare. 'You don't deserve Noel. It would serve you bloody well right if another woman walked off with him.'

She gave a tinkling laugh. Anne was being ridiculous. 'Not much fear of that. Noel's the faithful, domesticated type, and much too dull to be of interest to anyone else.'

'How long have you been married, Sylvia?'

She gave a satisfied smile. 'Eight years.'

'You'll be lucky if you make nine the way you're going.'

Sylvia's fingers tightened round a coffee cup. Anne had overstepped the boundary of friendship. 'Perhaps it would pay you to take more interest in your own marriage instead of mine.' Placing the percolator on the tray, she smiled. 'Bring the after-dinner mints, would you?'

Her passage through the door was blocked. 'What exactly is that supposed to mean?'

'It means you're letting yourself go, and Jeff has a roving eye when it comes to women.' The spark of alarm in Anne's eyes gave her immense satisfaction. That would teach her to interfere.

'We've been friends a long time, Sylvia. If there's anything I should know—'

'I'd tell you, of course, darling. What are friends for? If you and I can't be completely honest with each other after all these years – you do *want* me to be honest?'

Anne bit her lip, and nodded.

'It was probably nothing. You know what Caroline's like, and Jeff's friendly towards *everyone*. He means nothing by it, of course, though some might read it the wrong way.'

'I happen to trust my husband.'

'Of course you do, it's only gossip. Caroline imagines everything wearing pants is after her. I can't see Jeff being taken in by a pretty face and a nice body, when he so obviously prefers homely.' She gave a tinkle of laughter as she swept past. 'You really should take something for your pre-menstrual tension, Anne. It's getting a bit tedious.'

Her reward was Anne's miserable face for the rest of the evening. She was especially nice to Jeff, giving him a hug when they left. She heaved a sigh of relief when their car drove off.

About to ring the flat again, Noel forestalled her by ringing her. 'I'll be staying in town for the weekend. I have some work to catch up on.'

'You could have told me earlier. Did you forget Jeff and Anne were invited to dinner? I tried to get hold of you at the flat, but didn't get an answer.'

'I'm sorry. You know how it is, sometimes. I was dining with a client. I hope you apologized for me.'

'Of course.' She couldn't keep a tiny note of censorship from her voice. 'My parents did teach me *some* manners.'

'You have finishing school written all over you.'

'Thank you.'

Noel gave a heavy sigh. 'Look, why don't you go and see your mother this weekend. You know how much she enjoys your visits.'

'I think I might just do that.'

'Give her my regards. I'll see you on Monday.'

Her face brightened when she replaced the receiver. At least she wouldn't have to play the dutiful wife this weekend, and she could have the whole bed to herself tonight.

She yawned as she went through to the bedroom. She'd cook Noel his favourite meal on Monday to make up for having to spend the weekend alone.

Betony cursed when the phone rang. Rubbing the sleep from her eyes she was surprised to see the sun shining through a crack in the curtain.

Disappointment shafted through her when she saw Noel's side of the bed was empty. Panic edged in on her. What had she done? What must he think of her?

Her head ached, her tongue felt as if it was glued to her palate. She staggered downstairs, sculled a glass of water and snatched up the receiver. She croaked something resembling her name into it.

'Good morning. How do you feel this morning?'

She didn't question the tiny spurt of relief she experienced. She squinted at the clock. Christ, it was nearly ten! Her nose wrinkled. She desperately needed a pee, and a bath. 'I stink. Where the hell did you go?'

'Out to get something for breakfast. I just remembered I haven't got the key to get back in. I'm sorry if I woke you. I'd intended to bring you breakfast on a tray.'

A smile crept across her face. It was too late for regrets. Like Eve, she'd tasted of the apple and her appetite craved more. Perhaps it was a sign she was coming alive again. It was about time. Her finger rested against the leaping pulse in her neck. 'How long will you be?'

'Fifteen minutes do you?'

'Just.' She hung up on him and dashed into the bathroom.

Ten minutes later, and wrapped in a towelling robe, she swallowed a couple of tranquillisers with her tea. By the time Noel rang the doorbell, her headache had gone.

There was an awkwardness about him as he thrust a bunch of daffodils into her hands.

Just as awkwardly, she buried her nose into one of the golden trumpets.

'The end of your nose has turned yellow.' Pulling a tissue from the box, he tipped up her chin and brushed the pollen grains off.

'Are these your idea of breakfast?'

Their eyes met, and they grinned. He kissed the top of her head and turned towards the brown paper bag. 'Eggs, bacon, sausages, tomatoes, and bread for toast, OK?'

'You'll give us both a heart attack.'

He raised an eyebrow. 'If last night didn't give us one, nothing will.'

She grinned and blushed at the same time. 'I guess not.'

She poured herself another cup of tea and sipped it whilst he prepared the breakfast. Usually she didn't eat breakfast, but by the time he set it before her she was ravenously hungry.

Afterwards, she dressed and they went in search of a hardware store.

Betony knew exactly what she wanted. He just made the appropriate noises when she thought to consult him.

The market supplied them with camouflage army pants and T-shirts for painting in.

Betony seemed intent on hunting through second hand shops for bargains. Time seemed to hold no meaning for her, and everything proceeded at a leisurely pace.

In contrast, Sylvia had consulted interior designers, and had made up her mind with expensive speed. When the layout was delivered, she invariably spoiled its look with fussy additions of her own.

He found a comfortable old wing chair with a footstool and sank into it whilst Betony browsed.

Betony experienced an unexpected tenderness when she spied him stretched comfortably in the chair. A few minutes later she gently kissed him awake, and watched his eyes slowly focus on her. His abashed grin tugged at her heart.

'Have I been asleep?'

'Like a bear.' She ruffled his hair and added a coloured glass lamp to the parcels at his feet. 'Are you game to help me choose a new bed?'

He positively enjoyed the experience. Stretched out side by side, they held hands and grinned like idiots at each other as they tried each bed on display.

The shop assistant maintained a stiff upper lip throughout, and determinedly went through his sales pitch until the transaction was completed. Only then did he smile at them, offering his effuse congratulations, mistaken in his belief there was a wedding in the offing.

They laughed at each other's embarrassment, and didn't have the heart to enlighten him.

By the time they got back they were loaded down with packages. It was too late to start work. They ate spaghetti at the Italian restaurant, then fell into bed and made love half the night.

On Sunday, Noel stripped off the Indian shag wallpaper and painted the room a glowing buttermilk yellow.

Betony was determined to hang a cluster of framed flower prints above the bed. She had difficulty balancing on the soft surface. Her pants tightened against her curves her every time she moved from one foot to the other.

'Tell me when they're straight,' she ordered.

'The pictures are still crooked, but you have a gorgeous arse.'

Grinning, she leapt from the bed and launched herself into his arms. Her legs wrapped themselves around his waist and her nose touched against his.

'So have you, soldier. Fancy a little hand to hand combat before lunch?'

Monday came too soon. He rose early and smiled down at her sleepy face. 'I'll have to go home tonight.'

'It was fun, wasn't it,' she said wistfully. 'When will I see you again?'

'As soon as I possibly can. The weekend after next, perhaps.'

Propping herself up on one elbow she gazed at him, her smile, slightly anxious. 'No regrets?'

'Do I sound as if I have any?' He leaned down and kissed her. 'We could lunch mid-week, if you like.'

'I do like.'

'Then I'll reshuffle my appointments and ring you. Don't work too hard.'

'Nor you – and don't forget to take my file.' She yawned and snuggled under the covers when he walked away.

Stuffing the file under his arm, he strode out into the soft April morning, feeling like a different man.

CHAPTER FIVE

Dorothy Throsby waved her hand vaguely over the bedroom. 'You can give me a hand with these if you like. Someone's coming to pick it up for the church jumble sale this afternoon.'

'You're getting rid of daddy's things?' Horrified, Sylvia trotted across the room and, snatching up one of the leather-bound diaries, gazed tragically at her mother. 'How could you, mumsy?'

'They've been gathering dust for ten years. One can't mourn for ever.' Dorothy's glance was almost accusatory. 'You might as well know. I intend to offer this room in return for a little companionship.'

Sylvia flushed. 'You're taking in a lodger?'

'As if I would. I believe I said it was to be a companion. I get terribly lonely here all by myself.'

'Don't do anything hasty. I'm sure Noel will see sense eventually.'

'After all I've done to help him get established, too. All I can say is his sense of obligation is strongly lacking.'

Noel was proving obdurate at the moment. Resentfully, Sylvia shoved the diaries into a cardboard box. It was the one issue she was unable to wear him down on, but she would eventually, if her mother didn't keep pushing.

'It's been difficult for him this past year. I'm sure the accident preys on his mind.'

'Then it's about time he took himself in hand. Self-discipline is required to recover from these things, not self-pity. You might suggest that he consults a clairvoyant.'

'A clairvoyant?' She couldn't believe her ears. 'Since when did you believe in that sort of thing.'

Dorothy's voice dropped to a hushed whisper. 'When I went to stay with my brother for the weekend I attended a seance in the next village, just for fun. I tried to contact your father.'

She only just stopped her mouth from falling open. 'And did you?'

'Not exactly, but the woman gave me a message from him. Brian said I must leave the past behind and enjoy life.'

Sylvia's glance went to the diaries. Bound in leather, each had a silver lock. They used to stand on a shelf in her father's chambers, but she'd never been allowed to touch them. She tried to flick one open with her thumb, but failed. 'You can't give these to a jumble sale. He told me they contain information on cases he dealt with, and he was going to write a book one day.'

'He's hardly likely to do that now. Please take anything you want of his, Sylvia. The rest must go.' Dorothy picked up a suit and stuffed it into a bag. 'These clothes have got plenty of wear left in them. It's a pity Noel's so tall.'

'Do go through the pockets first. You know how careless daddy was with money.'

'I'll leave it to you then, dear. I'll go and make us some lunch.'

Sylvia's search produced ten pounds in change, a gold lighter inscribed with her father's name, a woman's handkerchief and a postal package in a yellow envelope. Her lips pursed as she stared at the address. Daddy's distant cousin, Alison Green. She'd embarrassed them at the funeral by sobbing throughout the service.

They'd never understood why he'd bothered with her, relative or not. He hadn't left her anything in his will, though she still occupied the house she'd rented from him, now handled by an estate agent. Since the funeral, she'd been dropped completely.

She threw the package amongst the diaries and the other mementoes she'd rescued. Daddy's pipe rack, a sterling silver ashtray with a dog on the side, several first edition books, which might, or might not have some value. They would look at home in Noel's study. There was a box made of inlaid walnut. It was a pretty thing with a curved lid and silver hinges and lock. There was no sign of a key.

She packed the discarded items into plastic bags, placing hers to one side. She intended to supervise the collectors herself.

As for her mother. She must find out more about this clairvoyant. Her mother had been left rather well off. One had to be careful of charlatans who preyed on wealthy and vulnerable old women. Not that she looked old, and her figure was surprisingly good for a sixty-three year old.

'You ought to change your hairdresser,' she said over lunch. 'That blue rinse is terribly ageing. Mature women go blonde these days, and it would suit your complexion perfectly.'

Dorothy's hand fluttered to her hair. 'Do you really think so, dear? I was toying with the idea of a facelift.'

Sylvia frowned as she leaned forward to examine her mother's face. 'You look perfectly all right as you are.'

Dorothy's smile was smug. 'As I've constantly told you, looking good takes self-discipline. It's dreadful how some women let themselves go.'

Anne came into Sylvia's mind. 'I went to a health farm for a weekend last February. It was terribly gruelling, but I dropped a whole dress size.' Anxiously, she gazed at her mother. 'You won't tell Noel, will you? He thinks I was here.'

They exchanged a conspiratorial smile.

'How a woman achieves her beauty should remain a mystery to her husband, especially where cost is concerned. Eat your lunch whilst it's fresh, dear.'

The spinach salad her mother had made didn't satisfy their hunger. They washed it down with lemon tea and a diet pill.

'I think going blonde is a good idea,' Dorothy mused. 'The clairvoyant said a change for the better attracts good karma.'

'She would say things like that, wouldn't she? It's expected.'

'Nevertheless, it was odd how accurate she was. During the seance she went into a trance. There were several messages for the people present, but she didn't get mine very clearly. She said I was nervous and had blocked the message out. She wants to give me a private tarot reading this weekend.'

Sylvia's hand covered her mother's. 'You really must be careful about this type of person, especially when daddy left you so well off.'

'Rose Monique came highly recommended. She writes for a woman's magazine, and they wouldn't employ someone who isn't absolutely above-board, would they?'

'Rose Monique from *Goddess* magazine?' Sylvia's eyes began to shine. 'Tell me about her.'

'She's really quite sweet, and she only charges twenty pounds for a reading. You should have a reading yourself, Sylvia.'

'We'll see. It might be fun if she can fit me in. I'm certainly not allowing you to go there unescorted . . . .'

The following day the two women drove through the gates of Little Abbot.

Pulling the car to a halt on the gravel drive, Sylvia stared enviously at the mellow stone walls of the house. It was a little shabby, but so in character for the country setting. She'd love to live in a place like this. 'Abbotsford is so pretty, and this house very imposing. Do you suppose Rose Monique owns it?'

'I shouldn't be at all surprised.'

There was a gardener working on one of the flower beds. The sleeves of his sweat-stained T-shirt strained against a muscular pair of tanned arms. His pants stretched tight across his buttocks when he bent over. She averted her eyes from the genital bulge pushing against the material. Men were so ugly and animal.

Suddenly he straightened up and, turning, strolled towards them. His eyes were a peculiar green under dark, arching brows, his mouth fleshy. His smile and direct gaze disturbed her. 'Can I help you?'

'We're looking for your mistress,' she said haughtily.

'Ah, I see.' He gave a soft chuckle and scratched his head. 'Is it Cecily you've come to see, or Rose?'

The earthiness of him made her recoil. It wasn't just his musky smell, but an underlying sensuality that repelled her. His voice was low and unaccented. The hand that opened the car door was broad-palmed, calloused and ingrained with dirt.

'Rose Monique,' she said tightly.

He didn't move an inch when she stepped past him. Unconsciously, she held her breath to ward off the ripe heat enveloping her. What was the matter with her? She exhaled in a rush of relief when he moved to the other side of the car. She pulled a handkerchief from her pocket to dab daintily at the moisture dewing her face. 'It's hot today.'

'That it is.' The man grinned familiarly at her. 'It's going to be a hot summer.'

Annoyed, she assumed a haughty expression and turned away.

'Such beautiful gardens,' Dorothy gushed. 'You have green thumbs, my man.'

'Thank you, missus,' he said humbly and, eyes alive with amusement, tugged at his forelock.

How dare the creature laugh at them! Sylvia turned away when a moist, pink tongue slid over his lips. Strange, but she felt almost faint. She felt exposed under this man's insolent glance, as if he'd stripped her naked. He was disgusting.

'There you are, Alex.' A tall, handsome woman came round the corner with a box of seedlings in her hands. She stared at them for a second or two, then smiled. 'It's Mrs Throsby, isn't it? Just go in, will you. Rose is waiting for you.' Her voice sharpened. 'Alex, there's work to be done.'

'When I'm ready.'

The woman gazed from Alex to herself. The smile stayed, but animosity flickered in the depths of her eyes. She wondered if they were married. Neither of them wore a ring.

Sylvia's glance towards her was disdainful. 'Thank you for your help, so kind,' she cooed to Alex. The green eyes held hers in a second or two of intimacy. The air between them rippled. Suddenly dizzy, she pressed two fingers against her forehead.

He stepped forward. 'You're not used to the heat. I'll help you inside.'

'I can manage.' On trembling legs she started to walk after her mother, feeling his eyes scorching against her back. Once inside, she leaned weakly against a table allowing her eyes to adjust to the changed light.

'Are you all right, dear?' a voice said from the top of a flight of stairs.

'I feel a bit faint.'

'Do pull yourself together, you're making a show of yourself,' her mother whispered irritably.

Rose Monique seemed to float down the staircase. She was clad in a long, flowing skirt covered in flowers. A purple blouse clashed desperately with her ginger hair. Sylvia's nose wrinkled. The woman stank of stale cooking fat and disturbed dust.

Rose's smile was expansive. 'So nice of you to come, dears. Follow me through to my den. A glass of dandelion wine will soon pick you up.'

Two Labradors lifted their heads when they went into the den. 'How many times have I told you not to come in here during the day?' Rose said sternly to them. 'Go and find Cecily.'

The pair slunk off the couch and headed for the door with their tails between their legs. The doggy odour in the room was partially disguised by a sickly incense stick. It made her throat itch.

Bits and pieces tinkled and glittered from the rafters. There were balls of coloured glass, fat wax candles and a crystal ball on a stand. The table was covered in a black fringed cloth covered with symbols.

All slightly obvious. Experiencing a sense of disappointment, Sylvia coughed to clear her throat of the clinging vapours.

A glass was placed in her hand. Rose whispered in her ear. 'This sort of nonsense is expected by the clients. Have some of this. It will help your senses adjust.'

Slightly startled, she gazed wide-eyed at Rose. The woman had read her mind. Rose smiled enigmatically.

The dandelion wine, oddly-flavoured and slightly bitter, was also refreshing. It worked magic on her throat.

'Another?'

'Thank you. It's rather nice.'

'My sister makes it. If you like it, you can buy a bottle or two before you leave. It's very good for the bladder.'

'I hope you don't mind me coming unannounced,' she said, feeling awed by meeting such a celebrity. Anne would be green with envy when she told her.

'I was expecting you.' Rose pressed two fingers to her forehead and gazed into her eyes. 'I'm getting the initial S, and let me see . . . is it T? No . . . no, it's something similar. D perhaps?'

Impressed, Sylvia tried not to gasp. 'It's Sylvia Dearborn.'

Strange how the room temperature suddenly seemed to drop. Rose Monique's smile faded. 'Ah . . .' she said.

Uncomfortable under the woman's silent scrutiny, she stammered, 'Is something wrong? It's become awfully cold in here.'

'I knew you were one of us as soon as you walked in.'

'I beg your pardon?'

Rose shuddered and seemed to gather herself together. 'We have a ghost. Isabella sometimes makes her presence known to sensitive people.'

Goose-bumps raced along Sylvia's arms. She gazed nervously round, expecting to see a vapourish figure hovering behind her. 'A ghost is here?'

'I didn't feel or see anything,' Dorothy said loudly.

Rose's smile reasserted itself. 'Hardly anyone does. She's gone now. She just popped in to take a look.' Rose smiled knowingly at her. 'Isabella liked you, so you needn't worry. You did sense her, didn't you?'

Being liked by a ghost wasn't all that reassuring, but better than being disliked, she supposed. 'Yes, I sensed she meant me no harm.'

'Now, who shall I read first? You, Dorothy? Would you wait outside Sylvia? Ask Alex to show you the garden. Having another person present blocks the vibrations, especially someone special like you, with latent psychic abilities. I'm sure we're going to have a most interesting reading afterwards.'

Sylvia wasn't so sure when she wandered out into the sunshine. Of the gardener there was no sign, but a perfectly formed red rose had been laid on the seat of her car. She held it to her nose. Its perfume was strong, heady and over-powering. It made her feel languid and relaxed. Sliding into the car she leaned back in the seat, closed her eyes and inhaled its perfume.

After a while her breathing slowed and her body warmed. Sweat trickled slowly between her breasts. The rose dropped from her fingers and slid into her lap.

The gardener came into her mind. Her tongue could almost taste the salt of his perspiration and her heart began to drum loudly against her ribs. Alex, the woman had called him. His odour filled her nostrils. Something about Alex reminded her of her father. Her eyes flew open in shock when a shadow moved across the window.

Alex peered at her through the window. 'Are you all right?'

'Yes. I'm just resting.'

He had her father's mouth, her father's eyes. He moved away, a spade over his shoulders, then turned and smiled at her, exactly like her father used to.

She gasped, then squeezed her thighs against the moistening gusset of her panties. Her fingers strayed towards it, hovered. Nice girls didn't touch the temple. Snatched away, her hand grazed across the stem of the rose. She winced when a thorn scratched across her palm.

Stepping from the car, she threw the bloom into the garden bed and washed her bloodied hand under the garden tap. There was a plaster in her handbag. She'd just finished fixing it in place when her mother came out of the house, a bemused smile on her face.

'Rose is waiting for you, dear. I've paid for both of us so you don't need to bother.'

There was reluctance in her to return to the house. Dying to go to the toilet, she felt edgy and soiled. But now her mother had paid she'd have to go, or the money would be wasted.

When she entered, she paused, standing in the curved arch of light spilling in from the outside. She wanted to turn and run. Most of all, she needed a bathroom. Suddenly, the door creaked shut behind her, plunging her into darkness. Terror strangled the scream gathering in her throat.

'You mustn't be afraid,' Rose said soothingly. 'Destiny has brought you to me. Take my hand and I'll guide you to the light.'

Trembling with relief, she allowed herself to be led upstairs to a small, sunny room. She seated herself on the couch.

'This is my private sanctum. I keep the theatricals for those who are more impressionable, like your mother.' Her smile had a sly, knowing edge to it. 'You know you're special, don't you?'

What was she supposed to say? Dumbly, Sylvia nodded.

Rose took her hands. 'Feel the empathy flowing between us. We must have been close in a previous life – sisters, I expect. You can feel it, can't you?'

Goodness, how strange, she could feel something. She smiled. 'Like warmth trickling between us?'

'Exactly.' Rose let her go. 'Would you like some tea so we can chat before the reading? I'll make it while you have a pee. The bathroom's over there.'

The offer didn't seem odd to her. Rose Monique was wonderfully genuine, and so friendly.

Flattered by her attention, she rose to her feet. 'Thank you, I do feel a little uncomfortable. I mustn't be too long though, my mother is waiting.'

'Cecily's showing her the garden.'

Sylvia's mind accepted the statement as fact as she balanced herself over the pedestal. She tried not to touch anything with her body. Germs lurked in strangers' lavatories.

She'd never felt so full. The relief she experienced was a pleasure in itself. Giving a delicate little shudder she tissued herself dry, adjusted her clothing and turned towards the washbasin.

A large, black spider was hunched over the plug-hole. Paralysed by shock, her throat squeezed over her scream. It moved swiftly, running over the edge of the sink and on to the floor near her feet. Shuddering all over, she flung open the door, snatched up a magazine from a table and slapped it over herself in case the beast was on her clothes.

A few seconds later she was more or less composed, despite the feeling her hair was standing on end. She smiled in embarrassment at Rose's amused expression. 'There was a spider.'

'She won't hurt you.' Coming to her side, Rose plucked something from her head and threw it towards the bathroom door. 'That's very naughty of you, Samantha. You mustn't frighten my guests.'

Sylvia turned in time to see the creature scuttle under the door.

She couldn't remember afterwards exactly what made her burst into tears. Gathered into Rose's arms, she experienced such a sense of belonging, she could have stayed there for ever.

The time Noel spent apart from Betony was purgatory.

He'd seen her once in the past two weeks, when they'd grabbed a quick lunch at the *Kings Arms* on the Chelsea embankment.

He smiled to himself as he stared through the kitchen window into the darkness. They hadn't noticed the view, but had gazed into each other's eyes, held hands under the table and wished they were in bed together. He wished they were in bed together now. He felt stifled in his over-stuffed house, living a lie with a wife he no longer loved.

He was wondering what excuse he could give Sylvia for spending the weekend in London, when she broke in on his reverie and provided him with a perfect opportunity.

'I've been thinking, Noel.'

Sylvia thinking, whatever next? Despising his own sarcasm, he turned and gazed at her, trying to appear interested. Poised in the doorway, she looked like a little yellow canary with its head cocked to one side. If he was a cat instead of a coward he'd get rid of her with one bite.

'Would you mind if I visited my mother more often? She's terribly lonely.'

Her transparency annoyed him. He wasn't going to play her game, neither was he about to give in over her mother.

'Why don't you go and stay with her for a couple of weeks?'

Annoyance crept into her voice. 'Two weeks is out of the question. I'll go down tomorrow afternoon and return on Monday. Someone has to cook your meals and look after the house. I also have committee meetings to attend.'

'I can cook my own meals, and we have a cleaning lady,' he pointed out. 'And you could put in your apologies for the meetings. It's not as if you're the president.'

He knew he'd scored a point when there was an audible sniff.

'The cleaning lady needs supervision, otherwise the work doesn't get done properly.'

'It looks all right to me.'

'Really, Noel. You have no idea of the work involved in running a house.' She busied herself polishing each item of cutlery he'd already dried, and placed it in the drawer. He hated the way she lined it up, each fork and spoon gently placed on its side to fit with precision one into the other. The cutlery had been a wedding present, and looked as shiny and new as the day they'd unwrapped it.

He wondered why he'd married her. They'd met at Jeff and Anne Sullivan's engagement party, where he'd been the guest of a guest. It was her dainty, doll-like looks that had hooked him. The fact that he'd never been able to get under her skirt had been a change from the easy-going females he was used to. It had branded her as different. She was different. She'd been created with an inability to consider anyone else's point of view but her own.

He must have loved her at one stage, but for the life of him he couldn't remember when. Had they ever had fun together, or had their marriage always been one of inhibited sex and dreary domesticity?

'You can help me go through daddy's stuff tonight. What doesn't suit your study can be packed in the loft. Thank goodness I was there to prevent my mother giving it all away. She can be quite vague at times. She really needs someone to look after her, don't you think?'

He gave a non-committal grunt. He didn't want an argument followed by a day of tight-lipped silence. He could have strangled her when she interpreted his grunt wrongly.

She gave a smugly complacent smile. 'You won't forget to trim the hedge this weekend, will you? It looks quite dreadful.'

'Another week won't hurt it.'

'That might be all right on a council estate, but a better standard is expected in this neighbourhood.'

She was in top, bitchy form tonight. Perhaps a tight-lipped silence would be preferable, after all. His modest upbringing hadn't rated a mention in months.

'I don't give an owl's hoot about the neighbours.'

'You should. A couple of them help provide our bread and butter.'

'I never realized a trimmed hedge carried such snob value.'

Her lips tightened. 'We should set an example.'

Feeling more bloody minded than usual, he said something designed to upset her even more. 'I was thinking of asking my parents down for a holiday.'

The cutlery drawer slid forcibly shut. 'I don't think that's a good idea. They were uncomfortable last time, though I can't imagine why. I did all I could to make them welcome. Your mother put everything in the wrong place in my kitchen, even though I told her to leave it to me. It just makes more work when guests *insist* on helping. After all, one wouldn't do it in a hotel.'

Tomorrow suddenly seemed a long way away. Just as suddenly, he knew he couldn't stand another minute of Sylvia's company. He managed to keep his irritation under control, but only just. 'Why don't you pop out and see Anne? I can manage to sort your father's things out by myself.'

'I suppose I could. I did want to talk to her, and Jeff goes to his Masonic Lodge tonight. I don't know why you refused to join. Daddy was a Mason, and it did wonders for his career. He was appointed as a judge very early—'

'Don't start that again,' he said, trying not to sound as savage as he felt. 'You're like a dog with a bone. I'm sick of you trying to manage my life.'

'Noel?' Her voice sounded bruised as he slammed out of the kitchen and into the study. 'I'm only thinking of what's good for you.'

Five minutes later the car drove off. Heaving a sigh of relief he headed for the telephone. Betony's phone rang and rang and he prayed she'd answer. He smiled when she did, mostly at the breathlessness in her voice, as if she'd run downstairs. 'What took you so long?'

Her gurgle of laughter made the hair rise at the nape of his neck. 'I was in the bath. I'm wearing a towel and dripping suds all over the floor.'

'You look great in a towel and suds. I'll be over Friday evening. Will that be OK?'

'More than OK,' she purred. 'I've finished painting the lounge, and I've got a surprise for you.'

He chuckled. 'Tell me what it is?'

'Probably not what you think it is. Pick up some pizza on the way over, would you?'

'Will do. Can I bring anything else?'

'Only yourself, Noel.'

'I've missed you.'

'Me too,' she breathed. 'We'll think of something to compensate for it this weekend, mmm?'

His heartbeat accelerated into launch mode when the door was thrown open.

'Anne wasn't in,' Sylvia said crossly. 'I wonder where she went at this time of night. Oh, who's that on the phone?'

'A client.'

He tried not to laugh when Betony said 'whoops' and smacked him a kiss down the line.

'Thank you, Mister Sutra. I look forward to doing business with you,' he said, battling the urge to laugh.

'Mister Sutra?' Sylvia made a face when he replaced the receiver. 'He sounds like a foreigner. A man in your position should be careful only to encourage the best clients to the practice. They add tone.'

'Believe me, Mister Sutra is *noted* for his position in society.' Mood much improved, he pulled one of the boxes towards him. 'Now, let's see what junk you've scavenged.'

It took two hours to get rid of Judge Throsby's effects. If Sylvia had been allowed to have her way the whole lot would have ended up in his study.

Photographs in silver frames were distributed around the house, making more work for the cleaning lady. Apart from some first edition books, the silver ashtray and the walnut box, he managed to persuade her the rest should be stored.

'I really don't know what to do with this,' she said, handing him the package. 'Perhaps we ought to open it to see if it's worth sending on. After all, it *was* written ten years ago.'

'It's an offence to tamper with private mail.' He slid it into his briefcase. 'I'll ask Joyce to look up her phone number tomorrow. If Mrs Green is still at the same address I'll ask her if she wants me to post it on to her.'

'She is at the same address. She rents the house from my mother. Whatever you do, don't encourage her to resume social contact. I don't know why daddy bothered with her.' She yawned discreetly behind her hand. 'It's getting late. I'm off to bed.'

'I'll be up later. I'll try not to disturb you.'

Not that there was any chance of that. The inclination to disturb Sylvia had left him now Betony had come into his life.

CHAPTER SIX

Heaving a sigh of relief, Noel ushered the last client of the day from his office. He said goodnight to the departing receptionist and turned to Joyce. 'Did you get that phone number for me?'

'Yes, but no one was in.' She handed him a slip of paper. 'She might be at work.'

'Thanks Joyce. I'll try her later.' He pocketed the number. 'I've just thought. If Ms Green was a relative of Sylvia's father, she's probably related to you as well.'

Joyce busied herself with something on the desk. 'I'm related through the female side.' She looked as though she was about to say more, but bit her lip when the door to Daniel's office opened.

'Have you got a minute, Noel?'

He checked his watch, impatient to see Betony. 'Is it important?'

'I thought you might like to see the summary of Mrs Nichols' file.'

Following Daniel into his office, Noel closed the door behind him and scribbled Betony's phone number on Daniel's memo pad. 'In this instance, I'd prefer it if you retained confidentiality. Make an appointment, you can discuss it with her.'

'She must be a special friend of yours.'

He met Daniel's curious gaze square-on. 'What makes you think so?'

Daniel's dark eyes smouldered with amusement. 'Not many people memorize the phone number of an acquaintance.'

He'd slipped up. 'I suppose they don't.'

'OK, I get the message. The three wise monkeys have nothing on me.'

'Thanks.' He didn't bother to explain his involvement. It was none of Daniel's business and the man was no fool.

It was raining outside. The air was soft, the pavements painted a liquid, glistening silver. It was good to stretch his legs as they conveyed him rapidly towards Betony's house.

He bought her a bunch of flowers on the way. Arms loaded with hot pizza and garlic bread, he rang her doorbell. She didn't give him time to deposit the parcels, just coiled her arms around his neck and kissed him, crushing the food and flowers between them. The warm fragrance of her chased the tension from his body. A man could thrive on a welcome home like this every night of the week. They were both laughing when she finally released him.

'You're late,' she said. 'I thought you'd never get here.'

'I couldn't get rid of my last client.' He handed her the flowers. 'See if you can rescue these. I'll stick the food in the oven.'

'Notice anything?' she said as they moved though to the living room.

He could hardly miss the changes. The soft, creamy paint blended with the new carpet. Under the window, a red leather couch with clawed feet took pride of place. Its gold and burgundy cushions matched the winged armchair he'd rested in at the antique shop.

He took a couple of steps forward, smiling as he ran his fingers over the new upholstery.

'Surprise, I had it tarted up for you,' she said softly.

'I love it.' Kicking off his shoes, he propped his feet on the matching foot-stool and relaxed. Within hand's reach was a round table holding the Tiffany lamp. He was touched by the depth of thought attached to the gift. 'This is a wonderful present. It must have cost you a fortune.'

She sounded almost offhand. 'I swapped the furniture in this room for it.'

'Even the picture?'

'An art gallery took it to sell on commission.'

'You're kidding?'

'You don't know much about art, do you?'

'I was brought up on a council estate,' he said, as if that explained it. 'Making ends meet took precedence over art education.'

She made a small, exasperated sound in her throat. 'If background was an excuse for ignorance you'd be pouring hot tar into holes in the road instead of running an accountancy business.' She returned his probing glance with a teasing smile. 'So, my dear Noel. It seems as if you have your touchy places too.'

He relaxed, accepting her challenge. 'Spoiling for a fight, are you? OK, so educate me about the sacked artist. I can see you're dying to show off.'

'He's an Australian, and was just making a name for himself when he overdosed on heroin. The gallery owner said the painting was not as good as his later work, but he should be able to get a decent price for it.'

She'd replaced it with a painting of a honey jar filled with daffodils, set on a window sill. There was something natural and joyous about the splash of bright colour picked up and reflected back from a rain-lashed window. The longer he looked, the more he saw. Paint flaking away from the putty, dust in the corners of the small window panes, a ladybird on the underside of a leaf, the remains of a label on the jar.

'I like the replacement. It has something special about it. Soul, I suppose.'

She slid on to his lap and rested her cheek against his. 'I feel the same way. It's a Renfrew. Her originals are expensive now and I couldn't resist it. I don't suppose you've heard of her.'

He kissed the side of her mouth. 'Hmmm, now let me see? First name Jane. In her youth she painted weird cult stuff under the name of Mistral. How's that, you patronizing little witch? Ouch!'

She removed her teeth from his bottom lip and sprang from his lap, giving a throaty laugh. 'You read that interview in the *Herald* didn't you?'

He nodded. 'I do read on occasion. You never know when such information might come in handy.' He ducked when she tried to box his ears, grabbed her hand. 'Let me buy the painting for you.'

She shook her head. 'A gift should be a surprise, and reflect what the giver sees in the receiver.'

He gazed at the fireside chair, and wondered what symbolism he should attach to that. They were too comfortable with each other for people in their position.

She waved towards an oblong alcove where the shelves had been. 'Surprise me with something for there. I haven't come across anything I thought suitable.'

'You're making this into a game. What if I buy the wrong thing?'

'Don't consciously look for anything special. You'll know when you see it.'

'Accountants are more logical than intuitive.'

'If you can point out anything logical about our relationship, I might believe you.' Sounding troubled, she slid her hand from his. 'I should hate you, but I don't. You're happily married, yet you're here with me.'

He winced at her reference to the accident, however oblique. 'Who said my marriage is happy.'

Her glance became curiously challenging. 'You aren't going to tell me a sob story, are you?'

'I guess not.' His smile became ironic. 'Would you like me to go away?'

'And spend the night in that khaki flat.' She gently kissed the top of his head. 'I'm sorry. Sometimes I feel as if I'm treading on razor blades.'

'Now who's telling a sob story?'

Her face closed up. 'I guess I should have seen that one coming. Let's go to bed. That's what we both want, isn't it?'

'Is it? I happen to enjoy your company as well. Shall we eat?'

'Damn you!' She stalked into the kitchen, her face flaming. The flowers were thrust savagely into a vase. 'You've made me feel like a tart.'

'That works two ways. I'm not some stud you've hired for the night.'

'Oh, God!' Her expression was horrified. 'Don't let's quarrel, Noel. I've been looking forward to seeing you all week.'

He crossed the floor in two strides and wrapped her in his arms, holding her against his body until she relaxed against him. Her mercurial moods were understandable under the circumstances. He could cope with them, but she'd have to meet him halfway. He wouldn't allow her to walk all over him like Sylvia had for the past eight years.

'You warned me this was going to be complicated,' she murmured.

'Even under normal circumstances our relationship wouldn't be easy.' He stroked the silken strands of her hair. 'Perhaps you need to talk to someone to get it out of your system.'

'I've been talking to a shrink for months. He's the best.'

'Does he approve of us?'

'It's none of his damned business! He tells me grief takes time to heal, that one day the pain will be bearable. You make it bearable, but I don't know why, and I'm terrified to do anything that might spoil what we have.'

'You expected a monster when you walked into my office, didn't you?'

'You are. You don't encourage self-pity. That makes me take a good, long look at myself. Self-confrontation isn't all that comfortable. I *am* using you, Noel, but it's not just the sex thing. I need your strength. I can understand and sympathize with your pain now. That's a giant stride away from loathing you.'

He tipped up her chin and, gazing into her eyes, said gruffly, 'That was quite a mouthful.'

An irrepressible grin rippled along her luscious mouth. 'You asked for it. Let's drop the miserable soul-searching and eat that damned pizza.'

He succumbed to the temptation to kiss her and, just when he'd decided he might be persuaded to head for the bedroom after all, the phone rang. She swore softly, and plucked the receiver from its rest, nestling it between them. 'Betony Nichols.'

'It's Daphne,' a voice said. 'Are you free tomorrow evening? Clive has invited a few people over and I thought you might like to join us.'

'I'd love to, but . . . .' Her eyes questioned his, and although she smiled when he shook his head, disappointment flared in their depths. 'I have a guest.'

'You're quite welcome to bring her along. Or is it a he?'

'I really don't think I'll be able to make it, Daphne,' she said lightly. 'Thanks anyway.'

'It *is* a man, isn't it?' Laughter entered the woman's voice. 'Don't be so damned mysterious. Who is he?'

'No one you know.'

'He must be something special if you want to keep him a secret. I'm intrigued. Do bring him along, Betony.'

'I'll see . . . .'

'Which means you have absolutely no intention of doing so. Ah well, you know where we are if you change your mind.'

'I have your address.' She dropped the receiver back in its rest and trailed her fingers across his lips. 'Now, where were we?'

'Deciding between bed and pizza.'

'And what did we decide?'

'That there was no contest.'

16th Day of February 1798

Sebastian was incensed when he discovered my act of defiance, but his cruel beatings will never make me reveal Katherine's resting place. I wept when he said he must burn her bones beneath the altar to give him power, and begged him to repent his evil ways. I'm driven to believe he's afflicted with insanity. He has imprisoned me within my chamber, subject to his will, and denies me the comfort of either priest or female companionship.

He has brought his mistress to taunt me. Her name is Lynette. Hardly more than a girl, she is great of beauty, but low bred. She is swollen with child. There is pity in her eyes for me, and fear when she looks upon Sebastian. I cannot blame her for my wretchedness, but she is dabbling in that which she cannot understand — the power of evil. I fear that he will use her for his own ends.

Sebastian mocks me daily. 'You are too pious, Isabella,' he taunts. 'The devil is stronger than God. Join us, and he will ease your pain.'

'Ah, the high priestess,' Rose said. 'It represents a feminine influence, mysticism and psychic ability. I did indicate the strong presence in you, dear This just confirms it.' Rose smiled when Sylvia gave a self-important nod. 'The two of swords. Oh, dear, oh dear.'

'Is something wrong?'

'It's reversed. You must guard against betrayal and malice.'

'What sort of betrayal?'

'All I can say is that you'll know it when you see it. Now, hush, Sylvia, I'm concentrating. This is interesting. It's The Lovers.' When a prim expression appeared on Sylvia's face, Rose's eyes sharpened. Something from her past, perhaps?

'You may have to choose between desire or duty. My advice to you is this. Let intuition guide you in matters of love.'

'I'm a happily married woman.'

The fool believes her own lies. Rose bent her head to the spread of cards. No man could be happily married to a woman like Sylvia unless ...? She flipped over the final card, and smiled. The tarot never lied. 'Why, here comes the Emperor. The Emperor is ruled by Aries. He depicts an influential man of ambition and high achievement who is always in control. Would that be your husband?'

Sylvia's laugh was almost scornful. 'Noel wouldn't fit into that image.'

Of course he wouldn't. Noel Dearborn was one of those dreary grey men with a conscience. His letter of apology to Betony a year after the accident had been almost abject. He wouldn't get away with it. Sylvia was the perfect tool to break him with.

Eyes narrowing, for Rose knew she must concentrate on the present if she wanted to achieve her goal, she continued her manipulation of Sylvia. 'Your father then ....'

'Daddy was an Aries,' Sylvia said thoughtfully. 'Yes, he would be the Emperor. He was a judge, and looked regal in his wig and gown. He's hardly in a position to control me though. He died many years ago.'

'Passed over, dear. A soul never dies.' *And control comes from many sources, including beyond the grave.*

Wrapping the cards in a square of black silk, she leaned back in her chair, closed her eyes and pondered on the stupidity of the woman sitting across the table. 'I sense you shared a special bond with your father. Why don't you tell me about him?'

'He was such a good father, and well respected by his peers ....'

Once Sylvia started talking she didn't know how to stop. Rose's mind absorbed the words like a sponge and she made encouraging little noises to keep her talking.

Within half an hour she knew all there was to know about Sylvia, which didn't differ greatly from what her mother had told her, except for Sylvia's strained sexual relationship with her husband.

It was an exhausting business being a mother confessor. Rose wondered how priests put up with it. Mother and daughter were stupid, selfish women. Dorothy

Throsby didn't matter. Rose had met many women like her: lonely, impression-able and willing to be milked of cash. She must find a way to use Sylvia though. She was ideal.

'It's odd, but your gardener reminds me so very much of daddy.'

Rose's eyes sharpened. Alex's animal earthiness didn't effect her in the slight-est, but he was probably screwing Cecily for want of something better. It was interesting that this woman equated him with her father, very interesting. 'In what way?'

'Oh, I don't know . . . .'

Rose observed the colour rise to her cheeks. Sylvia's lack of sensuality was probably something she'd been taught. It needed the right man to encourage it to emerge. Was that man Alex? What a delicious revenge it would be if she could bring them together.

'. . . it's his looks, I suppose. The resemblance made me feel quite odd when I saw him.'

The Emperor! Hiding her jubilation, Rose leaned forward and took her hand. 'Do you miss him very much?'

Sylvia touched a handkerchief to her eyes. 'We had a special relationship.'

'Would you like to try and make contact with him?'

'My mother said it was unsuccessful.'

'Perhaps he didn't want to talk to your mother for some reason. He might prefer to talk to his daughter.'

Sylvia's eyes widened

'Remember, you're one of the chosen. I believe he sent you a sign through the tarot. We could have a private seance the weekend after next. A select few, all sensitive.'

'I don't feel very chosen.'

'That's because your gifts haven't been developed. Would you like to give it a try? The seance could be a learning experience.'

'I don't know.'

'Think about it, dear. I'm quite prepared to take you under my wing at week-ends if you have the courage to explore your psychic abilities. It's not often one quite as gifted as you presents herself at the right time.'

'It's not a question of courage. I don't know how Noel will react if I come here every weekend.' She sniffed. 'Not that he's home very often himself.'

'Husbands can be neglectful at times,' Rose reinforced. 'It's odd how they expect to be consulted when a woman wants to pursue her own special inter-ests.'

Sylvia bristled like a dog with raised hackles. 'I don't consult him. Noel's not spiritual, like us. He'd ridicule the whole idea. I'll have to think of an excuse.'

She hadn't taken long to convince herself to deceive her husband. Rose hid a smile. A dissatisfied woman was ripe for exploitation. 'We must think of a legitimate reason.' She glanced towards the door then, lowered her voice. 'I'll let you in on a secret. Cecily and I have decided to open the garden of Little Abbott to the public next month. What if we dream up a nice little business venture . . . .'

Noel remembered to phone Alison Green on Saturday evening. She sounded like a nice woman, but appeared startled when he explained the situation.

'I don't understand. Brian died ten years ago.'

'My wife—' He glanced at Betony. She was slumped on the sofa reading a magazine upside down and pretending not to listen. 'Judge Throsby's daughter found a package addressed to you when they were disposing of her father's things. I thought I'd contact you first. I didn't want it to come as a shock after all this time.'

'Yes, it would have done. Thank you for warning me.' There was a short silence from the other end of the line. 'You don't know what's in it, I suppose?'

'It's sealed. I think he was just about to post it to you when he died. It was in his briefcase.'

'I was expecting a package at the time. I thought he'd forgotten his promise to us.'

Intrigued, he stared at the receiver. *Us?* He remembered Sylvia telling him not to encourage Alison, and reacted out of habit. 'I'll post it on to you, then.'

'That's very kind of you. I'll let you know when it arrives safely.'

Giving Alison Green his office phone number, he hung up.

Betony gave him a dreamy smile. 'I think it's romantic, receiving a missive from a lover ten years after he's croaked.'

'They were cousins, I believe, not lovers.'

'Pragmatist! I prefer my version of events.'

'Then I'll make a point of writing to you every day after I've gone.'

She crossed to where he stood, flung her arms around him and hugged him tight. Her heart thumped against his shirt. 'Don't even joke about it, Noel.'

He could have kicked himself. He tipped up her chin and kissed her. 'Let's go out somewhere. What about that party?'

Her eyes began to shine. 'Have you got your tux with you?'

'At the flat. I'll change on the way.'

It was dark by the time they arrived at the Harrington's town house, an elegant building in St John's Wood.

Daphne's glance swept over Betony, noting the elegance of the midnight blue satin pants suit. The change in her was remarkable. Her eyes sparkled, the tense lines had gone from the corners of her mouth and her skin was flawless. Her sole piece of jewellery was a silver crescent moon brooch inlaid with mother-of-pearl, and pinned to one side.

Daphne suddenly felt cheap in her designer label, short beaded tunic.

The man responsible for the change stood behind her on the step. Tall and dark, he had a pleasant smile despite his air of reserve. His looks weren't earth-shattering, but slightly medieval. There was a quiet strength about his face.

Betony introduced him almost defiantly.

Daphne's head nearly spun when the name registered. 'Hell,' she said faintly. 'No wonder you wanted to keep him under wraps.'

'If you're not going to be civil, we'll leave.'

'Don't go all frosty, when you knew damned well what my reaction would be.' She smiled and stuck out her hand to Noel. 'No offence, I hope.'

'None taken.'

'Then come and meet Clive while he's still sober.' Their relationship wasn't really any of her business, however many misgivings she had.

Betony slid her hand into Noel's as they followed Daphne through.

The gathering had reached the stage where guests were beginning to lose their inhibitions. She began to wish they hadn't come. The crowd was a mixture of the trendy and those who prided themselves on mixing with the trendy. They included a couple of actors and a politician or two. A popular singer toyed with the piano keys, his unenhanced voice thin and raspy. She winced as he attempted a high note.

Nobody seemed to be listening, except for a tall blonde leaning on the piano, who had an eye-catching display of cleavage.

Clive Harrington was a short podgy man of about fifty-five. His pale eyes were the coldest she'd ever seen, and set into features that merged one into the other. His mouth was a small pout.

So instant was her dislike, her initial instinct was to recoil. Her gaze shifted to Daphne, hovering at his shoulder. She gave a hardly discernible shrug and placed a hand on Clive's shoulder, displaying a sizeable diamond.

She tried not to shudder when he released her hand to pat Daphne's behind. 'White wine.'

'Soda water for me,' Noel murmured.

Clive's eyes flicked over him, dismissed him as a nonentity. 'Get the man a soda water, Daphne, and tell that damned faggot on the piano to shut his mouth for five minutes.'

'You hired him, you tell him.'

Clive watched her go, a smile edging across his face. 'Have you ever seen such a pert little arse? She's asking for a good spanking.'

He was disgusting. She exchanged an apologetic glance with Noel, who smiled and gently squeezed her hand.

'Excuse me.' Clive glided over to the piano and whispered something in the entertainer's ear.

All hell broke loose. The singer grabbed Clive by the shirt-front. 'Who the fuck d'you think you're talking to?' A camera flashed, the piano stool turned over and the tall woman screamed when the singer's fist connected with Clive's face.

'Serves the obnoxious little turd right,' somebody murmured when Clive sprawled on his back.

'I'll sue you for assault, you grunting creep,' Clive shrieked when the singer stalked towards the door.

'Just try it. My minders will cut your balls off and feed them to my cat.'

'Don't I wish.' Daphne appeared at their elbows, drinks in hand. She appeared calm, and in charge of herself. 'Do me a favour, darling. Play some music until I get Clive sorted out. He's had more than I thought.'

'I haven't played for some time.'

'Play something soothing.' She didn't give her chance to refuse. 'Hey, everyone,' she shouted as Clive struggled to his feet. 'This is my guest, the pianist, Betony Gifford. She's going to play something for you.'

There was a sprinkle of applause as she walked towards the piano. Hardly anyone took any notice of her because they were watching Clive stagger off, his nose dripping blood.

The conversation started again once he'd gone.

Betony glanced across the room, her mouth dry with nerves as she seated herself. Noel's eyes were intent on her. When he smiled and raised his glass in a toast, her nervousness fled. What did it matter if she was out of practice? This lot wouldn't know the difference, anyway.

She started with some simple Chopin *études* to warm her fingers, following it up with Liszt – *Sonata in B minor*. Totally absorbed in the music, she didn't notice the small crowd gathered around the piano until she'd finished.

The applause startled her. Panicking, she gazed shakily around her. Noel was at her side, instantly. 'Are you OK? You look pale.'

She managed a smile. 'I'm a bit dizzy. It's the smoke. I think I need some air.'

He helped her to her feet. 'Lean on me, I'll get you out of here.'

'I enjoyed your playing, Miss Gifford.' She turned, automatically smiling towards the voice. A camera flash blinded her.

'Get me out of here, Noel.'

'Play another,' somebody demanded. 'Do you know—'

'Not now,' Noel said shouldering them through the crowd. He nodded to Daphne who was just coming into the room. 'Sorry, we can't stay. Betony's not feeling too well. Is Clive all right?'

'Better than he deserves to be.' A kiss landed on her cheek. 'We're going to the village next week. I'll ring you when we get back, and we'll have lunch. It was nice to meet you, Noel.'

The fresh air began to revive her.

'Sit on the step for a minute.'

She snuggled against his shoulder, taking in great gulps of air. 'I'm sorry, that was unexpected.'

'You look as though you were having having a panic attack.'

She could have cried at the concern in his eyes. 'It happens sometimes. I'm supposed to take pills, but I think I forgot them today.'

'Have you got them on you?'

'In my bag.'

He found the pill box and thumbed it open. 'How many?'

'Two,' she lied, knowing she needed the larger dose.

'If you can't take them without water I'll go inside—'

'No, it's all right.' She swallowed them and smiled. 'See, they're gone.'

He placed her wrap around her shoulders. 'Stay here. I'll see if I can flag down a taxi.'

'I don't want to be left alone. Let's walk to Marylebone station. It's a lovely night and I need the exercise.'

It was a night made for lovers. A round silver moon played hide and seek with the clouds when they passed the cricket ground.

'It was a hellish party, wasn't it?'

Noel chuckled. 'It had its moments.'

'I can't imagine Daphne married to Clive.'

'He's probably different when he's sober.'

She experienced an annoying stab of jealousy when she wondered what Noel's wife was like. Did he touch Sylvia in the same way as he touched her? Did he enjoy making love to her?

She slanted him a glance. 'Noel?'

'Mmmm.'

She was being irrational. She had no right to ask him about his wife. 'I'm sorry the party was such a pain.'

'It wasn't your fault.' He drew to a halt and turned to face her. 'It gave me a chance to hear you play. I had no idea you were so good.'

Colour flooded into her face. 'I'm embarrassed. I played badly even though I chose simple pieces. It's been over a year since I practised.'

'It sounded lovely to me, but then, I'm not an expert.'

She hugged him close after he kissed her, overwhelmed by a stab of intense pleasure at just being with him. She didn't see the point of questioning the feeling. Sooner or later he'd come to his senses and leave her.

In the meantime, she intended to enjoy every moment she shared with him – and to hell with his wife!

CHAPTER SEVEN

'He looks a bit like you.'

Noel sighed when Sylvia thrust the social pages over the accounts he'd been going through. As his eyes riveted on the photograph his heart began to thump.

Betony was gazing straight at the camera, a smile on her face. Thank God he was turned away from it! He quickly scanned the caption. *Betony Nichols and escort.* It was next to a picture of Daphne and Clive.

'He's a dreadful little man.'

'Who is?'

'Clive Harrington.'

His heart went into overdrive again. 'Have you met him?'

'Someone who has, told me.'

Pushing the paper aside, Noel forced himself to concentrate on the household accounts. He frowned. 'Do we need all this kitchen stuff?'

'Oh that.' Her defensive manner put him on alert. 'I wouldn't have bought it if I didn't.'

'Why do you need sixty of everything? It's catering china.'

'I happen to be going into business.'

His stomach sank. 'You're what!'

Sylvia examined her immaculate nails. 'I've been asked to do the catering for public visitors at a stately home for the summer.'

'I see, and you didn't think to tell me.'

'Did you tell me when you took in a partner and changed office?'Her martyred expression was matched by her tone of voice. 'It's only at weekends, Noel. You're hardly ever home anyway.'

To say he was surprised was an understatement. Sylvia had never shown any inclination to work outside the home. Now she intended to run her own business?

'Have you costed it all out?'

'I saw my mother's financial adviser. She's going to invest some money into the venture.'

The look he gave her was mildly reproachful. 'You should have told me before you spent this amount of money, we've nearly gone into overdraft.'

'You would have tried to talk me out of it.'

She was probably right. 'You'd better tell me about it now.'

She launched into an enthusiastic account of her plans, a tea shop in a conservatory in some country house. His mind ticked over as he listened. If Sylvia took this on, it would leave him every weekend free to be with Betony.

'I'll do all the cooking myself, that's what the stackable trays are for. I'll go down on Fridays and make the cakes and scones ready for the weekend. I'll have a girl to help me, so her wage won't be very expensive.'

That meant he could spend Friday evening with Betony as well. A smile spread across his face. 'It sounds like a good idea to me. Do you want me to keep the books?'

'Goodness, no, you're much to busy.' He'd never seen her so animated. 'I'm sure I'll be able to manage them.' She kissed the top of his head. 'I was positive you'd be cross.'

'You're a wonderful cook,' was all he could think of to say. 'I'm sure you'll make a success of it. You'd better open a separate cheque account.'

'I'll make sure to leave you enough food for the weekends.'

Guilt surged through him when he observed the pleasure in her eyes. 'I'd better get the hedge trimmed,' he muttered, rising to his feet.

'Mow the lawn afterwards, would you?' Head cocked to one side, she stared at him for a moment. 'Have you seen Jeff lately?'

'No. Why do you ask?'

'I just wondered. I think they've been avoiding us since you didn't turn up for dinner.'

His guilt increased. 'I expect they're busy. Why don't you invite them all over for lunch tomorrow?'

Her face tightened. 'The children as well? They're not very well behaved.'

He stifled a sigh. They were just normal kids. 'It's going to be a nice day so I'll get the barbecue out. Look, I'll phone them if you like.'

'No, don't bother. I'm bored with them, anyway.' She picked up the paper and stared at the photo again. 'The resemblance is remarkable, only his hair is longer. He's shorter than you are. Betony Nichols? The name sounds familiar.'

'You look lovely in that outfit,' he said in desperation. 'Pink suits you.'

'Thank you, darling.' Dropping the paper to the table she wagged her finger at him. 'Trust you to remember it's Saturday. It will be nice to spend a weekend alone together. I suppose I should reward you for not being grouchy about my little business venture. It's been a long time.'

Not long enough, Noel thought, scuttling for the safety of the garden shed. It would be his turn to have a headache tonight.

The last pansy was planted. The border would look pretty when they bloomed. Straightening up, Cecily glanced at the house. Rose was fully occupied this afternoon, with one client coming after the other.

A quiet whistle reached her ears. She turned towards the high hedge that enclosed the lime tree walk, her body swaying as her tanned feet scrunched over the gravel pathway.

It was warm for May. Her dress clung to a body musky with perspiration. She didn't care. Alex liked her this way.

He was in their usual spot, leaning against the trunk of a shady tree whose branches swept the ground along the edge of the stream. High reeds and nettles lined the bank along the other side. Beyond that was Abbot's Field, once the site of an ancient monastery.

Although there was a slight danger from prying eyes, the thought added spice to their liaisons. But they were unlikely to be seen here.

Alex gazed at her and smiled. 'You're a slut to come running to my whistle, Cecily.'

'And you're a piece of trash. I saw the way you looked at Sylvia Dearborn. She's bad news, Alex, and if you think I'm doing what you asked, you can think again.'

'Rose said we need her, and Sylvia needs to be initiated to be of any use to us. You'll do it.'

'Why you? Why not one of the others?' She whimpered when his finger brushed down her throat. 'Sometimes, I hate you.'

'That's my girl.' He began to smile. 'You know how much you mean to me, Ces. Despite our age difference, I worship the ground you walk on.'

'So why her?'

'It won't only be me, Ces. You know that.'

His mouth was suddenly warm and tender against hers and a tiny shudder ran through her. She hated him for reminding her she was nearing forty. She hated the hands gently coaxing her body into life, hated the betrayal of her senses. Closing her eyes, she gave in to his demands, her hate overcome by an overwhelming need.

'Something has bitten you.'

Cecily secured the top button on her dress. 'A mosquito, I expect.'

Rose laughed. 'It must have had damned big teeth. You should stay away from Alex.'

'You were down by the stream, I should imagine.'

Cecily shot angrily to her feet. 'You bloody voyeur, you've been spying on us.'

Satisfied she'd got a bite, Rose smiled. 'I don't need to. You've got mud all over your face and hair.'

'Shit!' Cecily subsided back into her chair. 'Why don't you mind your own business. I don't interfere in your love life, and at least Alex isn't married.'

Rose's eyes glinted. 'Married men have got more to lose. It gives a woman an edge in the relationship.'

'Which one of the circle is it?' When she didn't answer, Cecily smiled. 'The master?'

'And if it is?'

'I don't give a damn. Just lay off me.'

'Alex is part of the inner circle. I don't want complications.'

'You could have fooled me. I know your plans for that blonde creature. I wondered why you took her under your wing.'

Rose hissed in annoyance. 'Someone has to pay for Ben's death.'

'Ben's death? Since when have you been judge and jury? You didn't even like the boy. You shouted at him, and sometimes clouted him when Betony wasn't around.'

'Rubbish. I just didn't like him touching my things.'

Cecily lowered her voice. 'Why don't you put the tragedy behind you like Betony's trying to do? No wonder she won't come home.'

'I hear she has a man friend.'

Despite her anger, Cecily's eyes widened. 'Oh, who?'

'Daphne Harrington clammed up and said she didn't know his name. She was lying, of course.'

'Perhaps not. Betony was never forthcoming about her personal life. We didn't know about Simon until a week before she married him.'

Leaning back in her chair, Rose closed her eyes. 'I know she's lying. Didn't you see the picture in the Sunday paper? Betony attended the Harrington's party with a man. I predicted she was going to meet her soul mate, but I hadn't realized . . . ?' She pressed her fingers to her forehead and began to shake. 'I can't get a grip on him, Ces. He's strong, very strong. He's her past and her present. The future is cloudy, but there's defeat, terrible defeat. I'm afraid of the path that's been revealed.'

'Then abandon it, and stop meddling with people's lives,' Cecily shouted.

'Especially mine. I'm not going to let you spoil my relationship with Alex like you did with Fiorenzo.'

'Can I help it if Fiorenzo's brains were in his balls. You forgot to tell him they belonged exclusively to you.'

Picking up a jug of water, Cecily hurled the contents at her.

When her sister stomped off, Rose buried her wet face in her apron and began to laugh.

The piano was the centrepiece in the window display of a shop specializing in junk. It was an old style upright, its surface painted with gaudy spring flowers.

Noel stared at it, smiling. It was crazy, but just the sort of gift she'd love? Caution kicked in. He didn't know anything about pianos.

A young woman placed a vase of flowers on top and threw him a sunny smile. She reminded him of Betony. 'Does it play OK,' he called through the window.

'Dunno,' she called back. 'It's what we call a conversation piece. Come in, I'll find out.' She glanced towards the back of the shop. 'Hey, Jude! Is there a tune left in the old Joanna?'

A young, arty type strolled towards him with studied nonchalance. 'It's not meant to be played, man. It's a work of art, an abstraction of *Spring* from Vivaldi's *Four Seasons*. Call it a statement, if you like.'

'Cut out the crap. Either it plays, or it doesn't.'

'Don't ask me, dad. Try it.'

Noel felt like ripping the scrawny beard from his chin. 'If you want to sell it, *you* try it.'

'Don't get yourself into a froth, man. Life's too short,' Jude whined. He climbed into the window, lifted the lid and launched into a jazzy rendition of three blind mice. It sounded OK to Noel's uneducated ear.

'Don't let him rob you,' the girl whispered in his ear. 'Three fifty, tops.'

Noel knew a con when he heard one. 'How much?'

The man's eyes sharpened as he took in his suit and briefcase. 'Five hundred.'

'It needs tuning.'

'Four then, not a penny less.'

Noel took out his wallet. 'Two fifty.'

'You've gotta be joking, man. I spent a week painting that.' His glance went to the banknotes Noel was counting out. 'Three fifty, then.'

'Three hundred, including delivery. It's not far, just a block or two.'

The girl shrugged when Jude sighed and held out his hand. 'Done, but you'll have to give me a hand, and I'm not taking it up any stairs. I've gotta bad back.'

*

It took twenty minutes to trundle the piano through the streets to Betony's house. The matching stool, a spotted mushroom of fairy-tale magnificence, was balanced precariously on top. Jude did a disappearing act as soon as he saw the step.

Thumbing the doorbell, Noel hopped on to the stool when he heard Betony's footsteps, and mashed at the piano keys when she opened the door.

Her reaction was more than he'd hoped for. Her dumbfounded expression was replaced by a grimace and she stuck her fingers in her ears. He raised his hands in surrender and grinned at her like a dog after a pat on the head.

'It's wonderful.'

'His name's Vivaldi. As a work of art, it's an abstract statement, or so I'm reliably informed.'

'The only abstract statement about it is the lack of tone. Let's get him inside before the neighbours call the cops and have him arrested.'

The piano fit nicely into the alcove. Arms around each other's waists they admired its gaudy splendour. 'It's perfect.' She suddenly giggled. 'Vivaldi? You're totally mad, Noel.'

'Aren't you going to try it?'

Her eyes met his for a few moments. 'There could be a hundred things wrong with it,' she warned. 'It might need a new sound board.'

'Whatever that is, if Vivaldi needs one, he'll get one. Just tell me.'

Giving a nod she seated herself at the instrument, lifted the lid and ran her fingers over the keys. Scales came, one after the other. She went through them again, head cocked to one side, faster – then faster again.

Chords came next, her fingers nimble flying over the keys, her head still in a listening attitude. Finally, she played one of the pieces she'd played at the Harrington's party. Even to Noel's untrained ear it didn't sound as good. He suspected he'd bought a lemon.

Hands in her lap, she swivelled round to face him and smiled. 'Don't look so anxious. This isn't bad. It needs tuning, and some of the strings will have to be replaced. It will never sound like a baby grand, though.'

'Exactly as I suspected, Maestro.' He couldn't keep his face straight when she laughed. 'OK. Where do I find a piano tuner and stringer-upper?'

Her brow wrinkled for a moment. 'I used to know one a few years ago, he's probably retired by now though.' Picking up the phone book she flipped it open towards the back and ran her finger down the page.

Within minutes, she was on the phone and conversing in some technical language he didn't understand.

'That's nice of you, Peter. I appreciate it. Why don't you stay for dinner? Oh, another time then.' She turned to him, her eyes shining. 'He's coming over now. Thank you, Noel. Vivaldi's just perfect – I love him.'

He'd never seen her bubbling with so much excitement. He wished the piano tuner wasn't coming quite so soon. 'You come here,' he said. 'You owe me a kiss.'

'How long does it take to get here on the tube from St Pancras?' she murmured, when she came up for air a few seconds later.

Sylvia dressed for the evening in a long, purple, jersey-knit tunic. Around her neck she wore a silver ankh on a long chain. Expertly applied purple eyeshadow and liner made her eyes appear mysterious.

She felt mysterious as she fastened a silver headband around her forehead. Excitement churned in her stomach. Tonight, she was going into the unknown, becoming a part of Rose Monique's inner circle. Her mother would have a fit if she knew. But then, what she didn't know wouldn't bother her, and Rose had sworn her to secrecy.

'There will be an initiation for you to undergo, but I'm sure you'll take it in your stride. Understand me. People like us are different, Sylvia.'

She'd always sensed she was different, of course.

'Some prominent people are part of the inner circle. If word of what occurs passes your lips the consequences will be quite serious. I'll ring a bell when you're to come down to the drawing room.'

Nose wrinkling, she stared critically at the room she was in. As the guest of honour, she'd expected something grander. The wallpaper was peeling, the floorboards bare and the curtains stained and threadbare. Carved pineapples decorated the long ridged poles of the wooden head and footboards on the bed.

The bedding seemed clean enough, but the mattress was lumpy. A dirty, cracked mirror with bevelled edges hung over the bed.

From the window she could see over the village. It was dusk, lights were beginning to twinkle in the houses. She was quite taken with the village. It had an affluent air and the houses were in perfect taste with their surroundings.

Idly, she wondered if she could persuade Noel to move down this way. It would be convenient for herself and her mother, and he'd only have to commute for an extra hour or so.

The stars had begun to appear when the bell rang. She shivered, but more with excitement than fear.

Slowly, she descended to the drawing room. Rose came to meet her, her eyes glittering. She looked dreadful with her fat hips straining against her gaudy skirt. Her breasts bounced under a red satin blouse.

Several people sat about the room with glasses in their hands. All of them stared when Rose led her in.

'My protégée, Sylvia,' Rose said. 'I'll bring her round and introduce you all individually.' Feeling like a celebrity, Sylvia glowed when murmurs of welcome reached her ears. Goodness, was that—?

'Gregory,' Rose said.

'I do so enjoy your novels, Mister Lord,' Sylvia trilled.

'As I told you, we don't mention professions or last names,' Rose reminded her quietly.

She coloured. 'Of course. I'm so sorry.'

Gregory Lord graciously inclined his head and they passed on to the next two guests, a politician followed by an ageing television star.

Then came Cecily, who returned her smile with a sour look. Two men who resembled scholars smiled at her. The names and faces became a blur.

'Clive,' Rose murmured when they reached a man lounging in an armchair. His face seemed familiar.

He scrambled to his feet and bowed. 'Charming.'

He'd been in the social pages a couple of weeks earlier. Clive Harrington with his wife. She couldn't see his wife anywhere.

'You've met Alex, of course.'

Alex looked splendid in a black polo neck sweater and pants. His eyes were shadowed and his mouth stretched into a faint smile. 'We meet again.' Her nerves began to flutter when he pressed his lips to her palm. 'I'll look after her while you prepare, Rose.' He pulled her down beside him on the sofa. 'Ces, fetch her a drink. She needs to relax a bit.'

Cecily scowled as she walked towards the table. She came back with a glass of fizzing liquid and thrust it into her hand.

Candles were lit, the lights lowered.

'The master, everyone.'

Shivers ran up her spine when a man in a black cowled robe joined them. Everyone bowed their heads until he was seated, including herself.

Rose settled herself behind a small round table, folded her hands in her lap and began to meditate.

The conversation became muted, then stopped all together when she began to rock backwards and forwards.

Eyes wide, Sylvia sipped rapidly at her drink, breathless with anticipation. The wine had lost its fizz and tasted peculiar.

Alex took the empty glass from her fingers and set it on the table beside him. 'Relax,' he whispered. 'Hold my hand, empty your mind of everything and concentrate on Rose.'

In the dim light a pale blue glow seemed to emanate from Rose. Her breathing became long, rasping gasps. *'I'm lost . . . I can't find my mummy.'*

Sylvia's eyes suddenly widened and the pit of her stomach cramped. Prickles spread up her arms and she clutched Alex's hand.

'Tell me your name, dear,' Rose murmured.

'The room's full of smoke. I'm choking, I want my mummy!'

'Oh, God! Can't you help her?' the actress choked out.

'What's your mummy's name, dear?'

'My pyiamas are on fire . . . it hurts . . . mummy . . . mummy!'

The child's voice trailed off, leaving Sylvia feeling slightly nauseated. A strange, faraway feeling engulfed her. Her limbs became lethargic and she seemed to be very small. She made a tiny moaning sound and closed her eyes.

'Sylvia?' The voice was a sibilant whisper of sound in her ear. *'Open your eyes. It's time for your initiation.'*

Were her eyes closed? Making a great effort she opened them a chink and smiled when her father's face came into her vision. 'Daddy, I feel so tired.'

'Take her upstairs,' a woman said.

Trust her mother to spoil things, but then, she'd always been envious of daddy's love for her. She snuggled against his chest when he lifted her in his arms. 'You love me best, don't you daddy. I'm your little angel.'

'Of course you are, darling.'

They seemed to drift a long way up the stairs. She kept her arms wound around his neck as he lowered her to her bed. 'I didn't mean to do those disgusting things.'

'What disgusting things, Sylvia?'

'You know,' she dropped her voice to a whisper. 'Touching my temple.'

'Do you enjoy touching your temple, Sylvia?'

She gave a small ecstatic sigh. 'Nice little girls don't talk about such things. Mummy said I must keep the temple pure for the man I love.'

'You love your daddy, don't you?'

'More than anyone in the world.' Cool air touched her skin when he pulled the dress over her head. She sighed. She loved it when daddy undressed her and put her to bed.

'You love me more than you love mummy, don't you?'

She felt funny and shivery when he whispered. 'Of course I do. You're my angel.'

'And you love me more than that horrible woman who was in mummy's bed.'

'What horrible woman, Sylvia?'

Tears slid from under her eyelids. 'You were kissing her temple.'

'Daddy will prove he loves you best of all. You mustn't cry out, however naughty you think it is, otherwise mummy will be cross. All right?'

Dreamily, she nodded.

A few minutes later she groaned with ecstatic joy. She'd always wanted daddy to do that to her.

Sylvia woke with a throbbing headache. It was still dark, the remains of a candle burned fitfully in a sconce. There was a crampy feeling in the pit of her stomach, as if she was getting her periods. But of course, they weren't due for another two weeks.

Then she saw Alex's head on the pillow and it all came back to her. *Oh God! What had she done?*

When his heavy-lidded eyes flicked open to gaze at her, she automatically covered her breasts with her arms.

'Don't cover them, Sylvia, they're perfect.'

'What are you doing in my bed?'

A silly question, when she remembered every intimate moment. She grew shamefully moist at the way he'd made her feel. In fact, she felt *different* to how she usually felt with Noel. Sort of hot and pulsating, in a manner which made her feel entirely wicked.

Alex grinned and gently pulled her arms down. 'Relax, the initiation isn't over yet, so you might as well enjoy it.' His glance went past her. 'Hadn't she, Clive?'

A movement brought her eyes up to the mirror – to a reflection of Clive Harrington. 'You've got a sensational body, babe,' he grunted.

The candle gutted out, leaving a rancid stench of hot wax. A raw and sensuous anticipation filled her.

CHAPTER EIGHT

'What have you planned for today?' Clive asked Daphne the following week. She tucked a stray strand of hair behind her ears. 'I have a hair appointment followed by lunch.'

'With whom?'

It was annoying having to account for every minute of her time. 'Betony Nichols.'

He stared over *The Times* at her. 'Is that the woman who came to the party?'

'I'm surprised you remember her.'

'Don't try to be smart,' he snarled. 'Tell me about her.'

'What's to tell. We were at school together and she's a widow.' Be damned if she'd tell him anything else.

'Who was the tall chap she was with?'

So that's what he was after? 'Why do you want to know?'

The cutlery jiggled when he thumped the table.

'Just answer, damn it.'

'I wouldn't have a clue, and if I did—'

He fisted her robe and dragged her halfway across the table.

'What's his name, Daphne?'

'What the hell do you think you're doing? Let me go.'

'His name.'

She glared. 'I can't remember.'

He thrust her back in her chair and grinned. 'Find out, OK babe?'

Pushing back her chair she adjusted her robe. 'Do that to me again and I'll walk out on you.'

His glance flicked over her. 'You won't. You've got too much to lose.'

'Not as much as you. That satanic thing in the village wouldn't do much for your career if it got out?'

The paper was lowered. 'I don't know what you're talking about.'

'No? I often wondered where you went on Saturdays, so last weekend I followed you.'

'And what did you see?'

'A bunch of stupid morons hanging on Rose Gifford's every word. Can't you recognize a con artist when you see one?' He became still for a few moments, then a smile inched across his face. 'Your friend owns that house.'

'So what? She never goes there.'

'Even so, I doubt if she'd thank you for exposing what goes on there. Imagine, someone might think she's involved.'

'Leave Betony out of it, she's been through enough.'

He shook his head from side to side, mocking her. 'You won't tell anyone.'

'Don't be too sure.'

'Did you know your gardener boyfriend's part of it?'

'I don't give a gypsy's curse who belongs to it.' Though seeing Alex had given her quite a jolt.

Clive pulled their joint credit card out of his wallet. 'Didn't you mention some trinket you wanted from the jewellers the other day,' he said, placing it on the table. 'Be nice to Clive and we'll see what we can do.'

When Clive was inclined to be generous, he was very generous. She was little more than a whore to him, despite the ring on her finger.

'Tell me how it was with Alex when you lost your virginity. Did he hurt you?'

She gazed pityingly at him. 'You can't get it up without someone else in the picture, can you?'

He backhanded her across the face. 'You bitch,' he snarled and his fist tangled in her hair, pulling her head back until her neck almost creaked with the strain. 'Tell me,' he shouted.

'Go to hell.' She began to laugh despite her aching neck. It was the first time he'd hit her, and it would be the last.

'Frigid cow,' he shouted. 'You're not the only woman who can turn me on.'

'Then go and find another, because you don't turn me on at all.'

She cringed, waiting for another slap. It never came. Instead, she was suddenly released and his feet thudded over the floor. The door crashed violently back against the wall. Dragging a napkin from the table she held it against her nose to staunch the blood whilst she listened to his footsteps thump overhead. Finally, he stomped down the stairs and the front door banged. God help the people who work under him, she thought.

Tears slid down her cheeks as she hugged her shaking body with her arms. After a while, she stumbled to her feet and stared into the mirror. At least her face wasn't marked.

About to go upstairs, she saw the credit card, lying where he'd left it. Her hand closed over it and she began to laugh. He'd pay heavily for his bullying.

It was late afternoon. Noel was immersed in his work when Joyce slipped into the office with his coffee.

'Alison Green is here. I told her you were busy, but she insisted on waiting.'

He gazed blankly up at her. 'Is she a client?'

'She's the woman of Judge Throsby's letter.'

'Ah ... yes. What does she want?'

'She wouldn't say.' Joyce fiddled with a pen on his desk. 'Shall I tell her you can't see her?'

Joyce obviously knew something he didn't about the woman. He recalled Betony's remark about getting a missive from a dead lover. 'Why would you want to do that?'

She shrugged. 'Mrs Throsby didn't approve of her, you see. Neither does Sylvia.'

Which provided Noel with a good reason to see Alison Green first hand. 'Show her in.'

'Are you sure that's wise?'

He took a stab in the dark. 'Are you worried I'll discover she was Brian Throsby's lover?'

'You knew?'

'I do now. Why didn't you tell me?'

'It was only rumour,' she said uncomfortably. 'I doubt if there was anything in it. Dorothy wouldn't have allowed her to stay in the house if it was true. She did demand that Alison Green pay rent after the Judge died, though. Dorothy wasn't sure how much was fair, so she asked me to find out.'

Noel grinned. 'What else was rumoured about her?' Joyce looked so uncomfortable he let her off the hook. 'Never mind. Show her in. I can spare ten minutes.'

He'd expected someone older. Alison Green was about forty-five. Her brown hair was dragged into an elastic band at the nape of her neck. Clear brown eyes gazed warily from a face that was finely boned and attractive. The navy suit she wore had seen better days. Scuffed, flat shoes completed the dowdy statement.

Rising from his seat, he smiled. 'Would you like some coffee?'

'No thank you.' Perched on the edge of the chair, she clutched her large navy handbag against her. 'I suppose you want to know why I'm here?'

'I imagine it's about the letter from Judge Throsby.'

'Yes, that's right.' She cleared her throat. 'You sounded nice over the phone.'

'I am nice.' He smiled encouragingly at her again. She managed a stiff little smile in return.

'He . . . Brian, left me something.'

'If this is to do with property settlement, hadn't you better see a lawyer,' he said gently.

'I thought we might be able to sort it out without resorting to that. We're related, you see, by your marriage.'

He felt sorry for her if she intended to take Sylvia and Dorothy on over property, but failed to see how he could help.

She delved into her bag, coming out with the package. She slid it across the desk. Inside, were the deeds to a house, a letter and a couple of keys.

He slid the letter towards him with his finger. 'May I?'

She nodded.

My dearest Alison,

I learned today that I have an acute heart condition. As I promised to care for you and our son, I'll be transferring the house to your name – and ensuring the legacy with a new will, the draft of which is in the walnut box you gave me. It also contains the precious mementoes of the love we share.

I enclose the house deeds, for your safe-keeping. As soon as the will is notarized I'll bring you my diaries and the box, which I keep in my chambers. God knows, their contents are too precious for me to commit to anyone's hands but yours. I will also bring myself. (If you'll have me).

I'm about to walk away from my marriage, and on the doctor's advice, my career. I intend to inform Dorothy and Sylvia of this tonight.

I would like Sylvia to know she has a brother, though I doubt if she will welcome the fact. She's growing to be too much like her mother for me to truly love her, though I do my best not to show it.

Dearest Ali, will you have me? The doctor tells me the end will come suddenly, and without warning. You must be prepared for that. My intent is to devote the time I have left, however short, to making you happy and getting to know my son.

I know now, I should have followed my heart instead of staying in a relationship from which nothing could be salvaged . . . .

Noel put the letter aside when it went into more personal details. Sometimes life just wasn't fair. He took a gulp of his coffee before he dare look at her again.

'All this time you've been renting a house that would have been yours if he'd died a few days later. You should take this to a lawyer.'

'Dorothy Throsby will fight it, won't she?'

'I should imagine so, but then again she might not want it to get out. I'd say you had a very good case.'

Alison's fingers twined painfully around each other. 'I'm not really bothered about anything but the box and the diaries. The box belonged to my grandmother. I gave it to Brian for his birthday.' She retreated into herself for a few moments, then whispered, 'He said he wrote a poem every day for me in the diaries. I'd really like to read them.'

'They're in my study.' His fingers touched lightly against the keys. 'I could bring them to the office tomorrow. Are you staying in town?'

Her smile was rueful. 'Do I look as though I can afford a hotel?'

'I have a flat you could use,' he suggested. 'It's small, but the bed is comfortable. It's not too far to walk.' He scribbled down the address and passed it to her with the key.

'Thank you so much, Mr Dearborn. I'm sorry to put you to so much trouble.'

'It's no trouble.' Until Sylvia found out, then there would be hell to pay. 'You really should consider consulting a lawyer about the house.' He smiled reassuringly at her. 'If you can prove your son is blood related, it will serve to strengthen your claim. There's such a thing as DNA testing.'

Heading home, he hoped Alison would push for it, for it had been obvious that Brian Throsby had loved Alison Green.

Something about Sylvia was different tonight, he thought, when she slid her arms around his neck and kissed him on the mouth.

There was something about her eyes, too. The faint smudges of darkness underneath was new. Whatever it was, he'd be expected to notice, and comment on it.

'New eye make-up?'

'What are you talking about?'

'Your eyes look different.'

'Don't be ridiculous.' Her glance shifted to the kitchen. 'I'll go and finish cooking the dinner.'

He went into the ritual as she walked away. 'How was your weekend?'

'Fine, and yours?'

His weekend had been perfect, wonderful and exciting! He gave his usual noncommittal grunt. 'So, so.'

'Good,' she said.

Going into the study he packed the diaries and the walnut box into a sports bag and placed it just inside the door. The box was an antique tea caddy, the lock designed to prevent servants stealing what was once an expensive luxury. It was a pretty thing.

He was taking the coward's way out. Unless Sylvia noticed they were missing he didn't intend to inform her about Alison until later in the week. By that time, the woman would have decided what to do.

After dinner, Sylvia surprised him by joining him on the couch. 'I'd like to talk to you, Noel.'

Just as the programme he'd wanted to see was about to start. 'Can't it wait? I want to watch the documentary about Michelangelo.'

She took the remote from his lap and aimed it at the set. 'Since when have you been interested in art?'

'It's never too late to learn.'

'Our marriage is more important.'

His heart gave a giant leap. *Please God, let her say she wants to end it.*

Instead, she kissed him on the lips again, something she hadn't done in years. It took every effort not to recoil. Whatever was she about? She was making him nervous. He was relieved when the door bell rang. He pushed her away and scrambled to his feet.

'Anne, Jeff, it's great to see you. Come in, come in.'

Sylvia looked put out. 'I didn't know you were coming round.'

'I promised Jeff I'd go through some figures with him this evening.'

'You could have told me. I might have had other plans.'

The atmosphere became tense. He gave Sylvia a sharp glance. 'Have you other plans?'

'No, as it happens.' The smile she gave Anne was totally false. 'I'm sorry, I didn't mean to sound unwelcoming. I've had a busy weekend, and I'm tired.'

Anne turned towards the door, obviously miffed. 'I can always wait in the car. Jeff's business won't take long.'

'Oh, my goodness, you'll do no such thing.' Sylvia took her arm. 'Why didn't you answer my phone messages? I've got heaps to tell you. I've started my own little business.'

For a moment it appeared as though Anne was going to refuse, then curiosity came into her eyes. She shrugged and followed after her.

'What's going on between those two,' he said, handing Jeff a whisky and soda.

'Damned if I know. You know what women are like.' He grinned comfortably when Sylvia trilled with laughter. 'See, what did I tell you?'

90

*

'Rose Monique thinks you're a sensitive?' Anne said, her eyes widening. 'What fun. Tell me, what goes on?'

'You mustn't breathe a word of this to anyone, Anne, not even Jeff. I don't want Noel to know yet. He wouldn't understand.'

'Will you give me a tarot reading when you've learned how?'

'Of course. I'm already learning, and I'll need someone to practise on.'

'What about now?'

'I'm not ready yet. Rose said I need to meditate for half an hour every day. Then the cards need to be handled and spoken to so they can familiarize themselves with me as a sensitive. Once I've learned the card layouts and symbol interpretations, she'll allow me to give some readings under her supervision.'

'The sorcerer's apprentice,' Anne said with a laugh. 'I'm surprised at you. Never in my wildest dreams would I imagine you had anything so mysterious inside you waiting to escape.'

Was there just a teeniest bit of irony in Anne's voice? Sylvia decided it was envy. 'Actually, it's a bit scary. There's more to being a sensitive than just reading tarot cards.'

Eyes wide, Anne leaned forward. 'Tell me.'

Sylvia bit her lip. If only she could. She'd felt so wicked and alive. Excitement quivered through her.

They hadn't been gentle like Noel. They'd made her feel powerless to control the cravings Alex had created in her. Her body still craved, but there was only Noel to satisfy her tonight. She hoped the Sullivans wouldn't stay too long.

'Sorry, I can't tell you, Anne. It's a secret that sensitives share. We have an awareness of each other that's sacred and remote from the understanding of ordinary people such as yourself.'

Anne had never heard such twaddle in her life. Eventually, Sylvia would tell her everything – she always did. She placed her hand over Sylvia's and smiled. 'If you need anyone to talk to at any time, you know where I live.'

Later, when Anne and Jeff had gone, Sylvia prepared herself carefully for bed. When Noel slid in beside her she left the light on, then sighed and snuggled her naked body against his back. 'It's been a long time since we've made love,' she whispered against his ear.

Surprised, and a little alarmed, he trotted out the excuse she usually made. 'I'm tired.' Her hand slid around his body and closed around him. Gently she caressed its length and the traitor responded. *Shit!* What had come over her?

'Give me orgasms,' she said in her best dolly voice.

She must have been reading erotic magazines, or something. It was so out of character he lost his erection. He tried not to laugh as he propped himself up on his elbow. 'I didn't think you knew the meaning of the word. What the hell's happened to you?'

'I've become what you've always wanted.' She didn't smile, just threw back the covers and looked coyly up at him. 'You can look at me if you like.' Her hip bones jutted out, her ribs were bold stripes beneath her skin. He couldn't remember her being this skinny.

Eyes glazing over she slid her fingers to her bush. 'This will make you want me, Noel.'

'You look dreadful, are you eating properly?' he said inanely.

'Go to hell,' she spat. 'I don't need you, anyway.'

'My pleasure.' He slid from the marital bed and headed for the spare room. He was still puzzling over her strange behaviour when she cried out a name.

It wasn't his.

They spent the remainder of the week avoiding each other. Both of them were polite when they were forced to speak until Sylvia noticed the box and diaries were gone.

'They belong to Alison Green,' he told her. 'Your father wanted her to have them.'

'*Alison Green!*' she shrieked. 'How could you, Noel? If daddy wanted her to have them he would have said so in his will. That box was an antique.'

'It was in his letter. Besides which, the box originally belonged to her grand-mother.'

'I told you not to encourage that woman.' Her face puckered into fury. 'She's lying, I demand you get them back.'

He put down the coffee he'd been drinking and rose to his feet. 'Demand all you like. I'm sick of being told what to do. I read the letter your father wrote the day he died. He intended to leave your mother to go and live with her.'

'Liar!'

The slap to his face jerked his head back with shock. He fought to contain his anger as he fingered the burning flesh. She packed a mean punch.

Her face drained of colour. 'Oh God, I didn't mean it, Noel.'

His face tightened. 'There's something else you should know before I leave. You have a half-brother. He's a year younger than you.'

Her eyes became enormous. She pressed her fist to her mouth and gave a strangled cry. Staggering to the couch, she buried her face into the cushions and began to sob.

Pity flickered through him when he was packing his suitcases. When he came down, he poured her a brandy and waited until she'd calmed herself. 'I'll be at the flat. I'll call you next week, OK? We'll try and sort this mess out.'

Her head jerked up and down a couple of times. 'If you leave, don't bother coming back.'

He nodded. Just as he reached the door, she hissed, 'And don't take the car. It's registered in my name and I need it for the weekend.'

Hoping he hadn't missed the last train, he dropped the keys on the hall table.

'Noel,' she screamed out just before he closed the door, 'don't you dare walk out on me.' The hedge needs trimming, he thought almost irrationally as he strode rapidly towards freedom.

Betony was almost asleep when the phone rang. She smiled and grabbed up the receiver.

'Noel?'

A man cleared his throat. 'Actually, it's Clive Harrington. I'm sorry to ring so late. Is Daphne with you?'

'I'm afraid not.'

'I thought she was lunching with you today.'

'I had to cancel. I had a doctor's appointment at the last minute. We've scheduled lunch for tomorrow, instead.'

'Ah, I see.' There was a moment's silence then he said smoothly, 'That's good. I found something at the party. I think it belongs to that chap you came with.'

'Noel Dearborn.'

'Was that his name? I'll give it to Daphne to bring with her.'

'Fine. What exactly is it?' Noel hadn't mentioned losing anything.

'A gold tie pin.'

'Noel was wearing a bow tie.'

'Was he? Oh, wait a minute, so he was. I'm so sorry to have disturbed you, Betony.'

'You didn't. I hope you soon find Daphne.'

He chuckled. 'She probably met some friends and went to a nightclub. The trouble with having a younger wife is that an old man like me can't keep up with her.'

'I wouldn't say you were *that* old.' Glancing at the clock, she yawned when he chuckled again. 'Goodnight, Clive.'

It was raining outside. She pressed her face against the cool, blurred glass of the window and stared out at the street-light. What was Noel doing now? Was he asleep, or making love to his wife? Jealousy shot through her and she wondered at it. Was she falling in love with him? Sometimes, she thought so. At other times, when Ben intruded, she knew it was impossible to even consider loving Noel. Ben's ghost would always come between them.

Noel had promised her nothing. Yet they were so good together, and not only in bed. The more she saw of him the more she liked him. Despite his quiet nature and gentleness, there was strength at his core, and honesty in his dealings.

His partner, Daniel Jacobs, thought highly of him. A worried frown furrowed her brow. Daniel had told her she couldn't afford to maintain Little Abbot indefinitely. He'd advised her to sell it whilst it was still in reasonable condition, and *before* it began to eat into her capital.

She would have sold it long ago if it hadn't been for her sisters. Their whole life revolved around it.

She must think about it for a while.

A figure appeared around the corner. 'Noel,' she breathed, recognizing his long, loping strides. Before he had time to knock at the door she pulled it open, dragged him inside and hugged him close.

'I was just thinking about you.'

'I'm tired and wet,' he said. 'It was crazy to walk all the way from the flat at this time of night, but I *had* to see you.'

Her heart gave a sudden, wild leap in her chest when she saw the expression on his face. 'What's the matter, you look exhausted?'

His funny, crooked smile was endearing. 'I've left my wife . . . I think.'

Thank God! Thank God! Tenderly, she kissed him. 'Go and dry off and get into bed. I'll bring you some warm milk.'

He was asleep when she went in, his hair damp against the pillow. She slipped in beside him, and being careful not to wake him, cuddled herself against his back.

CHAPTER NINE

'I had absolutely no right to barge in on you like I did last night. Can you forgive me?'

Sweet, lovable Noel. He must have let himself out early, because it was only just past eight now. A smile touched her lips. 'Why didn't you stay for breakfast?'

'I needed to unpack my suitcases and iron a shirt. Am I still welcome this weekend?'

His ego was badly bruised. 'Of course you are,' she growled, then trod carefully into the unknown territory. 'Have you really left your wife?'

He sighed. 'I rather think I have.'

'Is it because . . . did Sylvia find out?'

'The problem is completely unrelated to us. It's something that's been building up. I don't want you to apportion any blame to yourself.'

'Apportion?' She chuckled. 'That's an accountant's word if ever I heard one.'

'I guess it is.'

He sounded so strained, her heart reached out to him. 'Sorry, I didn't mean to tease you. You must feel terrible. If you need a shoulder to cry on you know where I am.'

'My life's liable to be messy for a while and I don't want our weekends together spoiled by personal drama. You . . . they've come to mean so much.'

He sounded as unsure of what he felt as she did. What had she started with her need for revenge? How many lives would be ruined and could their relationship survive in an atmosphere of guilt?

'Noel, don't make the mistake of shutting people out. It's too hard to pick up the pieces afterwards. Friends like to be leaned on at times.'

His voice warmed. 'Tell me if I become a bore.'

'You're a bore for going off without kissing me goodbye.'

A chuckle curled into her ear. 'Survival tactics. I wouldn't have been able to tear myself away if I had.'

'Then take this one to work with you.' She sent a kiss down the line before she hung up.

Noel's day took a turn for the worse when Alison Green rang. She'd been given four weeks notice to quit the house by Dorothy Throsby.

Sylvia's revenge had been swift. He raked his fingers through his hair, pondering the problem. 'Didn't Brian say he'd made a new will?'

'It wasn't notarized. I wondered if you'd talk to Mrs Throsby, or perhaps ask your wife to.'

'It would do more harm than good now. We've just separated.'

'Oh, I'm so sorry.'

'Thanks,' he grunted, accepting the standard reply for what it was. 'The only advice I can give you is to take any pertinent documents you have to a lawyer. It shouldn't cost much for advice, but I think they'll need an eviction order to get you out.'

He would need a lawyer himself if he was going to get out of his marriage with his business intact. Sylvia would go for the jugular once she'd recovered from her shock.

There was no question of reconciliation. His marriage had been over long before the showdown. He'd just been too lazy to do anything about it.

The enormous sense of freedom he experienced buoyed his confidence. Bites of guilt eroded it. The blow to Sylvia's self-esteem would be considerable. He shook his head to clear it when Joyce brought his first client through. The busy day he had lined up would distract his mind from the radical step he'd taken.

It was half past four when he called Joyce and Daniel into his office. Briefly, he informed them his marriage was over. 'I'll try not to let it disrupt the running of the business. I just thought I'd let you both know what was going on before I consult a lawyer.'

'I have a relative who specializes in divorce,' Daniel said with a grin. 'Considering my share of the business could be in jeopardy, I might be able to get you a discount.'

Noel grimaced.

'You can count on my loyalty,' Joyce said, promptly bursting into tears 'You poor, poor man.'

An understatement, since he actually felt quite liberated. He placated her as best he could, but when Daniel grinned at him over her shoulder and offered to drive her home, he accepted gratefully on her behalf.

Dying to see Betony, he could almost taste her on his tongue. Changing into the casual gear he'd brought with him, like a snake discarding its skin, he dropped his suit off at the cleaners on his way. His heart sank when he saw the car parked outside Betony's house. He hoped she didn't have a guest.

Enveloped in a cloud of breathless excitement when she slid into his arms, slowly, he inhaled her fragrance. Nothing could be as good as this. Her mouth sought his, all giving and loving. Or this!

She pulled away first, her eyes scrutinizing his face. 'You look tense. Have you had a bad day?'

'Seeing you has made up for it.'

Her smile became a tender curve. 'I thought you might need cheering up so I've booked a room in a Cotswolds pub for the weekend.'

'You're a gem.'

'The car's parked outside and ready to go when we are.'

Relief filled him. 'I didn't know you had a car.'

'It's kept in a garage round the corner but I don't drive it very often.' She moved from his arms towards the fridge. 'I thought you might like to eat before we leave. I'll make us a chicken salad while you have a good soak in the bath.'

A wonderful idea, he realized as he reclined up to his neck in bubbles. His eyes drifted shut as he measured the tension leaching from his body in heartbeats.

A few minutes later her hand drifted across his face. Without opening his eyes he brought it to his lips, sliding his tongue along its contours. It tasted of spring onions.

'Make some room for me,' she whispered.

He opened his eyes a chink, then opened them wider and smiled. Everything in him sprang to attention as he scrambled to oblige. Seconds later she was opposite him, her long legs draped over his, a teasing smile playing around her mouth.

Grinning, he grasped her ankles and slowly slid her up over his soapy thighs. 'Impossible,' she said.

'You think so?' It was a challenge he couldn't ignore, the mechanics of which were guided by intuition rather than logic.

Later, the chicken salad was good too.

They were still laughing about the soap bubble overflow when he guided the car on to the motorway.

A couple of hours later his eyes narrowed in on her when mine host of the thatched country pub greeted him as Mr Smith. Whilst she innocently smiled at him, he duly signed them in as such.

The weekend was perfect. The sun blazed down from a June sky as they explored the twisting lanes and scaled the hills. Their room had a sloping roof, and a small window under the eaves, allowing a distant view of the Severn River winding through a verdant valley towards Wales.

The sun shone down on them with benevolence, they gorged themselves on country cooking and made love in a bed built for togetherness. It was a good way to say goodbye to his marriage, Noel thought.

When they returned to London, Big Ben was chiming midnight.

His glance tangled with hers. 'I'm loath to leave you.'

'Stay the night.'

'My business suits are at the flat.'

Her arm stole around his neck. 'What's wrong with what you're wearing? You look dangerously sexy in leather.'

He gazed at his dark pants and casual jacket and grinned self-consciously. 'Nothing, I guess.' He didn't put up any resistance when she pulled him inside.

He hurried into the office an hour late the next morning, thankful his appointments were scheduled for later in the day.

Joyce intercepted his flight towards his office. 'Mrs Dearborn is waiting in your office.'

His heart sank into his shoes. 'How long has she been there?'

'Fifteen minutes. I've given her coffee.'

'Thanks Joyce. Was she difficult?'

A smile touched her mouth. 'She's always difficult.'

He gently squeezed her hand. 'You don't have to take her rudeness, you know.'

'I didn't this time. She seemed taken aback.'

He grinned as he headed towards the office. With a bit of luck, Sylvia would have been struck dumb by it.

Not a chance. 'Where have you been all weekend?' she hissed. 'I've tried to reach you several times.' Her glance wandered over his casual attire and her mouth pursed. Tense lines stitched at the corners, like inverted commas. Her eyes and skin were dull, despite the cosmetics.

If she mentions daddy I'll strangle her!

'There was an odd-looking old man loitering in the foyer when I came in. He was muttering to himself.'

'That would have been Mister Levi. He owns a chain of jewellery stores.' He glanced pointedly at his watch. 'I have a client due. What did you want to see me about?'

'I'd like us to sell the house in Essex and move to Dorset. It will be closer to my mother and easier for me to get to my business.'

He leaned back in his chair and stared steadily at her, cursing the heartbeat pounding alarmingly against his rib cage. It was obvious she hadn't taken him seriously when he'd walked out. What had been easy in the heat of the moment, now seemed a momentous task. He hoped she wouldn't make too much of a scene.

'The house in Essex will have to be sold anyway. It's early days, but I suggest we wait until our lawyers reach agreement on the divorce settlement.'

'Divorce? What, over that silly tiff we had?' Her attempt at laughter trailed into uncertainty. 'You *are* joking? My mother assured me there's nothing in that Alison Green business. The woman's just trying to stir up trouble.'

'I'm not joking, Sylvia. Alison Green has nothing to do with it. Our marriage has been a farce for years and I want out.'

'I see.' She stood up, her eyes glittering like ice. 'Perhaps it would be for the best. You never did quite measure up. Lord knows, I did my best to change you into something better. My mother warned me that a man with your background would find it hard to adapt to our standards.'

Pretentious cow! He almost felt sorry for her. 'Your mother was right, for once. Let me know the name of your lawyer.'

'You can be sure that I will.' Her mouth was stretched in a tight smile, her eyes boiled with fury. 'In fact, I intend to ruin you. I'll get the best legal representative available. Daddy had contacts.'

'Fuck daddy,' he said pleasantly, then laughed after the door slammed shut behind her. His laughter ceased when an odd thought popped into his mind. Hadn't she always wanted to?

A few minutes later Joyce hurried in with a cup of coffee. 'Is everything all right, Mister Dearborn?'

'Life is definitely looking up. Ask Daniel to give me a buzz when he's got a minute, and Joyce,' he said to her departing back, 'we've worked together a long time. Isn't it time you called me Noel?'

She turned, a smile lighting her face. 'It will be a pleasure, Mr . . . uh . . . Noel.'

The next morning, Daniel introduced him to a thin man of pale complexion. 'My cousin, Sam Gilbert,' he murmured. 'I'll make myself scarce.'

Sam was middle-aged, and elegantly scruffy. Noel was subject to an intent gaze when they shook hands. Sam then subsided with a grunt into a chair. An over-stuffed briefcase was thumped on to the desk, forms were shuffled out. 'Right, fill these in. I want to know what you're worth, right down to the door knocker.'

Noel grinned. 'Sylvia's welcome to the door knocker.'

A dark look shafted his way. 'Let's not make any concessions at this stage. Is there a third party involved?'

'A third party?' he said warily. He didn't want Betony drawn into this.

Sam leaned back in his chair and smiled for the first time. 'I need to know everything, whether it be fact or suspicion. That way, we won't be caught unawares. I'll spell it out for you in simple terms. 'Do you, or does your wife, have a lover?'

Sylvia had called out a name in the throes of her self-induced passion. His eyes narrowed and he suffered a twinge of uneasiness. It would be hypocritical to lay the blame on her. 'Could be. Look, can't we just have an amicable divorce and split things down the middle?'

Sam's expression hovered on the edge of derision. 'By all means, if you think your wife will be agreeable. In my experience, women are disinclined to be accommodating where property or other women are concerned.'

Sylvia agreeable? He shrugged. 'She won't be agreeable. Now, what do you need to know?'

'We'll get into the more personal aspects of your life later. Let's start with finance. You seem to understand that better, mmm?'

Noel grinned. 'You're a sarcastic sod.'

Sam's eyes flickered in acknowledgement. 'If you want a bedside manner you pay more for it. Personally, I believe in cutting through the crap.'

'It seems to be a family trait.'

Sam nodded. 'Daniel likes you too. Now, let's get down to business. Do you have joint personal accounts and credit cards? If so, I suggest you contact your bank manager straight away and—'

Noel reached for the telephone before Sam finished speaking. He just hoped Sylvia hadn't got there before him.

*

In Abbotsford, Fiona Bunnings was astride her chestnut mare, cantering along the lane bordering the Harringtons' property.

When Clive's car overtook her she slowed her mount to a walk, edging along the high, ivy-covered wall. A third of the way along, the wall had crumbled. Concealed by the spreading branches of a copper beech tree, she parted the branches of a shrub on the other side.

Clive was heading rapidly towards the house. She smiled and nodded. Yesterday, hidden at the same spot, she'd watched the furniture removal men carry their goods out.

Daphne Harrington had left her husband. Fiona had intercepted her at the gate, and she'd apologized for leaving the committee so abruptly. 'Clive hit me,' Daphne had confessed.

Shocked to the core by such brutality, Fiona had listened avidly when Daphne had hinted at her husband's involvement in witchcraft at Little Abbot. She wasn't surprised, and had in fact suspected the Gifford sisters were up to no good, for some time.

Eager for more, she'd invited Daphne to take morning coffee with her before she left. Daphne hadn't arrived. The only car that had left the village was Cecily Gifford's. The dreadful witch, Rose, had been in the passenger seat. Fiona couldn't couldn't work out how she'd missed Daphne.

'That fucking bitch! I'll kill her when I catch up with her!'

She tittered nervously when Clive stormed from the house, his face mottled with rage. The door slammed shut, the car started with a roar and squealed into the lane, scattering mud.

'The stupid little man,' she muttered, her hands gentling her skittish mount. Ducking under the branches, she reached the lane in time to see the car heading towards Little Abbot. Her eyes began to gleam. Setting the mare in motion she began to canter after the car. If nothing else, she might catch a glimpse of Cecily Gifford with the gardener.

Cecily was pulling the last few weeds from a flower bed when the car screeched to a halt.

Her face darkened when gravel flew in all directions. Alex would have to rake it all over again before the weekend opening.

Alex was painting the conservatory for Sylvia. Sick of being treated like a commodity, she'd refused him the night before. By now he'd be as randy as a stallion. She threw the fork into the wheelbarrow and strolled towards the conservatory.

He'd finished painting. Everything gleamed white. It was an energy-draining colour, but Sylvia wouldn't be told. Alex was carrying in some palms in pots, his muscular arms sweat-licked.

Stacked against the wall were white plastic tables and chairs. A counter had been set up. Underneath, towers of china were stacked. Next to the stacks were chintzy flowered tablecloths and crystal bud vases, just the right size for the customers to slip into their pockets. If Sylvia thought she'd be provided with flowers from the garden, she should think again.

Against one wall was a large glass cabinet. Cecily had intended to display aromatic oils and pot-pourri for sale, but Rose had said Sylvia needed it for her cakes and pastries. She smiled happily to herself. She'd heard the villagers were going to cash in on the garden opening with their own tea shop in the village, and she'd come up with a better idea for her own interests. She'd use the small garden pavilion for her shop. The further she was from Sylvia, the better she'd like it. She woman's bad vibes disturbed her.

'Still running after her like a lackey, Alex? I'll have to ask her to contribute towards your wages.' She lifted her hair from the nape of her neck, her breasts straining against her bodice as she let it run through her fingers.

He stared at her for the few seconds it took her to open the top buttons on her dress. His eyes were unfathomable as he crooked his finger, strolled past her and headed towards the lime grove.

A few moments later, she followed him into the cottage he occupied.

15th Day of March 1798

> *This month has passed slowly. I have been ill with fever and none but a maid has been near me for fear of infection.*
>
> *Sebastian has boarded up my chamber windows so I know not whether it be night or day. I will not yield to his dark power, yet it is hard to resist, for I am weak, and my faith in God has almost deserted me.*
>
> *My breasts have emptied of the milk that once sustained my dead infant. I feel her sweet breath against my face, hear her tortured cries of pain with every beat of my heart, but can never again experience the ease and joy of her sweet, suckling mouth.*
>
> *I despair. There is no room for the Lord in my heart amongst such suffering.*

'Poor Isabella,' Rose murmured, laying down the journal when the door bell rang. She sighed. 'Who the hell's that? I'm not expecting anyone.'

'I've no idea where Daphne is,' she said a few moments later to Clive. 'Does it matter?'

Clive was practically jumping up and down with rage. 'Of course it matters. She's run my credit card to the limit, stolen half the cash from our bank account and cleared the house of furniture.'

'How very enterprising of her.' Rose almost laughed. 'You shouldn't have slapped her around, Clive.'

His face became ugly with suspicion. 'How did you know that? You've seen her, haven't you?'

'The whole damned village knows. You can be so stupid, sometimes. I rather liked your wife. She has guts.'

He subsided into a chair, looking crushed. 'If you know where she is, tell me. I want her back.'

'I don't know, but I might be able to get a reading of your future together in the crystal when you calm down. Did you find out who Betony was seeing?'

The look Clive gave her was triumphant. 'Would you believe it's Sylvia's husband. Noel Dearborn.'

Shocked to the core, Rose pressed a hand against her breast. 'How could she, after what he did to her?'

'Some women like punishment, after all, you were right about Sylvia.'

Her mind ticked over. How could she use this unexpected turn of events? Suddenly, it began to make sense. Power filled her and her eyes began to glitter. Everything was coming together in ways she'd never predicted.

Clive watched her eyes draw evil to them and said, 'I wonder if Sylvia knows what her husband is up to.' A smile crept across his face. Overcoming Sylvia's inhibitions had been a real turn on. Rose had read her well.

It was the first time he'd been unfaithful to Daphne and he felt guilty about it. Everything inside him crumbled. Nobody had walked out on him before, it was usually the other way around. He shouldn't have hit her. He'd buy her everything she could ever want if she'd come back.

'Help me find her, Rose,' he said brokenly. 'If you do, I'll attend the ritual when it's arranged.'

Rose stared at him. Clive was a loathsome, pathetic creature – all men were. But she needed him to fulfil Isabella's destiny. Fate had delivered the means into her hands, as she'd predicted, and the master had promised to carry out the ritual.

She smiled as her hands reached out for the crystal ball. Clive was a great believer in mumbo-jumbo.

*

'Good God! What's Daphne Harrington doing here?'

Seething, Cecily crossed to Alex's bed and stared at the sleeping woman. 'Has she been here all night?'

'I found her car in the woods early this morning. She'd wandered off and fallen down the embankment. There was a half-empty whisky bottle in her car, and these pills. I'm worried. She hasn't come round yet.'

'They're sleeping pills. She's only swallowed one by the looks of it. Relax, Alex, she's not the suicidal type. Kneeling by the bed, Cecily felt for Daphne's pulse, then peeled back an eyelid. A red-veined eye stared back at her. Daphne groaned a protest.

Cecily's mouth pursed. 'She's still drunk. Give her a cold bath and some coffee, then send her home.'

'Help me with her, Ces.'

'Why should I? She's your problem.'

'There's blood on her clothes.'

'Not enough to worry about.'

When he undid the buttons on Daphne's blouse a pair of pointed breasts slung in black lace were released. He grinned. 'Bugger off then. I'm sure I can manage without you.'

Elbowing him aside, she snapped, 'Go and run the bath.'

She dragged off Daphne's clothes, then gazed at her in shock. She shouldn't have been so rough. The woman's body was covered in scratches. Her eyes softened. 'Make that a warm bath, Alex, then fetch my bag from the kitchen. Don't let Rose see you.'

Alex sucked in a breath when he saw the injuries. 'Poor Daphne.'

'It's nothing much, just scratches. But they must be cleaned.' She gently pulled the sheet over Daphne's body and gazed at him. 'How long have you known her?'

Alex shrugged. 'She attended the school where I was employed. It was a long time ago.'

'Did you screw her?'

His eyes were gentle against hers. 'Would it worry you if I had, Ces?'

She thought about it for a moment said briefly, 'I'm not expecting a lifelong commitment from you. One of these days you'll move on.'

He ran a finger down her nose. 'You're all right, Ces. Come on, I'll give you a hand to get her into the bath.'

Daphne muttered an obscenity when she was lowered into the water, but she didn't wake. Alex's arm supported her head whilst Cecily bathed her. Alex stayed long enough to help Daphne back to bed. 'My head feels like chilli beans,' Daphne muttered, waking up momentarily when Cecily gently towelled her dry.

'It serves you right. You're old enough to know that pills and alcohol don't mix.'

'Keerist! Why don't you witches come up with something useful, like a cure for a hangover,' she said, and went back to sleep.

Cecily laughed.

Alex didn't return for twenty minutes. 'What took you so long?'

Dumping her bag on the table, he grinned. 'Harrington's up at the house. He's trying to find her. Rose is about to give him a crystal reading.'

'Did you tell them she was here?'

He shook his head and gazed down at Daphne, lying on her stomach under a sheet, snoring. 'I figured I'd let her recover first, so she's got some say in the matter.'

She nodded as she blended oils of lavender, camomile and patchouli together. Alex stood at her shoulder when she uncovered Daphne's perfect body. Gently, she massaged the mixture into the bruises and scratches on her buttocks and back. Her skin felt like silk.

After a while his arms circled her. She bent slightly to turn Daphne over and repeat the process. Finally, her fingers travelled over Daphne's face and she cupped her hands over her nose, allowing the fragrance to do it's work. Flipping the sheet over her, she turned to face Alex.

'You're the salt of the earth, Ces. I'll always love you.' He took her face in his hands and kissed her with hungry intensity.

He would love her as long as he needed her. He would love her with the image of Daphne in his mind. It would make him potent, and she'd pray to the Earth Goddess for a child to fill her arms before it was too late.

Daphne felt like hell when she woke.

She was in a strange room with damp patches on the ceiling. Her head spun when she sat up, but her body felt relaxed. Fragrance surrounded her.

Someone had undressed her. Her clothes were folded neatly on a chair in the corner of the room. She was relieved to find herself alone in the bed.

Grabbing a towelling robe from a hook on the wall, she investigated the other side of a door, finding a bathroom to fulfil the pressing need in her.

Her glance ran over an old-fashioned lavatory with a cistern and chain, and a bath flaking rust. A pack of skinny-legged spiders jostled for position on the ceiling.

Afterwards, her stomach hollowed with hunger, she made her way through to the other room, following her nose to the smell of food.

The man standing at the cooker had his back to her, but she'd have known him anywhere. 'How did I get here, Alex?'

'I found you in the woods. You'd fallen over an embankment.' Alex turned, smiling at her. 'Hungry?'

His face hadn't changed, just matured. His body had become man-size. 'I'm ravenous.'

'There's tea in the pot and aspirin on the shelf. Help yourself.'

He set the table whilst she nursed her cup of tea and headache.

'Clive's looking for you,' he said, placing a plate of bacon, eggs and baked beans in front of her.

'Sod Clive. I'm through with him.'

He sliced a hunk of bread from a loaf, chuckling as he handed it to her. 'I thought you'd say that.'

They ate in silence for a while, then her eyes came up to his in curiosity. 'How did you end up here, Alex?'

'It's as good a place as any.'

She guessed he was up to his arse in the witchcraft thing with Clive. The Alex she'd known had flirted with danger. He'd been in tune with nature, though, especially human nature. She grinned at him. 'Did you run out of schoolgirls?'

His deep, throaty laugh was exactly how she remembered. 'Did you run out of gardeners?'

'One ran out on me and left me to pay the bill.'

'How much was it? I'll reimburse you.'

'My father paid it after he'd frothed at the mouth a bit.'

'Did you get into too much trouble?'

As if he cared. Her chuckle made him grin. 'As I recall, it was worth it.'

'We must do it again, sometime,' he said, his casual voice at odds with his intimate smile.

'Why?'

His eyes narrowed in on her. 'Because you have a great body, and you give me a hard-on.'

A sensual note wafted up from the depths of the robe she was wearing. She ignored it. Alex would complicate her life even further. She hadn't finished with Clive, yet.

'As I recall, everything wearing skirts gave you a hard-on. Did you bathe me?'

'Cecily did.' His grin was disturbing. 'She anointed you with oil afterwards. She's left some to use on your bruises later.'

Daphne mopped up the rest of her beans with her bread. 'I suppose you watched.'

He nodded, his eyes hooding over. 'Uhuh.'

She dissolved into laughter as she gazed at him. 'You haven't changed, Alex.'

'Have you?'

Rising, she walked towards the bedroom to dress. 'I don't intend to give you the chance to find out.'

CHAPTER TEN

When Alison received a letter demanding Brian Throsby's effects be returned, she rang Noel.

He was polite, but firm. He'd recommend her to the lawyer handling his divorce, but otherwise couldn't advise her. He said he'd be willing to verify the contents of the letter, should the need arise.

Her interview with Sam Gilbert intimidated her to start with. His casual and slightly outrageous manner soon thawed her, and she realized this was a man she could relate to.

She told him everything about her love affair with Brian, making no apologies.

He tapped a nicotine-stained finger on his desk. 'Your son should lodge a separate claim against the estate.'

'That might be difficult. I haven't seen him since he was seventeen and he doesn't know that Brian is his father.'

'Why not?'

'Brian registered his birth. When it came to father's name he put Brian Green.'

Sam frowned. 'It's illegal to falsify a birth certificate.'

'That's the name Brian used when he stayed with us. He was trying to protect him, I guess. I told my son that Brian had died abroad. I didn't know what else to say.'

Sam made a notation on his pad.

'Then someone phoned him and told him he was illegitimate. We had a row and he walked out. I haven't seen him since.'

'Or heard from him?'

'I received a letter shortly after he left. He told me he'd found employment and was going to make his own way in the world. I haven't heard from him since.'

'I suggest an effort be made to find him. Do you still have the letter?'

She dabbed a handkerchief to the corner of her eyes. 'Somewhere. I'll send it on to you if I can find it.'

'And a photograph.'

Opening her bag she slid a photo across. 'It was taken seven years ago.'

'A nice-looking lad.'

She straightened the creases from her skirt, wishing she had something smarter to wear. Her job at the supermarket just paid enough to cover the rent and her groceries. Her glance wandered over the luxurious office. 'You might as well know before we go any further. I haven't the money to pay your fee, at least, straight away.'

Sam smiled at her. 'I'll charge one or two of my wealthier clients extra. That should cover it.'

Her eyes flew open. 'I can't let you do that. It's unethical.' She flushed when he began to laugh. 'You were joking.'

'I never joke. I laughed because I rarely meet a completely honest person and this is the second time in as many days. I'll be delighted to handle your case for the following reasons. First, it involves another client of mine. Second, it's a case I can win. Thirdly, I like you.' His smile warmed her. 'I'm taking you to lunch . . . shall we go?'

Forgetting about her shabby suit Alison rose to her feet. She'd never met anyone quite like Sam Gilbert.

Betony left the consultation rooms in a bad mood. The locum had refused to renew her prescription. *Refused!*

'You're becoming addicted to them.' She'd only half-listened when he lectured her on the body adjusting to ever-increasing dosage. 'They're not a panacea. They're a potent drug and, as such, should be handled responsibly.'

'Are you suggesting Dr Beech is irresponsible?'

'I'm suggesting nothing of the sort. Your records suggest you have enough medication to last six more weeks.'

'I've mislaid the prescription.'

'Then find it. If you have trouble weaning yourself off them in that time, we'll try hypnosis.'

Hypnosis! She wasn't going to let that miserable Scottish leech into her head. She'd simply wait until Dr Beech got back.

She scowled as she let herself into the house. How could she wean herself off them when there was hardly any left? She couldn't believe she'd taken too many. She must have put them somewhere and forgotten about them.

Dashing upstairs to the small bedroom she scrambled desperately through the top drawer of the dresser, frantically pushing bits and pieces of underwear aside. Her eyes riveted on a tiny, yellow shirt.

'Oh God! Snooky's T-shirt.' She gazed guiltily at Ben's photograph, smiling at her from the dresser. His silky fair hair curled against his face, his plump baby legs straddled a gaudy plastic train. Snooky was clutched against his chest, as he always had been – as he'd been on that day.

He had no right to look so achingly alive, so ready to step out of the picture into her arms. He should be sepia-coloured, remote and gone from her, like photographs of her mother.

'I'm sorry, Ben,' she choked out, but didn't know whether it was because Snooky might be cold without his T-shirt, or the fact that she'd fallen in love with the man who'd killed him. She fetched the bear from the top of the cupboard and, thrusting his stumpy arms into the shirt, cuddled the toy against her face. She should have buried him with Ben.

A faint smell of baby powder clung to the bear. Whether it was real or imagined she couldn't tell. She was frightened to let Ben go, so perhaps she wanted it to be there.

The old despair slammed like a fist in the guts. 'Oh, Ben.' Sinking to the bed she curled herself into a ball around the bear and and began to sob.

She couldn't bear this pain without medication. She wasn't ready for it. For half an hour her life was how it had been before Noel: one big, despairing mess – until she remembered she had Rose to talk to.

Rose replaced the receiver and gazed thoughtfully at it. A few seconds later she snatched it up again, dialling the number of one of the inner circle.

When he answered, she said 'My sister, Betony Nichols will be making an appointment for a private consultation shortly. I want you to let me know her condition.'

'I'm afraid I can't divulge—'

'Nonsense, William,' she snapped. 'Your reputation depends on it.'

Later that day, Dr William George examined Betony thoroughly. She was healthy, but agitated as she reeled off a list of her symptoms. She had them down pat. Her eyes were filled with anxiety when she mentioned a friend's tranquillizers, and requested the same prescription.

William was aware of Betony's bereavement. Straight away, he guessed why she'd consulted him instead of going to her own doctor. She didn't mention her condition, which came as no surprise to him. People lied to themselves when they needed to satisfy a craving, often by omission.

William believed drug dependency was a state of mind – but the mind could be tricked. Acting on the side of caution, he gave her a repeat prescription for a harmless placebo, then trotted out a few platitudes and directed her to a nearby pharmacy to have it filled.

With great reluctance, he then contacted Rose.

Pregnancy being the last thing on her mind, Betony rushed straight home to swallow a couple of the pills. She sat at the ridiculously-painted piano whilst she waited for the tension to ease, her fingers tracing around a daisy. Noel had surprised her with Vivaldi. Lifting the lid she went automatically through the exercises, then into some Chopin.

She should start studying again. She was feeling much more in control of herself now. She'd reconciled herself to the fact that Ben had gone. He no longer dominated her every waking thought. Noel did.

As a child, she'd dreamed of being a concert pianist, and had thought her career to be set when she'd won a scholarship to the conservatoire.

Then she'd met Simon. She'd been about to give her first public performance, a concert arranged to raise money for charity. She'd been nervous, her fingers trembling because she'd chosen a difficult Prokofiev concerto which had demanded her full concentration.

She'd fluffed one of the passages at the beginning. Simon, who'd organized the matinée and was watching from off-stage, had frowned. From then on she'd been conscious of him. Although she'd managed to get through the piece with-out too many mistakes it was due to the expertise of the conductor, for the music hadn't received the concentration demanded by it.

She began to tremble as she went blindly into the andantino. Simon had constantly criticized her playing.

'You play well enough,' he told her. 'But you haven't got the confidence to be a soloist. You should teach.'

This from a man who'd failed so badly at being a guitarist the pop groups he'd headed had been laughed off stage. He'd gone into record producing, which, though she hadn't realized it at the time of their marriage, was also a floundering venture. Her money had propped it up.

She'd listened to him because she'd discovered the joys of sex with him in the back of his van, and mistaken it for love. He was always full of confidence, and seemed to know what he was talking about, so she'd believed him. She'd dropped her studies to become a piano teacher. Perhaps she should take in students again. Her life seemed so aimless at the moment.

Feeling jittery, she began the allegro. Simon had been right. She *was* too nervous to perform in front of an audience, even a small one. She'd nearly collapsed with fear at the Harringtons' party.

Why was she shaking? Mouth dry, she fought off the panic rising in her. What *was* that horrible buzzing noise! Was something wrong with Vivaldi?

Lifting her fingers from the keys she gave a shaky laugh. Someone was leaning on the door bell.

'So sorry,' Daphne said, dropping her suitcase on the doorstep. 'Clive's kicking up an awful fuss and I've got nowhere else to go.'

'Oh, I see.' Taken aback, she stood aside. 'You'd better come in, I suppose.'

By the end of the two weeks Betony's nerves had reached screaming point. Daphne was the untidiest person she'd ever come across.

She felt sorry for her, but she had enough problems of her own to cope with. She'd only seen Noel a couple of times, a few stolen hours at his flat.

She'd felt on edge, and he was too caught up with his own problems to notice hers. Their lovemaking had been mind-numbing and frantic.

Daphne was presuming too much on their acquaintance, she thought resentfully. Two days ago she'd tactfully mentioned the subject of alternative accommodation.

'Of course, darling. I'll start looking straight away.'

Desperately needing some privacy, Betony was on the point of throwing her out when the perfect solution occurred to her.

Noel wasn't quite as enthusiastic as she thought he'd be.

'I don't think living together is a good idea at the moment,' he said quietly. 'If Sylvia finds out, she'll use it against me.'

'If I don't care about that, why should you?'

There was silence for a moment or two. 'I don't want you involved. It could get messy.'

'For pity's sake, just save me from Daphne – or save her from me. I'm feeling decidedly homicidal.' Hearing the water gurgle down the plug hole upstairs, her voice dropped to a whisper. 'I'm desperate. If you don't help me out I'll take an axe to Vivaldi and never speak to you again.'

A warm chuckle whispered against her ear. 'You mean we'll have to make love using hand signals?'

'Right now I've got two fingers forked aggressively up,' she warned.

She knew she'd won when he gave a completely natural laugh. 'OK, but just for a couple of weeks until she sorts herself out.'

'Have you got any spare tampons?' Daphne shouted down the stairs. 'I've forgotten to buy any.'

She managed not to grind her teeth as she dashed upstairs. 'Tampons,' she muttered. 'Now where did I see them last? In the underwear drawer in the small bedroom, I think.'

The room was a shambles. Clothes covered every surface and spilled on to the floor. She'd probably have to clean the bathroom after her again, as well. Something in her snapped. 'This really has to stop, Daphne. I can't tolerate all this mess.'

'I'm sorry.' Daphne's contrite expression made her feel guilty. 'I'll try to be tidier. The room is so small and there's nowhere to hang anything. I've been looking for somewhere else to live, but everything's so hideously expensive.'

Betony shoved the packet of tampons into her hands, reminding herself to buy some more. She'd always been irregular, but she was bound to need them if she didn't have any on hand.

'Noel has a flat you can use until you find something. You can move in at the weekend.'

A small, wounded expression appeared on Daphne's face. 'I'm sorry I've been such a nuisance. You've been so marvellous, especially with you being so fraught and everything.'

Had she been fraught? Probably. She hadn't been sleeping at all well lately, and she'd lost her appetite. Well, not lost it exactly; her stomach was a bit queasy sometimes and she just couldn't face food.

That would change when Noel moved in. Hopefully, she would persuade him to make the arrangement permanent.

She managed a smile, not wanting Daphne to feel bad. 'It's not that I want you out so much as I want Noel in, if only for a few weeks.'

'I understand.' Daphne lightly kissed her cheek. 'I expect I'll be going back to Clive when he's suffered enough.'

Betony stared at her in amazement. 'After he mistreated you. How could you?'

Daphne grinned. 'He won't risk it again, it cost him too much the first time. Besides, I'm not a fool. When I leave him for good, it's going to be on my terms.'

For at least two weeks, Betony's life became happy and stable. She looked forward to Noel coming home after work.

Her culinary skills improved as she practised different recipes. She enjoyed the domesticity of her life in a way she never had with Simon. He'd kept her buried in the country with Ben whilst he lived a double life at her expense in London.

Daniel Jacobs had exposed a great hole in her capital from her time with

Simon. There was no chance of retrieving it. The record company had gone bust with no assets.

She'd been lucky he hadn't bought the London house in the company name, for it had appreciated in value considerably.

Then there was the problem of her father. Richard Gifford's frequent requests for money were a drain. It wasn't as if she could claim them as expenses against her tax. Richard Gifford had an annuity, which was adequate for his everyday living expenses.

Daniel had been quite forceful, telling her it was going beyond duty to support her father in his foolishness, or provide her sisters with rent-free accommodation. Little Abbott soaked up cash. She should get rid of it if she had no intention of living there, not wait for it to fall down.

But Rose and Cecily had brought her up, and loved Little Abbot. How could she turn her back on them? As for her father, he was seventy now. Soon he would be too old to gallivant around the world looking for relics to dig up. He'd expect to retire to the house he'd shared with her mother.

Every time she tried to discuss the problem with Noel he smiled and shook his head. 'Consult Daniel. We're too involved for me to be objective.'

He rarely discussed personal matters at all. She knew nothing about his marriage, his schooling or his parents, apart from the fact he'd been brought up on a council estate. He asked for no information about hers.

There was a barrier between them because of the accident. They lived on the surface of the relationship, without treading into areas that would probe wounds open and lead to dissent. She loved him, and she wanted more than their exquisite lovemaking and his patient understanding of her moods. She wanted closeness of soul and spirit, and needed to share his worries, hurts and thoughts.

'I've think I've fallen in love with you,' she blurted out one evening, surprising herself. She was sitting on the floor, her back against his legs, enjoying the sensation of his fingers trailing through her hair. If he laughed she knew she'd die a thousand deaths.

But he slid his arms around her and pulled her up into his lap. 'I love you too. When my divorce is through—'

'Move in with me, Noel. Don't go back to that horrible little flat tomorrow.'

'It's too soon to plan a life together.'

'You just said you loved me,' she pushed, edgy and uncomfortable.

'It's not that easy, is it? There are problems to overcome.'

'If you're referring to the accident . . . .' She sucked in a deep breath. 'I've forgiven you, if that's what's bothering you.'

His whole body tensed. 'Forgiveness, I don't want. I need you to accept that the accident wasn't my fault. Your husband had time to get out of the way. He just stood there, swaying back and forth.' His voice dropped to a whisper. 'I screamed at him to get out of the way. He just stared with this awful look on his face. And the child was in the pushchair . . . smiling.'

She thrust her hands over her ears and shot to her feet. 'I don't want to hear any more.'

His eyes displayed the despairing sadness he felt. 'Do you still think our relationship will work?'

How could he remain so calm when he was tearing her heart from her chest? 'You didn't have to prove your point quite so cruelly. I'm going to bed.'

She slept in the small bedroom, tossing and turning. Finally, she swallowed a sleeping pill and tumbled into a restless sleep, beset with dreams of a child's voice calling her name over and over again from the depths of a tangled forest. She kept catching glimpses of him as she went deeper into the trees. She caught up with him in the middle of a thorny thicket. His back was towards her.

'Ben!' she screamed, holding out her arms. He turned, his teddy bear clutched against his chest. Where his face should have been was a smooth, featureless mask.

An anguished scream of shock drove her awake. She jackknifed into a sitting position, her heart pounding, her tongue salted with adrenaline.

Noel was at her side in an instant, holding her against his chest, comforting her. 'It was a bad dream, everything will be all right in a minute.'

'Make love to me, Noel. Help me forget.'

And he carried her through to the other room, which had once been her husband's and was now theirs. He held her in his arms and tenderly kissed her. But he didn't make love to her, just spooned her into the shelter of his body and cuddled her. Safe and relaxed again, she fell into a deep, dreamless sleep.

Noel was gone when she woke. He'd left a red rose on her pillow.

She began to cry because there was dew on the rose and he'd risen early to buy it from the markets. And then she cried for herself, because she felt like hell and didn't consider herself worthy of him.

Only the pressing urge to pee roused her from her bed. Her mood was as grey and depressing as the day, and it worsened when she found his note on the table saying he'd see her again at the weekend.

She swallowed a couple of pills. An hour later she swallowed a couple more because the others hadn't had any effect. Perhaps the locum had been right and her body was getting used to them. Still in her dressing gown, she fell asleep on the couch. It was mid-afternoon when she woke, dragged out of her stupor by the insistent ringing of the telephone.

She pressed her hand to her aching head as she listened to her sister's request. 'No Rose, I really don't think I can manage any more money at this time. The remains of my allowance barely cover my living expenses as it is.'

'You could sell the house in London and come home. Cecily and I miss you quite dreadfully. We could use your help with the gardens at the weekend. It would give you something to do and take your mind off your bereavement.'

How simple bereavement was to those who'd never experienced it where it counted. 'I have no intention of moving back, not ever.'

'I don't know how daddy will get home, then. We can't just leave him in Mexico to rot.'

'He's returning to England? Why didn't you say?'

'I thought I had. Look, I know you haven't seen him for years and hardly know him, but he's your father.' Her voice adopted a chilly note. 'Still, if you can't help, you can't. Cecily and I might be able to manage his travelling expenses if the garden opening is a success.'

Guilt nearly swamped her.

'Ces could sell her shop, she's had an offer for it. She said trade has picked up considerably of late and it's her sole source of income, so she's reluctant. I suppose we can put off the car repairs for a little longer.'

When Rose mentioned the car Betony remembered hers was rarely used. 'I think I might be able to manage it,' she said.

The positive pregnancy test threw Sylvia into a complete spin. Talking about being a mother was one thing, being it was another altogether. It was a nuisance coming at this time. The fact that it might be Alex's child bothered her. Having a gardener for a husband was not quite socially acceptable, yet her child must have a father.

The baby could be Noel's at a pinch. She grappled with the mathematics, then abandoned the project, vaguely remembering indulging in marital relations with Noel not long before he'd left her.

Typical of a man to slake his appetite on a woman and then abandon her. He wasn't going to get away with it. It would suit her much better if the child was his. She wouldn't have to go through all the trouble and expense of a divorce. Noel would never abandon his own flesh and blood.

She could still see Alex at weekends, though sometimes she felt ashamed when she realized how uninhibited she'd become with him. By the end of the day she'd talked herself into believing the father couldn't possibly be anyone but Noel. It would be a girl, she decided, with blond hair and blue eyes. She'd call her Charlotte, which had quite a nice ring to it when combined with Dearborn.

She informed her mother, who was ecstatic once she'd got over the shock. Then she called Anne. Anne's voice was cool when she congratulated her, as it had been since her split with Noel.

She warmed when she told Anne she'd be reconciled with Noel. 'A stupid misunderstanding, that was all,' was the way she put it.

Anne went on to say she had stacks of baby furniture and clothes in the attic, and would sort them out for her. As if she'd put her child in second-hand clothing.

She shuddered. 'Thank you, dear, but no. This is my mother's first grandchild. She insists on buying everything new. You do understand?'

Noel's mobile was turned off. She dialled the number of his flat and was greeted by the answerphone. She left Noel a message informing him she was expecting his baby.

She sat by the phone half the night, waiting for an answer that never came. The next morning, she drove to her mother's house and had a fit of hysterics.

Sylvia pregnant! Noel grinned. What was she trying to pull? He hadn't touched her in months, and would be willing to submit to genetic testing to prove it.

So, who was the father? He tossed it about in his head for a few moments, tempted to return the call and ask.

No. He'd take Sam's advice and communicate only through lawyers. That way, anything he said couldn't be taken out of context.

Dorothy Throsby called him at work the next morning, knocking him for a loop when she said imperiously, 'You do realize divorce is completely out of the question now? The baby's due in February, so you must forget your pride and work things out. I'm prepared to overlook your interference regarding Alison Green. Despite the damage you've done we'll accept you back into the family for the baby's sake.'

'Nice try, Dorothy,' he said pleasantly. 'I know you think Sylvia's perfect, but her maths are sadly lacking. Unless she has a twelve month gestation period, the child can't possibly be mine.'

He hung up on the affronted noises coming down the line and began to laugh. It was hard to believe Sylvia would try to pin this on him. A baby. How very convenient of her!

Still laughing, he rang Sam Gilbert.

CHAPTER ELEVEN

The row between Sylvia and her mother had been raging for several minutes. 'Your father would be ashamed of you,' Dorothy hissed. 'Not only did you lie to me, you made me appear foolish.' Subsiding into a chair she fanned her heated face with her handkerchief.

'I didn't ask you to interfere,' Sylvia ground out. 'I would have convinced Noel, eventually.'

Her mother's mouth fell open. 'So what he said was true, the baby isn't his? The poor man. Have you forsaken your marriage vows and laid with another.'

'Oh, for pity's sake, don't be so archaic. It's done all the time.'

'Sylvia! How could you? What would your father say?'

Her mother's outrage made her smile. A few months ago she'd have reacted in the same way. She'd been brainwashed by her mother. *Temple!* What a stupid word. No wonder Noel had left her. Now she'd discovered the pleasure of sex, be damned if she'd listen to it any more. As for her father, it was time her mother faced facts.

'I promised daddy I'd never tell you about the time I caught him in your bed with the au pair but it doesn't really matter now he's dead. Cheap labour, you called her. Daddy certainly got his money's worth.'

Dorothy gave a strangled cry. 'Your father would never have done such a disgusting thing.'

'He had his head between her legs, and it wasn't a cross examination.'

'Don't be so vulgar.'

Mouth puckered in disgust, her mother's hand lashed out.

Catching it in mid-air, Sylvia thrust it back at her and taunted, 'Did you know about Alison Green's son?'

Her mother's face suddenly aged. 'She's lying.'

'Is she? You do realize he could have a claim on daddy's estate. We could lose everything.' Having gained a new perspective on human nature in recent months, the scales had fallen from Sylvia's eyes with a vengeance. 'Daddy was a man. If men are denied, they seek satisfaction elsewhere.'

'Only when there are immoral women to encourage them.' Her mother's glance raked her stomach. 'What's obvious is you're more like your father than I thought.'

Her mother suddenly admitted, deflated, 'I suspected Brian was having an affair with her. I'm sure the boy isn't his, though. Noel's making mischief because of the divorce. He never liked me.'

'Don't be ridiculous. He read the letter daddy sent to her. Noel might have his faults, but dishonesty's not one of them.'

'An honest man would acknowledge the child you're carrying. Are you sure you can't convince him.'

Tears gathered in Sylvia's eyes when she realized what she'd lost. 'This isn't Noel's baby, but it could have been if you'd kept your damned nose out.'

'I was trying to protect you. Will the father of your child marry you?'

'I haven't told him yet.' She grimaced, wondering what her mother's reaction would be to having a gardener as son-in-law. But did she want to marry Alex? Being a single parent was quite acceptable now. Termination was an option, but dangerous. She shuddered. It might not be so bad married to Alex. Once the divorce settlement was through, she would buy him a small business. A plant nursery or something.

'Are you going to tell me who the father is?'

'Not at the moment.'

'Very well, Sylvia, there's nothing more to be said. Close the door on your way out.'

The air was stiff with affronted pride when she left.

She drove straight to Little Abbot and headed for the kitchen. Excited, she began to prepare for the opening of her tea room.

Rose joined her, her grubby fingers breaking off bits of pastry and scones, and stuffing them into her mouth. 'Come to my private sitting room later,' she said between bites. 'We're having a small private seance, and I want to tell you a little bit about our main subject. Oh yes, and I'm arranging a meeting of the inner circle to try and contact Isabella the Sunday after next. She obviously feels close to you, so I thought you might like to act as medium for the event.'

'Isabella. How thrilling!'

Sylvia was proud the unhappy spirit had singled her out. She often sensed her presence, going so far as to talk to her when no one was listening. Isabella's was such a tragic story. No wonder she'd cursed the house of Dubeney.

'There's something I want to tell you, too, but you must promise not to tell

Cecily. It will be *our* little secret.'

As if she would, when there was so much animosity between herself and Cecily. Afterwards, she intended to seek Rose's counsel with her own little problem. Rose was the one person she trusted enough to confide in.

It was nearly seven o'clock when she finished preparing the conservatory. It looked pretty with the potted palms, flowered tablecloths and the white china.

Cecily came in, gave the place a cursory glance then helped herself to a scone from the glass cabinet.

'Those scones are for sale in the tea room. I won't have time to make any more.'

Taking a coin from her pocket, Cecily dropped it into her hand. 'That should cover it. Just remember, this isn't your house, and as far as I'm concerned you can keep your bloody airs and graces to yourself.'

She tried to intimidate her with a glare. 'It isn't your house either. I understand it belongs to your younger sister.'

'Ah yes ... Betony.' Cecily's smile had a mocking edge to it. 'By the way, I've heard that the villagers are providing cottage teas in the village hall over the weekend, so don't expect many customers.'

Dismay ripped through her. 'I'm not worried. I'll ask Alex to paint a sign for the gate when I see him later.'

'You won't see Alex tonight. He had to dash off.'

Her eyes hardened. 'Where did he go?'

Lazily, Cecily scratched her stomach. 'How would I know? He received a phone call and said he'd be back in the morning in time for the opening. Perhaps he's got a girlfriend in town.'

Bitch! Sylvia smiled but she'd rather have scratched her eyes out. Cecily was running after Alex. As if he'd pay any attention to a woman fifteen years older than himself. It was ludicrous.

She wondered how Cecily would react when she learned about the baby, and was tempted to call her back and tell her. Then she remembered Rose was going to take her into her confidence – and it was something Cecily wouldn't be a part of.

Dropping the coin into her pocket, she took one last look around, smiled with satisfaction and headed towards Rose's sitting room.

The weekend had been a disaster. Alex hadn't come back for the opening and Cecily had insisted that the girl Sylvia had hired for the tea room must sit in the pavilion and sell her rubbish.

Not that she'd needed her. Sylvia went through the figures again in case her calculations were out. She reached the same total.

She'd made a loss, and it was the fault of the damned village committee. It had been underhand of them to set up in opposition, and mean of Cecily not to let her know until the last minute.

Furiously, she chewed the end of her pen. After a short while a smile slid across her face and she reached for the telephone book. She might be able to do something about it.

A few minutes later, after checking that her mother was taking her usual promenade along the Bournemouth sea front, she dialled the number of Dereck Wallwark, a local councillor and a member of the inner circle.

He was an ordinary-looking, middle-aged man with sparse, ginger hair and astute, blue eyes hidden behind round glasses. During the seance he'd stared at her, making her lose concentration just as Rose made a connection through her.

Thank goodness Rose had given her some information about the main customer. Somehow, she'd managed to fake the trance, and the woman had left, well pleased with the outcome. Although she'd fooled Rose and the others, she'd formed the impression Dereck had seen right through her.

'Dereck,' she cooed a few moments later. 'I've got a small problem I thought you might be able to help me with.'

'Sylvia, my dear. How delightful to hear from you.' His voice dropped a fraction. 'A problem you say, a personal one?'

'It's to do with the rival tea shop in the village. I wondered if the villagers have got permission to run a business from the village hall. Has the place been checked out by the health department or anything?'

He gave a fruity chuckle. 'I might be able to help you out, my dear. Perhaps we should discuss it over a lunchtime drink, hmmm?'

'Lunchtime drink,' she said stupidly. 'Couldn't you just—'

'I could, of course. However, that means I'll have to scratch someone's back and you'll have to scratch mine,' he said bluntly.

'I see.' Her mouth tightened. 'I wouldn't have thought you were the type to suggest something of this nature. Perhaps I'll just contact the proper authority.'

'My dear Sylvia, I am the proper authority. I'm surprised by your prudish attitude. I was hoping to see more of you – alone.'

She coloured. 'I'll think about it.'

His voice became cool. 'By all means, think about it, but not for too long. Just remember, the council can take a long time over decisions. If you want swift action, meet me at the Nelson Inn. They have private rooms upstairs where we can discuss it, in depth.'

She shuddered as she slammed down the receiver. Who did he think she was, some common little tart he could push around?

She sighed when her mother came in and stalked past her. There had been an atmosphere since their blazing row. She wished she wasn't obliged to live with her, but now the Essex house was on the market she *had* to live somewhere. At least it was convenient, and cheap.

Things banged in the kitchen, then her mother came through with a cup of coffee on a tray. She was being quite difficult and childish. She shuddered at the thought of how she'd react when she found out who'd fathered the baby. She would have to tell her, of course, but not until after Alex knew. She frowned. She'd been looking forward to seeing him, and was feeling quite restless. It would serve him right if she *did* meet Dereck.

Of course, it would only need to be the once . . . . An hour and a half later she walked into a seedy little pub in Poole.

'I knew you'd see sense.' Dereck picked up a bottle of red wine and two glasses from the table then headed through a door. After a momentary hesitation, Sylvia followed him.

In the shop opposite the pub, Cecily served the last customer, then made her way through a confusion of hanging objects to the door. The air smelled fresh after the sweet, musky odour of the interior.

She was almost tempted to take a walk along the quay, but the expected arrival of a consignment took her to the pub opposite, from whose vantage point she could keep a look out for the delivery van.

Ordering a salad sandwich and a half-pint of bitter, she seated herself at the window on the chair Dereck Wallwark had just vacated.

The week had not been easy for Alison Green. Seeing her son again had been a rude awakening.

Gone was the unsure and troubled teenager she remembered. In his place had been someone, not only contemptuous of her, but someone violent as well. Fingers trembling, she touched the bruise on her face. He'd slapped her when she'd finally told him the name of his father, then walked out of the house.

He'd come back later, white-faced, apologetic and full of repressed rage. She'd accepted his apology, even whilst knowing it lacked sincerity. Her son was a stranger now, a stranger she didn't like. She doubted she'd ever see him again.

'He's donated blood for testing,' Sam told her, sounding unimpressed when he rang her early on Monday morning. 'He said he's going to move abroad when he gets what he's owed.'

'It might be the best thing under the circumstances. Do you think Dorothy Throsby will settle out of court?'

'It's possible. There's a considerable sum of money involved. Mrs Throsby hasn't spent a penny of the capital sum invested. She has her own money, of course.'

Money had brought her son home to her. He didn't give a damn about their relationship.

When the phone call ended, she picked up a framed photograph from the mantelpiece and gazed at it. It was a school photograph. He'd been fifteen then. His hair was neatly trimmed, his smile self-conscious and his half-hooded hazel-eyes looked directly into the camera.

'Damn you, Alex,' she whispered, trying not to cry over the years she'd wasted worrying about him. 'Damn you for making me despise you.'

Betony was just about to make a salad when Daphne contacted her.

'You'll never believe what happened,' she said in disgust. 'Rose has invited me to a seance with Clive next Sunday. She's going to try and communicate with the spirit of one of your ancestors.'

Plucking a cocktail onion from a jar Betony stuck it in her mouth, shuddering at its deliciously sour taste. 'Which ancestor?'

'Someone called Isabella.'

'Ah, poor tortured Isabella.' She grinned. 'Rose has a bit of a fixation about her.'

'Why? Is she a skeleton in the family closet.'

'Sort of. She had a short and unhappy life.' She glanced up as Noel came in and, smiling, lifted her face to his to be kissed.

'You taste like pickled onions,' he whispered, chuckling when she popped another into her mouth and huffed a breath at him.

His arms slid round her waist from behind and she leaned back into the support of his body with a sigh of contentment. 'Look, I can't tell you about Isabella now, but be warned – take anything Rose says with a pinch of salt.'

'Oh, I intend to. I'm not really into that spiritual crap of hers.' She gave a throaty laugh. 'Have lunch with me before the weekend and tell me about Isabella. I don't want to appear ignorant if she happens to put in an appearance.'

'I promise you she won't. But all right, make it Wednesday at the usual place.'

Dropping the receiver back to its rest she twisted in Noel's arms and hugged him tight. 'I've missed you.'

His face lit up in a smile. 'You saw me yesterday.'

'That was ages ago. Move back in with me, Noel.'

'Once the divorce claims are agreed to, perhaps I will.'

'How long will that take?'

He shrugged. 'So far, all that Sylvia's agreed to is I keep the flat, which was bought before we met with a legacy from my grandfather, anyway. She's demanding the family home and contents, half the investments, half my business and the car.'

'Mercenary cow!'

He gave a faint frown, obviously uncomfortable with the analogy. 'Sorry,' she muttered. 'Slap me down if I tread on private territory.'

That brought a smile to his face. 'Sylvia's mother did advance the money to buy the house. The trouble is, they've never let me forget it.'

'But you paid her back, didn't you?'

'With interest.' He shrugged again. 'As far as I'm concerned she's welcome to the house and half the investments. The car's in her name anyway. Sam Gilbert disagrees, of course. He thinks I should go for the throat.'

'What's the use of hiring a lawyer if you're not going to listen to him?'

'Sylvia's pregnant,' he said quietly.

Her heart sank like a stone into a pond. *Christ, the woman certainly knew how to pick her time!* 'Are you thinking of going back to her?'

He shook his head. 'I don't know who the father is, but I do know it's not me.'

She'd forgotten he wasn't able to father a child. Relief made her head spin. 'So this could go against her when it comes to the divorce settlement.'

'Only if I let it. I don't see the need to penalize the child by destroying her character. All I want is my business left intact and half the investments. If Sylvia agrees to that she's welcome to the rest, which is roughly the same value.'

His face adopted a serious expression. 'I was thinking, I might sell the flat when the settlement is agreed on, and buy half of this place, providing you intend to make an honest man of me.'

So wide did her grin stretch, she thought it might split her face in half. Dear, idiotic Noel. How beautiful and honest he was, and how she loved him. A lump caught in her throat and tears filled her eyes. 'Try and stop me,' she said, and illuminated by the great rush of love engulfing her, kissed him long and hard. 'Now we've sorted that out, let's celebrate this weekend.'

'Uhuh. What do you suggest?'

How transparently secretive his eyes were, his barely-disguised smile a dead giveaway.

'A naked dip in the Serpentine by moonlight?'

'Unfortunately, there's no moon.' He patted his pocket and grinned hugely at her. 'What about dinner followed by a show?'

'It sounds pretty conventional to me,' she mused, allowing him to milk his surprise to the fullest.

'Can you speak French?'

'Like a native.'

'Good, because the event takes place in Paris tomorrow night, so you can do all the talking.'

Now he had surprised her. She giggled when he chuckled in triumph. 'You must be the nicest man I've ever met.'

One eyebrow lifted in ironic agreement. 'Didn't I tell you that right at the very beginning?'

CHAPTER TWELVE

Sylvia hummed to herself as she drove back to Essex, pleased with the outcome of the settlement meeting.

She hadn't expected Noel to be quite so thoughtful as to consider her baby's welfare. She'd always known he was decent, but he possessed depths she'd never imagined.

Her conscience had twinged when she'd set eyes on him again. He'd looked happier than she'd ever seen him. His manner towards her had been civilized, but distant. He'd been eager to get things settled, and had declined her invitation to take coffee afterwards.

'Be happy, Sylvia,' he'd said, then walked off without a backward glance, whistling to himself as if everything had been finalized – which of course it had. The rest was just a matter of course.

Feeling slightly depressed after the meeting, a visit to an estate agent to find out how much the house was worth lifted her spirits considerably. Once it was sold, she'd make sure her mother didn't give in over the Alison Green affair. As her heir, she *did* have a major interest in her estate, and was determined to preserve it.

She might decide to marry Alex. She didn't love him, of course, but that didn't matter. What mattered was that the child had a father. She intended to tell him about her pregnancy this weekend, and now she had access to money, discuss with him a more suitable career choice.

She was still keen on the plant nursery idea. Once summer was over she'd have the profits from the tea room at her disposal, especially now she'd done something about the opposition.

Feeling powerful, she let herself into the house, making a mental note that the hedge needed a trim and the lawn a mow. The estate agent had told her first appearances were important.

She'd just got inside when Anne called her.

'Anne, darling,' she said gaily. 'I've just walked in.'

'How did the meeting go?'

'Better than I expected. Noel was quite sweet about everything.'

'He's a nice guy. You'll never find a better one.'

She ignored Anne's comment. 'I've got the house and contents, the car and half the investments. Noel gets the other half, that awful flat and his business. I'm putting the house on the market straight away, then I'll move in with mother for a while.'

'If there's anything Jeff and I can do to help . . . .'

'There is. Do you think Jeff would trim the hedge and cut the lawn?'

Anne voice cooled. 'Just a minute, I'll ask him if he's got time.' There was a mumble of voices in the background.

'*Why doesn't the little bitch hire someone?*'

'*Shush, she might hear you.*'

'*Give me the phone, woman.*' Jeff came on the line, full of the false bonhomie he used with women. 'How grateful?'

'You men are all the same,' she said, the malice she felt towards him spilling into her eyes.

'I was angling for a chocolate cake. For crissakes, Sylvia, since when did you take up flirting? I understood you to be the original ice maiden – *ouch!*'

'I'm sorry about that,' Anne said, and she could hear laughter in her voice. 'He's had a couple of drinks.'

Obviously, she'd kicked him for opening his mouth too wide. She flushed to think Anne had discussed her private life with Jeff. They'd probably laughed about it behind her back. How perfectly horrible of them. One thing was certain, she'd never trust Anne with a confidence again. In fact, she might get her own back by showing Anne just how trustworthy husbands were.

'Has the new diet had any effect on that cellulite of yours?' she cooed.

'Actually, I've lost quite a bit of weight,' Anne said, almost defensively. There was some background talk, then. 'When do you want Jeff to come round?'

Sylvia knew Anne's schedule as well as she knew her own. 'What about Thursday evening, then it will look nice for weekend viewing.'

'Oh, OK. I can drop him off before my pottery class and pick him up afterwards.'

On Thursday, Jeff brought with him a motorized hedge trimmer. Although noisy, it neatened the hedge in a fraction of the time Noel used to take with the shears.

It was nearly dark when he finished the lawn. Sylvia watched him stow the lawnmower in the shed and make his way towards the kitchen. As a man, Jeff wasn't really the type who attracted her. He was tall and boyish, his friendly, puppy-dog manner irritating.

He gave her a friendly smile, displaying his perfect teeth as he flopped on to a chair. 'I hope you've baked my cake. There's nothing like manual labour to work up an appetite.'

'I made your favourite.' She cut him a generous slice of chocolate cake and turned to pour him some tea.

'I'm going to miss the dinner parties, Sylvia. This was the best place in town to get a meal.'

She came up behind him, reaching round to set his tea on the table. Her breast pressed against his back, her free hand came to rest on his shoulder. 'Would you prefer something stronger. I have some malt whisky.'

His hand came up to pat hers. 'Now you're talking.'

Half an hour later, and slightly inebriated, he leered roguishly across the table. 'I'm going to miss you.'

'It's only my cooking you'll miss.' She wagged a reproving finger at him and smiled. 'I don't think you like me.'

He cleared his throat. 'I'm really sorry about you and Noel. He's a nice guy.'

'It was a bit of a blow. I always envied Anne having you for a husband.'

The smile he gave was smug. 'I guess we are pretty compatible.'

'Whereas, Noel and I always had problems in certain areas of our marriage. I used to think it was my fault.' Squeezing tears to her eyes, she gazed at him, and said hesitantly, 'Noel would never discuss the problem, so I don't suppose I'll ever know, now.'

He placed his hand over hers. 'Know what, Sylvia?'

She dabbed at the tears, careful not to spoil her make-up. 'Excuse me for being blunt, Jeff, but you'll understand. After all dentists are almost doctors. What I meant by having problems, is that I've never experienced an orgasm. It must take a special sort of man to consider a woman's needs, especially if she's been brought up to be shy.'

His glass stopped in mid-air. He mumbled something in his throat, but his eyes told her he was halfway to being hooked.

Gently, she fluttered her eyelashes before gazing at him, wide eyed. 'What a shame you're happily married to my best friend. From what I gather, you're quite a man.'

His smile was intimate, his voice low as he clarified the position. 'Is this a proposition?'

'What if I said it was?'

The glass rocked as he set it on the table. His eyes strayed to the clock. 'Anne will be picking me up in just under an hour.'

Fifteen minutes. She'd put the clock back. 'Ah, I knew you didn't like me.'

Her heart lurched when he leered at her. 'It's not that. I've always had the hots for you, but I don't want to hurt Anne.'

She rose to her feet and slid on to his lap. 'As if I'd tell her. It would be our secret, something I'd treasure for the rest of my life.'

His finger hooked under the tie of the wraparound dress she'd worn for the occasion. He sucked in a breath as his eyes took in the black satin underwear she wore, garments Anne would never get her hips into.

'You have a fantastic arse,' he muttered as his hands slid under her buttocks. With her legs wrapped round his waist like a pair of pincers, he carried her up the stairs and kicked open the bedroom door.

Jeff's nervousness caused him to hurry. She thought it would be over too quickly, but then the headlights of Anne's car beamed into the room as it turned into the driveway. She whispered a warning against Jeff's ear.

He didn't have time to complete the act. Eyes wide with alarm he pulled away from her, then eyes wide with alarm scrambled into his clothes.

'You bitch,' he whispered when she laughed.

By the time Anne walked in he'd bolted to the bottom of the stairs. 'I was helping her move a wardrobe,' he garbled, sounding as guilty as hell.

'You've been drinking.' Anne glanced to where she stood at the top of the stairs, her eyes smouldering with suspicion and dislike.

Sylvia smiled at her, deliberately tightening the belt on her satin robe. 'Thank you, Jeff,' she said. 'I appreciate your help.'

She'd been feeling much better lately.

Pulling on a pair of cream slacks, Betony zipped them up, sucking in her stomach for the last inch or so. She seemed to have gained a little weight since the last time she'd worn them. She pulled the matching jacket over her olive green shirt, grabbed up her bag and headed out.

Daphne was already at the restaurant, seated in the secluded corner table they usually used. 'You look as though you've just spent the morning in bed with the greatest lover on earth,' she greeted her with.

Betony laughed. 'No such luck, I'm afraid.' The change had been brought about by sleeping all night without resorting to pills. As a result, she felt less groggy in the mornings. 'How's Clive?'

'He's a pain in the arse. He's started gargling every night and morning and it drives me nuts.' She picked up the menu. 'What do you fancy to eat?'

'A salad. I could hardly do my pants up today.'

'It serves you right for falling in love. Just the other day, I read that women in love gain weight.' She gave the order to the waiter then leaned forward. 'You're not pregnant, are you?'

'I wish I was.' There was more than a little yearning in her voice.

Daphne's hand curved over hers. 'Me and my big mouth. I reminded you, didn't I?'

'I can't expect people to pussy foot around the subject of children because of what happened. In fact, I feel more comfortable if they don't.'

'Will you and Noel – ?'

'One day, perhaps.' She wasn't about to tell Daphne a baby was impossible. Though come to think of it, Noel had only said it was unlikely. She tried to remember when she'd had her last period. Months ago, but that didn't signify anything. The shrink had told her that shock might cause her cycle to cease indefinitely.

'Tell me about Isabella, then I'll tell you a nice, juicy bit of gossip.'

Betony sighed. She'd been brought up on Isabella stories, and found them infinitely less fascinating than Rose did.

'She lived at Little Abbot over two hundred years ago. She became pregnant to her twin brother, Sebastian, who just happened to be lord of the manor, then.'

Daphne's eyes widened. 'Her brother made her pregnant?'

'So the story goes. I don't suppose she had much choice in the matter. She was seventeen when their daughter was born. Apparently, Sebastian was into devil worship and sacrificed the child. Isabella killed herself.'

'What happened to Sebastian?'

'He died an agonizing death after his mistress poisoned him. Sebastian was survived by a wife and three children, who were cast out. After Sebastian's death, she accused the mistress and her son of witchcraft. Her father was a magistrate. They were tried, and hanged.'

Daphne shuddered. 'How romantically macabre.'

'There's nothing romantic about it, believe me. The boy was only three years old at the time.'

'So, you're descended from the terrible Sebastian.'

'As ancestors go, they're not worthy of pride,' she said lightly.

'No wonder you don't want to go back there to live.'

'Rose scared me witless with tales of Isabella and Sebastian when I was small.'

'She didn't strike me as being all that terrifying.'

'She's not really, but she's enamoured by witchcraft, and she's a tad unstable.

Sometimes she gets strange ideas in her head. Cecily is the steady one, but she's a bit of a loner. If you're ever in need, Cecily is the one to go to.'

'I believe I've already experienced her help once. When Clive beat me up I went on a bender. I ended up in Abbotsford and tumbled down an embankment. Guess who rescued me?'

'Cecily?'

'No. Remember Alex, the gardener's assistant at school? He works at Little Abbot and lives in the old cottage at the end of the garden. Cecily treated my injuries apparently.' She gave a throaty laugh. 'Alex is still as randy as ever. He wanted to screw me for old times sake.'

'Did you let him?'

'If I hadn't had such a foul hangover, I might have been tempted. Alex looked like a Greek God after being with Clive.'

The conversation was suspended whilst the waiter served their lunch.

'This inner circle thing,' Daphne said a little while later. 'What goes on there?'

'I've no idea. Though I'm sure it's just fun more than anything else.'

'Did you know Noel's wife is involved in it?'

Betony's eyes flew open. 'In what way?'

'She runs a tea room in the conservatory, I'm told. Fiona Bunnings rang me. She said Sylvia kicked up a fuss with the council and the village committee has to stop selling teas for the church restoration fund.'

Noel hadn't mentioned his wife's involvement with her sisters, Betony fumed on the way home. What else hadn't he told her? She couldn't ask Rose about it. Rose missed nothing, and would be curious about her interest in it. She'd never been able to lie convincingly to either of her sisters. She decided to contact Noel at work. 'I want to ask you something.'

His warm voice caressed her ear. 'You sound very serious.'

'Why didn't you tell me your wife is running a business from my home in Abbotsford?' she asked.

There was a short silence. 'I didn't know about it.'

'How could you not know?'

'I knew she was working at a country house, but to be quite honest, I wasn't interested enough to ask where.'

She didn't know whether to believe him or not. 'You *are* telling me the truth, aren't you?'

His voice cooled a couple of degrees. 'Can you think of any reason why I should lie?'

She sighed. 'I guess not. What are we going to do about it?'

'What do you suggest?' he said. 'As far as I'm concerned Sylvia and your sisters can do as they damned well please.'

'It's going to complicate our lives.'

'Life is always complicated. It's your house. I guess you have the option of going down there and chucking them all out if it worries you.'

'Don't be sarcastic,' she snapped. 'I phoned you for help.'

'That's not the way I read it.'

'Bastard!' she hurled at him and hung up. Half an hour later she cooled down enough to call him again. 'I'm a pig.'

He grunted at her.

'Shut up,' she said.

He laughed. 'I love you.'

'Tell me that again.'

And he did, the words a soft shiver against her ear before he hung up.

As she replaced the receiver a tremor rippled gently across her stomach, a sensation strange, yet familiar. *Oh God! Could it be? Please let it be!* She rushed into the bedroom, stripped off and stood sideways, looking at her stomach. Was it her imagination or was there a slight curve? She pressed her hands against it.

When she'd been carrying Ben it had been five months before she'd shown. How long had she known Noel? It was September now. They'd been lovers for five months.

Her eyes became dreamy as her hands stroked over her stomach. She wouldn't tell him yet, she'd wait until she'd seen the doctor – and she must stop taking those pills.

Her heart missed a beat when sensation came again, a soft, delicate ripple under her hands. A smile drifted across her face. Their baby, if it was a baby, was very much alive.

Cecily was working in the lush green foliage of the peony border under the window.

Her tanned fingers removed the cigarette ends, chewing gum packets and matches dropped by the careless. There was damage to repair, too. Heads had been torn from flowers by children. Bare patches had to be planted, replacing plants which had been stolen. She scowled. The people who visited the garden thought nothing of snapping off stems to take home for cuttings, leaving the plants damaged and open to disease.

Alex should have been doing this, Alex with his broad back, his muscles and his overactive libido. But he was sitting in his cottage, his face as black as thunder.

Glancing at the rose bed, she sighed. The spent blooms had to be removed before the weekend, and the lawn needed cutting. Alex had been back for three days. He was being paid to work, not sit on his backside. Rising to her feet she strode to his cottage and rapped at the door.

'What is it?' he shouted out.

'I need help.'

'Go away.'

She thrust the door open and walked inside.

Slumped in the armchair, he glowered at her. 'Didn't you hear?'

She wondered if he'd found out about Dereck and Sylvia, but decided against it. He wouldn't care, anyway. Women were a commodity to him.

'I heard perfectly. Now hear me. I pay you to work, not skulk in the cottage all day.'

'You pay me to screw you,' he said.

Looking into his stormy eyes, she smiled. 'This time, you pay me, then.'

He threw back his head and laughed. When the laughter stopped, the eyes gazing into hers were full of tears.

'You're the only one who's ever understood me, Ces,' he whispered.

Heart thumping, Fiona Bunnings backed away from the cottage window.

Cecily Gifford came as no surprise. But she hadn't expected Daphne Harrington to visit the cottage, nor that nasty, blonde Dearborn creature who ran the tea shop. And Judy Cross had told her she'd seen Sylvia Dearborn with Councillor Wallwark last week. The whole place was a den of iniquity.

She could see the attraction where the gardener was concerned, of course. The mares always enticed the stallions with the biggest tackle – and the gardener had quite a set on him. She experienced a flicker of regret for the lost attention of her husband. All that had been finished with years ago. He'd just fizzled out one night, shortly after he'd joined the Masonic Lodge.

He'd moved into the spare room, and he kept out of her hair by fiddling with the computer he'd bought himself. She saw so little of him she might as well not be married. Sometimes she wished she wasn't.

Crawling through the reeds and nettles, she reached the safety of her horse and was soon back at the stables.

Two girls were coming for their riding lessons, silly creatures who talked in high-pitched voices. Neither of them had the seat for a horse, but their parents were wealthy, and riding was an accomplishment expected of them.

'Good morning, Pamela . . . Millicent. A lovely morning for a ride.'

They giggled as they mounted the two placid horses she kept for beginners.

They giggled when their bottoms jogged up and down on the saddle, turned pink and giggled when their mounts relieved themselves, and giggled all the way back to the stable.

'They've both improved enormously,' she lied to their mother.

Mrs Smythe-Witherington bared her teeth and pink gums in one swift lift of the upper lip as she ushered her darlings into a white Mercedes.

Pamela and Millicent were still giggling when she drove off.

When she arrived home she made a pie for dinner from leftover mince and mashed potatoes, boiling some sprouts to go with it.

Her husband left for his meeting with hardly a grunt. Watching him go, she thought of the women who visited the cottage. Life suddenly seemed dull compared to the goings-on at Little Abbot.

Perhaps she should go and have her fortune told by Rose. But no, she'd rung for an appointment before and Rose had said she was too busy. Resentment burned in her. What did they have to be so snooty about? They and their odd friends lowered the tone of the whole village, and she intended to do something about it.

She thought for a while, turning things over in her mind whilst she watched an Australian soap opera on television.

When it finished, she fetched a writing pad and envelopes from the drawer, and listed several names. She stared at them, then shrugged and drew a line through the list.

She stared thoughtfully into space for a few moments, trying to think of something more effective. A smile drifted triumphantly across her face, and she began to write.

Revenge would be sweet.

CHAPTER THIRTEEN

The 16th Day of March 1798

> *There is much pain in my head and I am taking fits. I have made my own pact with this devil of Sebastian's, offering my soul to burn in eternal hellfire if my spirit can reside in this house to guide that of my infant Katherine.*
>
> *My head aches so. Sometimes, I think I am going insane.*
>
> *Sebastian brought his mistress to see me. There was a boy child at her breast, and love in her eyes for the infant. She wore one of my silk gowns, and the necklace my mother gave me on her deathbed. The rubies were like drops of my daughter's blood against her throat. I envy her not for all her bright boldness and laughter, for her eyes are haunted and she will know sorrow after I am gone.*

Rose shoved the journal under a cushion when Cecily strolled in. 'Why didn't you knock? The client might have still been with me.'

'She left fifteen minutes ago.' Hands on hips, she gazed at her through bleak eyes. 'Why did Alex go off in such a hurry?'

'How should I know?'

'You know everything that goes on around here.'

Taking it as a compliment, Rose smiled, 'I don't know this time. If I did, would you expect me to break a confidence?'

'If it suited you. I want a straight answer, Rose. What the hell's going on?'

Her eyes narrowed. 'Everything's coming together.'

'Coming together. What's that supposed to mean?'

'It means I'm going to try and contact Isabella on Sunday night.' Excitement beat at her breast when the room seemed to pulse. 'Imagine the power that will be present.'

Rose almost felt sorry for Cecily when her face paled. Despite her involvement, she'd never been a true believer. She was a daughter of the earth, not of the spirit.

She gave a disgusted snort. 'Give it up, Rose. It's dangerous.'

'Don't be such a baby,' she scoffed. 'Now, I need your help. I want you to make one of your concoctions. Sylvia needs to be able to focus, and she's still self aware.'

'Sylvia?' The expression in her eyes became derisory. 'You're not using her, are you? She nearly passed out the last time I gave her something to relax her.'

'She's stronger now. Her appetite for excitement and depravity has grown beyond my wildest dreams.'

Cecily's lip curled. 'You know Isabella won't make contact, she never has.'

'I need to know where Katherine's bones are. Isabella lied. I've searched every inch of Abbot's field.'

Cecily's face closed up. 'I expect a fox dug the child up five minutes after she was buried, and ate her. This witchcraft thing has become an obsession. Forget it, unless you want to end up in the funny farm like our mother did – and forget me, I don't want any part of it.'

'Only if you forget your obsession with Alex.' Amusement filled her eyes. 'Did you know Sylvia's pregnant to him. The child in her womb will draw Isabella to her.'

Cecily looked sick. Her hand went to the table for support, her eyes became anguished. 'You're lying!'

'Ask her.' She shuffled a pack of cards and smiled to herself. 'Would you like a reading?'

'Does Alex know?'

'She's telling him at the weekend. If you really want him, Ces, I could cast a spell.'

Her sister began to turn away.

'You might think it won't work, but it will. I'll cast one anyway, because I want you to have what your heart desires. Just make me a concoction for Sylvia in return.'

She hesitated. 'It might be dangerous in her condition.'

Rose stared hard at her back. She'd never known Ces to be so difficult. 'I'll make one myself, then. I doubt if Alex will be happy about it. He trusts you with that sort of thing.'

'I suppose I'd better do it,' she said quickly.

She beamed a smile. 'And you'll be at the seance? The more power there is, the more chance we'll have of being a success.'

'I'll think about it.'

'By the way,' Rose said when her sister reached the door. 'I think dear Fiona's spying on you. There was horse dung in the field, and a footprint on the bank by the big elm. If I were you, I'd take Napoleon and Josephine with you next time you go that way.'

Cecily slowly turned, only to grin at her. 'One of these days Fiona Bunnings might get a bigger shock than she bargained for.'

Rose began to laugh. 'It will serve her right.'

Betony was fizzing over with happiness. A baby! It was confirmed. Flipping up the lid of Vivaldi, she played the *Minute Waltz*, then laughed with sheer exhilaration.

She'd cook something special tonight. Roast beef perhaps, with roast potatoes and all the trimmings. Then apple pie and custard to follow.

The baby was due late in January. She'd been given an ultrasound scan image, a tiny, perfect baby curled up inside her. She'd cried and laughed at the same time and, not caring if it was boy or girl, fell in love on the spot.

She'd rung the shrink, cancelling further appointments. 'I'm feeling great now,' she'd said, 'I don't think I need to see you any more.'

He'd argued of course, saying she could relapse into depression again without warning. He *would* say that – he had a lifestyle to maintain.

She didn't need him, she didn't need anybody but Noel and their child.

She hadn't told the shrink why she felt so strong. It wasn't his business, and she didn't want to be constantly reminded of Ben now. Nothing was going to spoil her happiness.

Noel was smiling so widely when he arrived, she thought he might have already heard the news. But no, he had news of his own. 'Would you believe it? I got an offer for the flat two hours after it was listed.'

'Of course you did. This is London and it's central. A tree house made of packing cases would fetch millions.'

He took her in a hug. 'Before I accept the offer, are you quite happy about me buying into this place?'

'There's all the more reason for you to buy into it now.' The news burst from her in a rush, because she was on such a high she couldn't wait until after dinner to tell him. 'I saw the doctor today. We're having a baby. In January.'

He stared at her silently, his eyes dark and uncomprehending.

'A baby,' she said slowly and patiently. 'One of those small people who dribble from both ends and cry half the night.'

'Good God!' he muttered.

'Is that all you can say?'

'I think I misheard you. Let me get this straight. Did you just say we're having a baby?'

She smiled encouragingly at him. 'Well done.'

His smile was tentative at first, then his whole face became incandescent. 'A baby. I'll be damned.'

She had no need to ask if he was pleased. 'You will be if you don't kiss me.'

It was nice being kissed in such a gentle, loving manner. She closed her eyes afterwards, hugging him, enjoying the synergy between them. She would spend the rest of her life with him in contentment. He would care for them in a way Simon never had. He'd always be there for her.

Tears trembled on her lashes. Choked by her overwhelming love for him, she whispered, 'Thank you, thank you, my darling.'

'You're crying.'

'I'm so happy, that's why.'

'We'll have to get a bigger house,' he said, practical all at once.

'But not yet. Not until he can walk. We can use the spare room as a nursery. I'll clear it out and buy some pretty wallpaper and stuff . . .'

He held her at arm's length, laughing whilst she prattled on about bassinets and cots, and should she paint the woodwork pink or blue. Eventually, he stopped her with a kiss.

'I'll come with you to choose the paint and wallpaper, because I want to be involved in this in every way, and I'll do the work. I'm not – repeat, *not* having you lift a finger.'

'But, Noel—'

'Don't waste your breath arguing,' he warned. 'If I so much as see you lift a paintbrush, I'll tan your backside with it.'

They stared at each other, grinning inanely. Gradually, the smell of scorching pastry drifted into the room.

'Oh, God,' she wailed, tearing herself from his arms. 'I forgot about the apple pie.'

They ate it anyway, the black edges scraped off, and the rest smothered in thick, yellow custard.

The evening was spent making plans for the future.

She was indescribably happy when Noel decided to accept the offer on his flat and move in with her the following weekend.

'I'll ask the estate agent to give us a market valuation of this place. I'll pay my share as soon as the sale is settled.'

'There's no rush.'

'There is for me. If I'm going to be a father I intend to do things properly, and that means providing for my family.' A grin spread across his face when he said that.

'You're a funny, old fashioned thing, but I love you, anyway,' she said, laughing at his pleasure, and certain she did love him, then.

It had been a beastly day. There had been a bunch of men and women occupying most of the tables for the second weekend in a row.

They'd criticized her pastries, made fun of the surroundings, and had her running backwards and forwards with bucket and sponge to mop up spilled drinks. Sylvia scowled. She was exhausted. The hired girl had burst into tears when she'd told her sharply to get on with her work instead of daydreaming, and had walked out on her.

It was nearly nine before she finished preparing for the next day. Her back and legs ached, and she still hadn't seen Alex, not to talk to, anyway. He'd walked past the conservatory without even glancing her way. He seemed to be avoiding her, and she intended to find out why.

It was nearly dark as she made her way to his cottage. She shuddered when she nearly walked into a spider spinning a web between two trees. 'Nasty brute,' she muttered, splattering it against a tree trunk with one of her shoes.

Cecily's voice made her jump a mile. 'You didn't have to do that. It wouldn't have hurt you.'

'What are you doing here?'

'Walking the dogs.'

'I can't see any dogs,' she said.

Cecily's whistle brought two shapes hurtling out of the dusk to quiver and pant against her legs.

She felt like a fool. 'I wanted some fresh air.'

'Who are you trying to kid? You've come to tell Alex you've got a bun in the oven.'

'If I have, it's none of your damned business.'

'If I were you I wouldn't bother him with it.' She gave a short laugh as she pushed past her in a mixture of body odour and sandalwood. 'The last time I saw him he wasn't in a receptive frame of mind. In fact, I'd be surprised if he was at home.'

Sylvia ignored her. The light was on in his cottage. When she knocked, nobody answered. She went inside, anyway.

Grimacing at the littered kitchen area, she started to clean the place up, then went through to the bedroom. She stopped in shock. Alex was lying on his back in the middle of the crumpled bed, his body glistening in the light from several candles. The room smelled of sandalwood. Cecily's bag of aromatherapy oils were open on the dresser.

Outraged, Sylvia shrieked. 'That bitch has been here!'

He woke with a start, his expression darkening. 'What the hell do you want?'

Her hands went to her hips. 'I'll tell you what I want. I'm pregnant, that's what.'

He stared at her, his face turning the colour of putty. 'You're lying.'

'Do you think I'd lie about something like this.' She gazed derisively at the candles. 'OK, you've had your fun, but it's got to stop. We have a baby to think about.'

He propped himself up on one elbow, his eyes dark and unreadable. 'Get rid of it.'

The suggestion was as unexpected as a blow, and twice as shocking. 'Alex,' she choked out. 'This is our baby, born of our love.'

'Grow up,' he said harshly. 'This isn't a soap opera. Get rid of it.'

'It's gone to far for that. I'm not going to put myself in danger just so you can wriggle out of your responsibilities.'

He swung his legs over the side of the bed and pulled on his jeans. 'You must get rid of it.'

'I don't see why. We could get married when the divorce comes through.' She hated the pleading note in her voice. 'I've already decided on a plan. I could set you up in business, a plant nursery perhaps. That way you would be acceptable to my mother.'

He pushed roughly past her, bitter laughter tumbling from his lips. 'I'll never be acceptable to your bloody mother.'

'Really, Alex, there's no need to be offensive. I'm sure I'll get her to accept you in time, despite the differences in our status.' The mixture of despair and anger in his face brought her up short. 'From the moment we met there was something special between us. You felt it too, you said so.'

The grin he gave was twisted and bitter. 'I never said a truer word. There *is* something special between us.'

'Then what's the problem?'

'Not what – but who?'

She stared at him with growing alarm. 'I suppose Cecily put you up to it. What's she got that I haven't, except for wrinkles.'

'You stupid cow,' he snarled. 'The baby mustn't be born. I'm Alison Green's son.'

For a moment she stared at him, uncomprehending, then a pulse started hammering in her head. Her hand fluttered to her chest, trying to contain her soaring heart beat. 'What are you saying?'

'You're my half-sister,' he said flatly.

'You bastard!' she shrieked, refusing to believe it. The room began to spin about her and somebody started to scream. The sound went on and on until she could hear nothing else.

Someone slapped back and forth across her face and the screaming stopped. Her body felt like ice. She couldn't see anything but a shimmering, red haze. She knew her eyes were open because they twitched and jerked uncontrollably against her lids.

There was somebody else in the room. 'Pass the blue bottle,' Cecily said calmly from a distance. A sharp, acrid smell raced up her nostrils to her brain, jerking her eyes back into position and herself into painful consciousness.

'Oh God.' She burst into tears against Cecily's chest. 'What have we done?'

Cecily's voice was soothing as she rocked her back and forth. 'No one is to blame. I could give you something to start contractions of the uterus.'

'Perhaps the kid's not mine,' Alex suggested. 'Clive Harrington took part in your initiation.'

Shuddering, Sylvia sat up to stare numbly at him. 'Of course. Who else could the father be?'

Ignoring Cecily's pitying expression, she stood to straighten her shirt. 'Goodness, look at the time. I must get to bed. I need my rest. I've got a hard day ahead of me now that dreadful girl has walked out.'

'We must talk,' Alex said. 'Sort things out. There's no need for us to hate each other over what our parents did.'

She glanced at him before she left. He was staring at her through her father's eyes and smiling with her father's sensuous mouth. Liars, both of them! How could she ever have loved her father? How could she ever have thought she loved Alex?

When her hands pressed against her stomach she saw distaste fill his eyes. He'd betrayed and soiled her, as his father had before him. She wanted to kill him.

As for Cecily. She'd known, and had been laughing at her all the time.

Composed now, Sylvia smiled at her and thought – just you wait.

'Well,' Cecily said softly after Sylvia had gone off into the darkness. 'You didn't handle that too well.'

'What was I supposed to do?' he mumbled, dropping his head to his hands in abject misery. 'You should have told me. You knew about the baby, didn't you?'

She nodded. 'If you hadn't planted a seed of doubt in her mind I might have been able to convince her to get rid of it.'

143

'She said it was too late.'

How weak he was. She reached out to touch his hair, then drew him, unresisting, against her breast. 'It could have been achieved without surgical intervention.'

'Oh God, Ces, what a mess. What am I going to do?'

'Nothing. Sylvia's resourceful. Once she's thought things through she'll come up with a solution to suit her. My guess is, she'll convince herself it didn't happen with you.' Her hand stroked soothingly through his hair. 'Why don't we go away together? Leave everything behind us.'

'What about the money?'

She sighed. 'You were quite content before you knew about it. Forget about the money.'

'Brian Throsby owes me. All my life I've been poor. While Sylvia was strutting about with her airs and graces, I was scratching for a crust.' The self-pity fled and his voice strengthened. His eyes came up to hers, shining with greed and insincerity. 'The money will give me a new start. Just be patient, Ces. We'll go away then, far away where nobody knows us. Canada perhaps.'

He would leave her, like Fiorenzo had. They were a pair, two sensual, shallow men who lived only for their passion. She should have learnt the first time. What she hadn't learned, was how to live alone with the desire Fiorenzo had awakened in her. She always fell in love with losers.

When Alex pulled her down on to the bed, she thought of the time she'd caught Fiorenzo with Rose. Rose has been squealing like a joyous pig, her flabby white thighs wobbling as his skinny olive bottom had bounced up and down between them.

Disgust filled her. 'Have you ever screwed Rose,' she murmured against his ear.

He lifted his head and gazed at her, anger deepening his eyes as his desire fled. 'Rose serves no one but the master.'

It sounded as if he'd tried. She pushed him away and rose from the bed. Gathering up her things she left, closing the door quietly behind her.

'Clive, can we talk.' Sylvia drew him away from the crowd and into a quiet corner of the corridor, where she informed him she was pregnant.

He shrugged off her clutching hand and stared at her, his eyes cold and thoughtful. 'Why are you telling me?'

'I don't know quite how to say this.' Tears came to her eyes. 'I think you might be the father.'

He began to chuckle. 'Jesus, if I thought it was mine, I'd ditch Daphne and marry you tomorrow.'

She put her hand on his arm. 'Would you, would you really, Clive?' It would be a feather in her cap to marry a man so wealthy and powerful. *A pity he was old.* She smiled as she pictured herself standing by his graveside, a black veil over her face, her hand clasping that of a small girl. He dashed cold water on the image.

'Nice try, Sylvia. We'll have a test done when it's born. If the kid's mine I'll marry you and make it legal.'

'You know you can't deny the possibility of fatherhood out of hand,' she snarled.

His smile was loathsome. 'Why don't you put the hard word on Dereck. He's comfortably off, a bachelor, and besotted with you.'

She'd almost forgotten Dereck's existence. She shrugged. 'He's a bore. Besides, I'm certain the child is yours. I feel it deep in my soul, and you know how special Rose thinks that is.'

Clive moistened his lips. 'I'll think about it.'

She gazed calmly at him, feeling more sure. 'You wouldn't want your own flesh and blood to grow up without a father, would you? What would people say?'

'I'll think about it?'

She nodded and moved away from him, excitement bubbling in her. 'I must prepare myself for the seance.'

'Are you sure the kid's mine?'

She nodded, knowing she'd hooked his interest.

He put out an arm to bar her passage, curiosity in his pale eyes. 'Can you really bring Isabella out of hiding? Rose has been attempting it for years.'

Her eyes narrowed. 'My power is greater than that of Rose, and I'm already in contact with Isabella. She'll come forth when I summon her. Just you wait and see.'

'About the kid,' he said. 'I've been married three times and never managed to score. If it proves to be mine—'

'Excuse me,' she said, 'I must go and join Rose in preparation for the seance.'

She left him standing in the hall, the seed she'd planted taking root in his mind as firmly as the seed planted in her womb.

The celebrities attending the seance surprised Daphne. There were eleven altogether, including one or two she'd met in her own drawing room.

Sylvia Dearborn was different than she'd pictured her. Her ethereal looks

145

were stunning. She sat in the centre of the circle in a trance-like state, the pupils of her blue eyes distended and unseeing. Her gown was little more than clinging layers of black silk. Everyone's eyes were on her, including those of Alex. Daphne felt uncomfortable.

He moved to stand behind them when Cecily handed out glasses of wine, bending to exchange a whispered word with Clive, who glanced her way and nodded.

Cecily caught her eye. Her face was expressionless, but her eyes dipped once to the glass in her hand. There was a wealth of meaning in the gesture – a warning. Something was going on she hadn't been told about. Uneasily, she pretended to sip the drink, her mind in overdrive.

It was obvious Sylvia was drugged to the gills. Daphne didn't want to be part of this macabre scene. Conjuring up a dead person was bad enough, people getting high on the event was obscene. The room was charged with tension.

'Drink up,' Clive said.

She put the glass to her mouth, then when he and Alex were distracted by the door opening, she tipped the contents down the side of the cushions.

Bloody hell! Rasputin had arrived with Rose on his arm. The candle flames flickered when Rose took a seat. The black monk stood behind her, his hands tucked into his sleeves in the fashion of medieval film monks.

Daphne grinned when the lights dimmed. What a farce! Who would believe these supposedly sane and powerful people were trying the raise a spirit. It was ludicrous. Her strong sense of the ridiculous took over and she experienced the urge to giggle.

'Tonight, we will all join hands and concentrate on the soul of Isabella Dubeney,' Rose intoned.

Daphne did giggle, a little snort she turned into a cough. Clive turned an annoyed glance on her. He looked like a greying ape with his brows hanging over his eyes. She gave a hoot of laughter.

Rose exchanged an exasperated glance with Alex. A hand was slipped under her elbow. The next minute she was being escorted out. When she glanced back, the circle had joined hands. Rose was rocking back and forth humming to herself and Sylvia was still staring into space. Light glinted in the depths of the monk's cowl. He was wearing glasses.

'What's the kooky blond on, hash?' she said, as soon as the door closed behind them.

'The same as you had in your drink.' Alex's weird, green eyes were locked into hers, a half-smile played across his lips 'How are you feeling, Daphne? Do you need me to help you upstairs for the initiation into the circle, or can you make it on your own?'

A lowered glance showed her exactly what form that initiation would take. There were at least eight men in there. Her eyes narrowed. Clive would get his rocks off watching it take place. The bastard! It was his revenge for her leaving him.

Drugged, was she? Like hell! It might be fun to string Alex along, though. She slid her elbow from his grasp, cocked her head sideways and smiled dreamily up at him. Her hand slid to his fly and pulled the zip down. He sprang into her hand, all warm and throbbing.

He was all engine, with a body attached.

'Not here.' Sliding his arm around her waist he led her towards the stairs. 'We have a room prepared.'

'I can't wait, Alex,' she panted as soon as they were out of earshot. She fell to her knees, yanked his pants down round his ankles and pushed him back against a wall. She drove her knee sharply upwards.

His eyes flew open, incredulous and shocked. He doubled over and gagged for breath. She drove her other knee up against his face, shuddering when something crunched.

'Be thankful I didn't maim you for life,' she spat out and, speeding down the stairs, she snatched up her coat and let herself out.

The circle was chanting when she closed the door quietly behind her. Creeping under the window she nearly tripped over someone standing in the flower bed. 'Shit!' she said, her heart pumping sparks. She clapped a hand over the frightened squeal Fiona was about to make. 'All hell's about to break loose in there,' she whispered, 'I want to hang around to see the fun. After that we'll high-tail it back to your place like a couple of cowardly custards – OK?'

Showing the whites of her eyes, Fiona nodded.

Sylvia could see Isabella. Her dress was a shimmer of gold silk as she floated towards her. Her hair floated about her shoulders.

'You're amongst friends,' she said, smiling at her.

An excited murmur filled the room until somebody shushed it.

'Ask her where Katherine's buried,' Rose hissed.

Isabella came closer. Her face was pale and unhappy, her eyes ringed by shadow. She'd never experienced such suffering. It filled her body and mind. She rose, extending her arms to the other. *Sebastian is angered.*

'We need to know where Katherine's bones are buried.'

Sylvia smiled at the assembled faces. 'Isabella will only communicate through me, Rose.'

Through the wavering form of Isabella she saw the door beginning to open.

Candles flickered in a draft, several were gutted. The inner circle shifted uneasily.

'Ask her where the baby's buried,' Rose shouted.

'Shut up, you stupid cow,' the actress said angrily. 'You'll frighten Isabella off and she'll break contact.'

Beware, Sebastian is angry.

She became one with Isabella. Through her eyes she saw a dark form stagger into the room. Blood covered its face. Adrenaline pounded through her. Her brother! Lifting her arm she pointed at him. 'Sebastian is here. Kill him!'

'Sebastian. Oh my God! How wonderful! She's brought forth Sebastian!' the actress screamed.

The dark spectre gave a terrifying groan. They turned as one towards the door when it crashed against the wall. Several of the women screamed. The men converged on the figure. The remaining candles blew out, pitching them into darkness. Pandemonium took control. Furniture was overturned, there was the sound of blows against flesh, curses and screams.

Terrified, Sylvia fainted.

Daphne was hysterical with laughter as she cantered through the night, her arms clutched about Fiona's waist.

A bloody horse, for crissakes! Betony would die laughing when she told her. She couldn't go home now. Clive would never forgive her for making a fool of him.

'Yee har!' she yelled in Fiona's ear. 'Ride 'em cowboy!'

CHAPTER FOURTEEN

Clive hadn't seen Daphne since she'd fled from the seance the previous month. She sat across the table from him with her lawyer now, looking like a dream. He pressed the blade of a paper knife against the blotter, wishing it was her jugular vein.

'If I agree to a cash settlement I'll expect you to sign an agreement not to claim anything else.'

She nodded.

'Furthermore, you must undertake not to reveal details of a personal nature occurring during our marriage?'

'Would I do that to you?' she purred.

'My client wants her jewellery and the personal items specified on the list,' the lawyer said smoothly.

Daphne had him by the balls. He couldn't fight it in court, she knew too much. She'd asked for a large amount of money, but it wouldn't break him. His glance assessed the list. Obviously, she didn't know about the Swiss bank account and she'd ignored the two houses, opting for cash in hand. His eyes narrowed in on the last item on the list. How had she found out about the Kensington flat?

'The tenant has a lease,' he murmured, loath to part with it. He'd spent many an enjoyable evening being entertained on the premises.

'The lease is due up for renewal,' she shot at him. 'And it specifies four weeks notice. The tenant only uses it to entertain his *guests*.' Her smile took on the consistency of cream. 'Shall I ring his wife to ask if it would inconvenience her if I moved in straight away?'

He scowled. She'd been through his personal papers.

'If this goes to court, my client would be awarded more.' Her lawyer slid some papers across the table. 'You'd be required to reveal your income from all sources, as I'm sure Mr Barclay will tell you.'

He glanced at Barclay, who nodded. Damned lawyers, they'd agree to anything to save their own skins. What the hell, he had too much to lose if he didn't agree. Much as he regretted losing her, and he did, Daphne was expendable.

An image of Sylvia flashed into his mind. Her role in the circle gave her too much power, but at least they'd have something in common. If genetic testing proved he was the father, he'd marry her. A pre-nuptial agreement was the way to go though, if marriage was on the cards. He could jettison her if it didn't work.

He picked up the gold fountain pen Daphne had given him for Christmas. 'Where do I sign?'

Dorothy received the anonymous letter just before Sylvia arrived home.

Dear Mrs Throsby,
I feel compelled to inform you that your daughter is having relations with the gardener at Little Abbot. She's also involved in the black magic rituals taking place there.
A well wisher.

Sylvia denied it, of course. 'Don't be silly. You know what goes on there is just harmless stuff. Goodness, you've had a tarot reading yourself.'

'And what about this accusation concerning the gardener?'

'Malicious lies. Someone in the village has got it in for me over the tea room affair.' She crossed to where her mother stood, gazing down at her pensively. 'Now you've mentioned the gardener, I really feel I ought to tell you. Alex is the son of Alison Green.'

'Sylvia,' she reproached. 'How could you associate with such a person?'

'I didn't know until last weekend. If I had, I'd have told you earlier.'

'It's all lies. I'm sure he's not Brian's son.'

Sylvia tried not to laugh at her mother's stricken face. She was beginning to look like the dried-up old hag she was. 'Then you have nothing to worry about if he files a claim.'

'He already has,' she said bitterly. 'The investment accounts are under investigation, even my personal ones. I'm to be given an allowance until it's settled. *An allowance!* As if I'm a recipient of government benefits. It's a waste of time. That labourer is *not* Brian's son.'

'Alex looks very much like him. You must stop believing daddy was a saint, when I know he wasn't.'

'No wonder Brian never really took to you, though he did his best not to show it. His concern was justified. He'd be upset to know how you'd turned out.'

'Oh, I don't know.' She smiled sweetly as she examined her fingernails. 'I expect he'd be overjoyed to know I'm engaged to marry a secretary to a cabinet minister. Position meant so much to you both.'

Her mother stared at her for a moment. 'Who is this man?'

'The father of my child.'

'I see.'

'He has a house in St John's Wood and another in Abbotsford. He's fabulously wealthy.'

'Does he come from a good family? I don't want you to make the same mistake twice.'

She thought of Alex, and smiled. Her mother didn't know the half of it.

'You can ask him that yourself. He's dropping in shortly to be introduced. I thought I'd prepare you first, but not a word to anyone. Both of us are in the middle of a divorce, and we don't want our relationship to get out.'

Dorothy realized Sylvia hadn't prepared her at all when Clive arrived. He was old enough to be her father. Nevertheless, her frosty expression changed to a gracious smile.

Clive knew that old-fashioned courtesy never went amiss when dealing with older women. Dorothy was soon eating out of his hand. Given half an ear, she talked graciously about nothing in particular for ages. Constipated with morality and steeped in traditional values, Clive knew that a laxative wouldn't purge the ghost of a fart from the woman.

She reminded him of his own mother.

He laughed at Sylvia's petulant face when they left. 'You forgot to tell me Alex is your half-brother.'

'I didn't know until last weekend, and neither did he. Anyway, it's not proven yet.'

'What was it like with him?'

'I want to forget about it, Clive. It's in the past.'

He turned into a deserted lane, drew the car to a halt and said silkily, 'You enjoyed his attention the night of your initiation. Tell me what it's like with him.'

Tears sprang to her eyes. 'I don't want to.' But he bullied it out of her, making her recite every shameful second before pulling her out of the car and behind the hedge. It was over quickly, leaving him satisfied and her still wanting.

Straightening her clothes, she got back into the car, her face sulky. He surprised her by showing her a diamond ring and watched her eyes sparkle with greed.

'In the morning, if you're a good girl. I expect more of you than that,' he said as he slipped it into his pocket. She'd have to learn the hard way that he was the one in control.

Daphne made everything sound so sleazy.

Although the episode on the horse had made her laugh, Betony didn't want to be bothered with the rest. All she wanted was have her baby and live a life of quiet domesticity, like thousands of other families.

A black magic coven at Little Abbot, with her sisters and Noel's wife at the centre of it? It was preposterous. She wouldn't tell Noel. It would be stupid to let outside influences jeopardize their happiness.

Needing to be reassured, she phoned the house, hoping she'd get Cecily. Rose answered.

'How strange, I was just going to ring you, dear. Is everything all right?'

'Why shouldn't everything be all right?' It was odd how edgy she felt talking to Rose.

'I thought you might have some news for me,' Rose said. 'You'll never guess what I saw in my crystal, but then again, you might.'

'No doubt you're going to tell me,' she said carefully.

'I saw you with a child in your arms. She was dark-haired and blue-eyed, and her name was Katherine.'

Betony said nothing, she didn't dare.

'Are you pregnant, dear?'

She felt cheated. The sparkle drained from her. Just the thought of Rose knowing in advance soiled it somehow. 'What if I am?'

'That's wonderful. Is it that accountant? You really must bring him down to meet us.'

She stifled her gasp. 'How did you know? And don't tell me you saw it in the crystal, because I won't believe you.'

'It wasn't hard to put two and two together after you took him to the Harringtons' party. You should be more discreet if you want to keep things a secret.'

'It wasn't really a secret, it's just . . . he was living with his wife at the time.'

'Did you know she's my protégée? A pity you saw fit to get your revenge by taking her husband from her. It will make things difficult for me when she finds out.'

Betony's knuckles tightened on the receiver. 'It might have started out that way. But I certainly didn't encourage Noel to leave her. His marriage was already in trouble.'

'If you say so, dear.'

Only Rose could show her displeasure by being so distant. She took a deep breath. Her relationship with Noel was none of Rose's business. She brought the conversation round to the reason she'd phoned.

'I've heard rumours of odd things going on down there.'

'Daphne Harrington, I suppose.' Rose sighed. 'She and her husband had a fight. Since then, she's been making trouble.'

'Why would Daphne make trouble for you, Rose?'

'I introduced Sylvia to Clive. Now they're an item. You really shouldn't remain friends with Daphne. She'll be a bad influence on you.'

Her temper began to simmer. When she'd been growing up Rose had subtly eroded her self-esteem, and Cecily had constantly built it up again. She'd ping-ponged back and forth between the twins like a ball between two bats, as if they were engaged in a contest for possession of her.

'How's father these days?'

'His condition's improving. He should be well enough to travel by Christmas. How lovely it would be if we were all together.'

She left the barely disguised hint hanging in the air. They were going to spend Christmas in Nottingham with Noel's parents. She was looking forward to meeting them. 'Is Cecily there?'

'Not at the moment, dear. She's gone to tend Ben's little grave. She's planting red chrysanthemums. I did tell her yellow might be more suitable. He always looked so sweet in yellow. She said red would make a warmer blanket.'

Betony wanted to scream. Ben was dead. He felt neither warmth nor cold. Why did Rose go on about him, making her feel empty and racked with guilt?

'I do think it odd you've found it in your heart to forgive the man who put him there.' Her voice contained a reprimand. 'I'll tell Ces you rang. She'll be sorry she missed you.'

She squeezed her eyes shut when pain clutched at her heart. Then the baby inside her quickened, as if jealous of the memory of its dead sibling. She placed a reassuring hand over her stomach. 'It's all right darling, it's all right.'

'Did you say something dear?'

'Nothing. Goodbye Rose.'

'Goodbye is so final. I have a strong feeling we'll all be together again soon.'

Not if she could help it, she thought as she hung up. She didn't want to set foot in Little Abbot again. In fact, she might take Daniel Jacobs' advice and sell it in the New Year.

From habit, her hand reached towards the pill bottle. Quickly, she withdrew it. She hadn't taken any since she'd found out she was pregnant, and she wasn't going to start. It was hard. She still had days when she was irritable, and nights when she was jerked out of sleep by dreams of Ben calling her. At least she had Noel to hold her close and tell her it was all right, now. The dreams were becoming fewer as her dependency on the pills decreased.

She wrenched the lid off the bottle, ran upstairs and tipped the remaining pills down the toilet. When they'd flushed away she felt proud of herself. Then her hands began to tremble and she regretted the action. Stumbling down to the lounge she crossed to Vivaldi and ran her fingers over the keys. They were clumsy, like cold, sausages hanging from her hands.

Discipline yourself, practice! She began to play scales, one after the other. The sausages became flexible, the notes sharper and clearer. She forgot the time, forgot everything as she began to play the *Allegro vivace* from the Schumann piano concerto. It was breathtakingly light and vibrant. She closed her eyes as her fingers wove the intricate threads of the melodies together. Though the funny little piano didn't do it justice, her mood was quite lifted when she finished.

She turned at the sound of applause, giving Noel a brilliant and loving smile. 'I didn't hear you come in.'

'You were too wrapped up in your music.'

His arm circled a plant wrapped in coloured paper. Crossing to where she sat, he bowed, then lifted up her hand and pressed his lips against it. 'A bouquet for my favourite soloist.'

The blood ebbed from her face when he placed it in her arms. 'Red chrysanthemums!'

She hadn't realized her smile had faded until Noel's did. The concern in his face twisted at her guts. 'What's the matter?'

It wasn't his fault. He couldn't have known Cecily was planting red chrysanthemums on Ben's grave. Rose had done this! She'd somehow got into his mind and played this cruel trick on her. She sucked in a deep breath. She was being irrational.

He took the flowers from her trembling arms, set them on the floor, and taking her hands chaffed them between the warmth of his. 'What is it, Betony love?'

She felt like bursting into tears. 'Nothing, the flowers are lovely. I felt a bit faint, that's all.' She forced a smile to her face, feeling the colour return now she was thinking straight. 'I rang my sister earlier on. She knows about us and the baby.'

'And that upset you?'

'In a way. I didn't want them to know, not yet.'

His eyes were dark against hers. 'Why?'

'I wanted it to be ours, something we share. Rose knowing sort of spoils it a bit.'

'Not for me.' His grin warmed her. 'I'd like to climb to the top of a mountain, beat my chest like an ape and holler it to the world.'

She giggled. 'What's stopping you?'

'A more experienced father might stand at the bottom and yell up at me, "So what, you're just a beginner".'

She dissolved into laughter and kissed him. 'You're going to be the greatest father who ever lived.'

'I'm going to try.' Looking slightly sheepish he slid a book out from inside his pocket. 'I bought myself a manual. *The A to Z of Pregnancy and Parenting*.'

'Oh, Noel.' Her whole body seemed to be one big grin. 'I don't know whether to laugh or cry.'

'Follow your instincts,' he said dryly. His lips twitched into a self-deprecating grin. 'I guess it was a daft idea, at that.'

'No, it wasn't . . . it wasn't! It was a lovely idea. We'll follow the manual closely and raise a perfect child who will grow to be loving, kind, and serious, just like her father.'

He wiggled an eyebrow. 'She sounds a bit of a prig to me. What about the dribbly bits you told me about? I haven't got those.'

The laughter she'd tried to keep inside, erupted. She laughed and laughed until her body ached with it. Noel's inane grin made her laugh more. 'You've got no idea how much I love you,' she gasped out.

He began to laugh, too. Throwing the book at the waste-paper basket, he snatched her up in his arms and they danced around the room in a mad euphoria until they were giddy and exhausted.

Later, when she told him his ex-wife was involved with Clive Harrington, she watched his face anxiously.

He looked pained. 'Your sister seems to thrive on gossip.'

'You don't mind, then?'

'I don't care what she does, or who she does it with.' As if sensing her anxiety he took her face between his hands and gently kissed her. 'I care only about you and our baby.'

Contentment spread through him like warm butter on bread. She snuggled her head into his shoulder. She'd never felt so safe and happy in her life.

Sylvia was very much on Noel's mind the following week.

He glanced up when Joyce came in with his morning coffee.

'There's a man waiting in the office to see you. I told him you were busy all morning, but he said he'd wait until you're free. His name is Jeff Sullivan.'

'It's all right, Joyce. He's a personal friend. I'll talk to him during my break.'

He hadn't seen either of the Sullivans since he'd left Sylvia, preferring not to put them in the unenviable position of taking sides, though Anne had phoned him to say how sorry she was to hear of the break up.

Jeff looked harassed when he came in. Briefly, they shook hands. 'What can I do for you, Jeff.'

'Anne's left me.'

Shocked, Noel stared at him. 'I don't know what to say. You seemed to have an ideal marriage. What happened?'

'Your wife happened, that's what. I know it's no excuse, but she threw herself at me. I'm convinced she did it on purpose, and planned it so Anne would be suspicious.'

Noel gave a mirthless smile, remembering the suspicion he'd dismissed about Jeff and Sylvia. 'How long did your affair with Sylvia go on?'

'Affair? There was no affair.' Jeff stared at him. 'Good God, Noel, if she told you that she was lying. This happened ages after you left.'

'You didn't spend the weekend with her when you were supposed to be at that Newcastle conference at the beginning of the year?'

His eyes widened. 'What do you take me for? Good God, you're my friend.'

Noel believed him. 'OK. I'm sorry.'

'The thing is, I want you to talk to Anne. Persuade her to take me back. Sylvia set me up. She fed me malt whisky followed by a sob story, just to get at Anne.'

'Are you telling me you were the victim, Jeff?'

'OK, so I should have kept my pants zipped. It's the first time I've been offered it on a plate – and from Sylvia of all people.'

'You'd better tell me exactly what happened.'

His face darkened when Jeff briefly outlined the event.

'I might flirt a bit, but I had never cheated on Anne before this.'

'Did you admit it to her?'

'Hell no. There's no way I'd hurt her deliberately. Things have gone from bad to worse since then. I'm so ashamed of myself, and I miss Anne and the kids.'

'I'll see what I can do.'

'Do it soon, Noel. I'm just about at the end of my tether.'

Noel did it later that afternoon.

Anne sounded as miserable as Jeff had been.

'Give the guy a break, Anne. He's never loved anyone else but you!'

'I'm sure he went to bed with her.'

'I doubt it. Between you and me, Sylvia was never exactly enamoured with that kind of activity.'

Anne, suddenly recalling a conversation she'd had with Sylvia relating to exactly the same thing, was convinced. Jeff hadn't even liked her. Why, he hadn't even wanted to go round to help her out that night.

'I've been a fool,' she said, beginning to sniffle. 'You were a saint to put up with Sylvia for so long, especially with this occult thing she's involved in. It's quite gone to her head.'

Noel frowned. It was the second time Sylvia had been mentioned in this context. 'I'm not sure what you mean.'

'Some woman who writes a horoscope column has taken her under her wing. They're into tarot card readings and seances.' She sniffed again. 'I suppose it's quite harmless.'

'Unless she uses it as an excuse to cause mischief to others. She always had a spiteful streak.'

A muffled sob reached his ears as the meaning of his words sank in. There was the sound of a nose being vigorously blown.

'Sorry,' she mumbled, sounding absolutely wretched. 'I hope you find some-one more deserving of you in the future.'

'I have,' he said, hoping the sob didn't develop into a fully-fledged session. Much as he liked Anne, his last appointment of the day was due.

The sniffles ceased. 'That's great! Why don't you bring her over for dinner next week, or is that being too obvious?'

When he chuckled, so did she.

'I'll give you a ring.' He hesitated slightly, but knowing if he didn't tell some-one, he'd burst. 'And Anne, there's some other news. I'm going to be a father at long last.'

'That's wonderful,' she said warmly. 'You *must* bring her over now. We've missed your company so much. What's her name?'

'Betony,' he said, tasting her name like wild honey on his tongue. 'It's Betony Nichols.'

He smiled to himself as he hung up.

Dorothy Throsby suddenly relented over the house.

There was no sense of triumph in Alison's heart – no feeling of pride. As she'd said to Sam, in gaining the house she'd lost her son. Worse, she'd lost her illusions about him.

Sam had said it was probably a good thing. Now she could think of herself and her future.

Getting the house hadn't changed her life all that much. It simply meant she didn't have to pay rent. Her job at the supermarket seemed to stretch into a drab, meaningless and boring future. She stared at herself in the mirror. A middle-aged woman with greying hair stared back. Her navy suit had been her best one since she could remember. Even the new blouse she'd made couldn't lift its drabness.

Why on earth did Sam want to take a woman like her out? He deserved someone cleverer, someone smarter. Not that he was much to look at himself. He was thin-faced and balding. His manner was cynical and sometimes off-putting. But he made her laugh and she always enjoyed his company.

'A dinner to celebrate your good fortune,' he'd said when he rung her that morning.

She made a face at the suit and turned a critical eye on her hair. Perhaps she *could* give him someone better. If she got her hair styled? And if the Oxfam shop had something better than what she was wearing now?

Her glance fell on the walnut box with its pretty silver hinges. It was probably worth something, enough to buy a new outfit with, at least. She couldn't remember the last time she'd bought anything new.

'I was wondering,' Sam said the following evening as they lingered over their coffee. 'Would you consider staying in London?'

'With you?' She was a bit miffed he hadn't noticed the effort she'd made on his behalf.

He shrugged and his eyes came up to meet hers. 'I've just bought a new television, and I'm sure my cats would like you.'

'That's a blessing.'

He grinned engagingly at her. 'Would you consider staying?'

'I suppose one night wouldn't hurt if you've got a spare room.'

'I haven't got a spare room. Well, I have, several in fact, but they're full of junk.'

She stared at him, more self-assured than usual in her new blue dress and matching jacket. 'Are you asking me to go to bed with you?'

He leaned forward, his expression serious now. 'I guess I am, but not for one night. I meant permanently.'

A grin flitted across her face. 'Ah, I see. You want me to live with you, watch your new television, feed your cats and clear out the junk from your spare rooms.'

'We could get married.' He gave a twisted grin. 'Though I must warn you, my mother will have hysterics.'

'Why?'

'She's been trying to marry me off for years to nice Jewish matrons.'

'Are you Jewish? I hadn't noticed.'

'Like I haven't noticed your new hairstyle and outfit. You look wonderful.' His hand covered hers, the expression in his eyes was serious now. 'I'm half and half.'

'Ah, a mongrel.'

'Does it worry you?'

'It obviously didn't worry your mother, so how hysterical can she get?'

They began to laugh.

CHAPTER FIFTEEN

A storm heralded the onset of October.

For three days, Sylvia stayed inside, watching the remaining leaves beaten from the trees and churned into mud by the rain. The driveway and lawn were littered with debris, a branch had snapped off a tree.

Living in the village had turned out to be boring, but at least she didn't have to put up with her mother's displeasure.

She wanted to change the inside decor of the house, make it cosy with her own things. The uncluttered, cool, ivory interior wasn't to her taste. Clive refused. 'I've just paid an interior decorator to replace the goddamned furniture,' he'd snarled.

She didn't see much of Clive. He wouldn't allow her to live in the London house – not until after the birth. He said her stomach would cause gossip.

It didn't embarrass Dereck, who she sometimes invited down, because she was lonely and frustrated. Dereck brought her flowers.

God, she hated being pregnant!

'Get to know the neighbours,' Clive had said when she'd complained about the isolation. 'Daphne was on the village committee.'

Only, the villagers didn't want to get to know her. The women ignored her and, after recognizing one or two as those who'd caused the fuss at the tea shop, she knew why. The problem could easily be fixed. When the weather improved she intended to approach Fiona Bunnings with a proposition.

The baby pushed against her bladder, urging her to pay one of her many visits to the lavatory. Pregnancy was tedious, February ages away. In the meantime, she must prepare herself for the revelation of the master. She had to learn the rituals and they were going to sacrifice a pig on the altar.

Her relationship with Rose was getting a bit strained. Dereck had told her that Rose was jealous of her, and he'd begged her not to have anything to do with the rituals.

She smiled to herself. After the rituals Rose would be discredited, then she'd set up on her own. There was easy money to be made from tarot card readings and seances.

She toyed with the idea of asking her mother down to see her, then decided against it. Her mother was becoming decidedly strange and vague. Sylvia wondered if she was becoming prematurely senile. Her mouth set into a grim line. If she was, she'd have to go into a home.

With a baby coming, she couldn't possibly look after her.

Lost in thought, she almost missed Alex turning into the gate. His nose had set a little crookedly, but the bruises he'd received from the beating had faded. The men had turned on him like a pack of thugs, at her command. If Rose hadn't intervened, they would have killed him.

She'd gained the upper hand now. Rose couldn't do without her, and come February, she'd be the most important person in the circle. When the master was revealed, it would be she who would summon Isabella and Sebastian into his presence, not Rose. A thrill of excitement raced through her, but it was tempered with envy when she realized nobody but Rose knew his identity.

She waited until Alex rang the bell, then smoothed the loose smock down over her stomach. 'Rose sent me down to see if there was any storm damage you wanted fixing,' he muttered, without looking at her.

'Ah, my baby brother,' she said. 'How nice of you to visit.'

His eyes blazed green at her. 'Our peculiar relationship wasn't my doing.'

'Nor mine. Does anyone besides Cecily and Clive know?'

'No, and they're not going to. Ces knows how to keep her mouth shut, and so does Clive if he knows what's good for him.'

She shrugged, strangely discontented. 'Come in and have some coffee. I'm bored to tears.'

'I'd rather not.'

'I could tell you about our mutual father. Have you got a photograph? You're like him.'

He hesitated.

'Oh come on, we need to talk anyway.' She turned towards the kitchen. 'Remove your boots first. I don't want mud tramped all over the carpet.'

'You've become quite the queen of the castle,' he said, ignoring her words and following her through as he was.

She shrugged. What the hell, it wasn't her carpet.

She'd just finished making the coffee when he dropped his first bombshell. 'Did you know your mother has handed over the house to mine.'

'The hell she has!'

He grinned. 'It isn't much of a place. I'd imagine the initial investment has been repaid in rent over the past ten years.' His glance fell on the fruit cake she'd just taken out of the oven. 'That looks good.'

Silently, she handed him a plate and a knife. 'I made it for Clive, but it will probably be stale by the time I see him again. Help yourself.'

'I'm surprised you moved in with him. He's bad news.'

'Someone's got to take responsibility for the baby.'

He looked uncomfortable for a few seconds, then he took a deep, shuddering breath. 'You should have let Ces help you. There are enough bastards in this world.'

Which reminded her about the photo. Opening her bag she shoved it in front of him.

He studied it, his greenish eyes oddly indifferent. 'He looks exactly how I remember him. I didn't know he'd died until the end of term, when mum fetched me from the school. By that time, he'd been buried.' He gazed up then. 'You were going to tell me about him.'

If he expected a romantic image to cling to he would be disappointed. Her laugh was bitter. 'All my life I competed for his affection. First, I was jealous of my mother. He traded on that, playing me off against her. Then I caught him with the au pair in mother's bed. I promised not to tell, and he repaid me by becoming more affectionate.'

'How affectionate?'

'Nothing untoward. I thought he'd finally begun to love me more than my mother, but all he was doing was buying my silence.' She cocked her head to one side, studying the face that looked so much like her father's. 'He didn't love either of us, he only loved himself.'

'And my mother.'

She gave him a scornful look. 'He needed someone to cling to while he died. My mother would have hired a nurse. I think I was the only person who would have cared enough to have died in his place, and he didn't like me enough to ask me.' Her laugh was harsh. 'Like father, like son. Christ, Alex, it's hard to believe it took my own brother to show me how to enjoy sex. I really fell for you.'

Sliding the photo into his pocket Alex stood up, his eyes troubled. 'And you think I didn't feel anything at all?'

She walked round the table to stand in front of him. 'I know you felt something.'

'You're my sister, it's natural to feel something. I just got the signals mixed. A relationship between us is wrong, and it won't happen again.'

His hands caressed the growing mound of her belly and he smiled. 'I wonder if it will look like its grandfather.'

163

'I hope it will look like Clive.'

His earthy heat seemed to wrap around her. Giving a little cry she moved against him. 'Does one sin compound a sin?'

'When you know it's a sin, yes.' After a moment, his arms came around her and he whispered against her hair. 'Poor little Sylvia. Nothing can change things now.'

'I left my husband for you,' she whispered. 'He was a good man.'

He began to laugh softly against her scalp. 'Why lie to yourself? Your husband left you for another woman.'

Her blood ran cold and she pushed him away. 'What are you talking about?'

'Your husband is living with Betony Nichols. She's the owner of Little Abbot.'

The breath left her lungs, leaving a sharp pain in its wake. Eyes wide, she stared at him. 'You're lying.'

Pity flared in his eyes. 'Ask Clive. The two of them went to his party before you split up. Ask Rose. She's known for ages. It's odd really,' he mused. 'Your husband killed Betony's kid, now they're expecting another. He must be quite a guy.'

She tried to clutch at him for support as the room began to spin round, but he moved away. When she came round she was lying on the floor. Alex was sitting on the edge of the table, eating cake and watching her. 'You bastard,' she whispered, struggling to her feet.

He washed down the remains of the cake with his coffee, smiled, then rose to his feet and strolled from the room.

'*You damned bastard!*' she yelled after him. He didn't answer as the door clicked shut. Picking up the remainder of the cake she threw it against the wall and watched it explode into crumbs.

Betony was as content as the cat who got the cream. Even the sullen November day couldn't keep the smile off her face when she saw Daphne.

She'd dressed in a blue denim shift, designed to accommodate her altering shape. A black, ankle-length raincoat was slung over her arm.

Daphne gave her a cursory inspection. 'I expected you to be enormously fat by now. Are you sure the baby's due in eight weeks?'

'Absolutely.'

There was an air of excitement about Daphne, as if she was bursting to tell her something. She managed to wait until lunch had been ordered.

'Fiona Bunnings rang. Apparently, Sylvia has offered to rent out the tea rooms to the village committee for next summer.'

She slid him an exasperated glance. 'If we do, we can watch television instead.'

It had reached that stage with Sylvia, Noel thought in surprise. The first thing he'd done when he'd got home after work was to switch the television on, rather than talk to her.

'Can we discuss this without resorting to sarcasm?'

'You want me to discuss your wife with you?'

'What I really want, is for you to stop avoiding certain subjects.'

Her eyes crackled with affront. Guessing the conversation was heading towards a row, he sought to diffuse it. 'Look, it's not important. Let's forget about it.'

'What, after you accused me of avoidance tactics? Exactly what subject am I avoiding?'

'Anything to do with family,' he said mildly.

'And by that, you mean the death of my son,' she blazed at him.

Her reaction horrified him. 'No! I didn't mean that at all.'

She shot to her feet, and the argument suddenly flared out of control. 'You know more about it than I do, Noel. You were *there*!' Anguish flooded her eyes. 'I don't want to talk about it. I'm over it.'

Now it was his turn to be angry. 'You're not over it, you're trying to deny your feelings. It's a case of out of sight, shoving it out of your mind. You find that a damned sight easier to cope with than admitting you're hurting like hell.'

'Shut up!' she screamed, pressing her hands against her ears.

He pulled them down. 'You'll never be over it, Betony, not until you go back and face it.'

'That's easy to say when you've convinced yourself of your innocence,' she hissed. 'It must be nice to be able to detach yourself after you've killed some-one.'

Shocked, he stared after her as she fled for the stairs, tears streaming down her face. She turned at the top, her face contorted with the need to hurt him. 'If you want to know about your precious wife, rumour has it she's pregnant to her own brother.'

'Sylvia hasn't got a brother.' His face drained of colour when he remembered Alison Green's son.

'Yes she has. He's the gardener at Little Abbot.' Heading into the bedroom she slammed the door behind her.

He slumped in the chair for what seemed like an age, listening to her sobs and despising himself. When the crying subsided he went upstairs and knocked on the door. 'Are you all right'

'Go away,' she muttered. 'I hate you.'

'We can't leave things like this. We have to sort this out.'

'I know, I know.' The door was suddenly yanked open and he staggered backwards when she flung herself into his arms. 'I don't deserve you, and I hate myself.'

His fingers trailed soothingly through her hair. 'I love you. If you don't want to talk about it, fine. We won't let it spoil our relationship.'

The tear-stained face she turned up to his sent a quiver of tenderness and love into his heart. Then her lips sought his in a frenzied kiss and she pulled him into the bedroom.

'Make love to me,' she whispered, 'I can't stand it when we argue. I didn't mean what I said.'

This was her way of forgetting, to lose herself in the act of love. Although he made love to her carefully and gently, his heart filled with pain. Was this all he meant to her? But afterwards, when she took his hand and placed it against the gentle swell of her belly, he felt the miracle of their baby quicken inside her and understood the depth of her pain.

'Rose dreamed I had a baby girl called Katherine. Do you like that name?'

'If we have a girl I'd like to call her Lavender.'

'Lavender?' She propped herself on one elbow and managed a watery grin. 'Why?'

'Because she'll have eyes like her mother.'

'Hmmm. Lavender Nichols.' She made a face. 'They'll call her lav when she goes to school.'

'Lavender Dearborn,' he said with a grin.

The second anonymous letter dropped on the mat whilst Dorothy was on the receiving end of an abusive phone call from Sylvia.

It was impossible to make Sylvia understand she'd given Alison Green the house rather than have Brian's name dragged through the mud. All her daughter could do was shout her down. She flipped the envelope open with her thumb whilst Sylvia continued her diatribe. Every word she uttered made her dislike her a little bit more.

Dear Mrs Throsby,

Be aware. The child your daughter is carrying is the result of an incestuous relationship. As well as Clive Harrington, she is also involved with Councillor Dereck Wallwark.

A well wisher.

The room spun around her.

'Sylvia,' she said quietly when her daughter finally ran out of breath. 'Have you told me the truth about who the father of your child is?'

'You haven't listened to one word I said,' she shrieked. 'What do you want me to tell you, that I don't know who fathered the brat?'

'I want the truth.'

'Since when have you wanted the truth? You don't even believe I have a brother.'

'I've been convinced otherwise. I've received copies of documents and medical tests. I've faced the fact that Brian was unfaithful to me.'

'And you want me to admit the baby might be my brother's. You're sick in the head. You should be in a home for the senile.'

'What do you mean by *might be?* Is he or isn't he?'

Sylvia gave a malicious laugh. 'It's possible, of course.' Her voice rose. 'There were a few others. Would you like me to name them?'

'I don't think that's necessary.' Drained, Dorothy hung up on her. She rested for a while, turning things wearily over in her mind. Her life had been one long lie and Sylvia had become an anathema to her. She was totally out of step with this graceless new age.

Noel was justified in walking out of his marriage to her daughter. Despite his unfortunate background, she'd been unjust to consider otherwise. Tearing the anonymous letter into tiny pieces, she flushed it down the lavatory pan, where it would join its predecessor in the sewer where it belonged.

After making a phone call to her lawyer, she wrote a letter. A little while later, she carefully made up her face, donned her best coat and hat and went out to keep the appointment she'd made. It was two hours before she returned, her face glowing from the cold. She'd enjoyed her walk along the promenade, despite the wind.

The tide had been coming in, the sea was rough and grey as it hissed over the sand towards the cliffs below the house. She had taken her daughter to build sandcastles there when she'd been small.

She could hear the breakers from her bedroom – the bedroom she'd shared with her husband for the first happy year of her marriage. How pleasant life had been after her disciplined and rigid upbringing. How quickly it had crumbled around her in the face of Brian's infidelity. It had been easy to draw on her train-ing, to hide behind a façade of genteel respectability.

Brian had recited a poem to her when the tide was in. He'd been fond of poetry, she remembered, and her brow wrinkled in thought. Tennyson, she mused, as she poured herself a glass of milk and carried it through to the bedroom. Something about breakers.

It seemed odd to be going to bed in the middle of the day. Placing her jewellery carefully in her padded jewellery box, she locked it in the safe. Shoes set neatly beside the bed, she arranged herself against the frilled pillows and shook the sleeping pills into her hand.

Tennyson had never been her favourite poet, and she could only remember the last verse. *Break, break, break, at the foot of thy crags, O sea! But the tender grace of a day that is dead, will never come back to me.*

There was no tender grace left in her life, so it seemed fitting for the occasion, somehow.

The letter arrived with the morning mail.

Up to his eyes in work, Noel threw it into the in-tray and concentrated once more on the screen in front of him. He smiled with relief when he spied a vagrant zero he'd pressed instead of the nine. The printout was satisfyingly neat, and accurate.

He glanced at his watch. He was taking Betony to the Ritz for lunch. She'd been depressed since their argument. Her quietness disturbed him, as did the sadness in her eyes. A special lunch was an effort to cheer her up, and show her he loved her.

He waded through the pile of mail, frowning when he reached the small blue envelope at the bottom. It was Betony's handwriting.

Noel, my darling,

I didn't have the courage to tell you this face to face. I'm going away for a while to sort myself out. Please don't worry about me or our baby, darling. Just know that we love you, and will be back.

Yours, Betony.

Don't worry? He gave a short, incredulous laugh to stop himself from bawling. Christ, what did she think he was made of, stone? He'd do nothing but worry until she returned.

CHAPTER SIXTEEN

Daphne was as mystified as Noel.

'If you hear from Betony, you will let me know.'

'Of course.' She swooped in a breath. 'I hope she hasn't gone down to Little Abbot.'

He managed a chuckle. 'She seemed to think you were over-dramatizing the situation.'

'I know, she nearly bit my head off. But, Noel, if you'd seen Sylvia.' He could almost see her biting her tongue. 'Sorry, I forgot you're married to her.'

'Not for much longer.' Perhaps he should take Sylvia's activities a little more seriously. 'Tell me what you were about to say.'

'They were all high on something. Sylvia was sitting in the middle of a circle of people. She was in a trance. The others looked as though they were worshipping her.'

This time he laughed outright. 'They must be out of their tiny minds.'

'Don't laugh. This lot are deadly serious about what they're doing. Most of the inner circle are high-powered slobs. And there was a man in a black robe and cowl. If I hadn't laughed and stuffed things up, I would have found out what was going on.'

His eyebrow rose a fraction. 'You laughed?'

'They thought I was high. Alex led me away, muttering something about an initiation. I'll leave that to your imagination. I managed to disarm the randy little sod with a well-placed knee, and ran.'

'Ouch,' he muttered.

'Then when I got outside I nearly tripped over Fiona Bunnings who was spying on them through a window.'

'Fiona Bunnings?'

'One of the Abbotsford wives. We took off like a couple of bats out of hell on the back of her horse.'

When he burst into laughter, she giggled. 'Shut up Noel, I haven't finished. When we got to her place we downed half a bottle of brandy between us. I think Clive would have killed me if he'd caught up with me. He's scared I'm going to open my mouth to the newspapers.'

'And are you?'

'Hell no. I wouldn't do anything in the world to hurt Betony.'

'This Alex,' he said. 'Is this the man rumoured to be Sylvia's—'

'It's more than a rumour. They've been seen together.'

'By whom?'

'Fiona. To be quite frank, Alex is the type of man who needs to be chemically castrated. He's also involved with Cecily Gifford.' She gave an embarrassed cough. 'I knew him myself when I was still at school. He's, um . . . hung like a camel.'

He bit back his laughter. 'I can't see Betony going there. She said she'd never go back. Perhaps I ought to ring them and make sure.'

'Don't do that. Betony's been a bit unstable since she stopped taking those tranquillizers. She might resent it.'

Daphne was right, but what she'd said had him worried. 'I can't just twiddle my thumbs.'

'I'll ask Fiona to keep an eye out for her. Nothing moves in and out of the village without her knowing. My guess is, Betony's holed up in a hotel somewhere.'

'You're probably right,' he said, unable to disguise his doubt as he voiced his main concern. 'What if she's found someone else.'

Her voice softened. 'She isn't shallow like me, Noel. She loves you. She'll be back.'

'And you're not as shallow as you think you are. Thanks Daphne.'

He dashed home at lunch time to see if she'd returned. Everything was neat and tidy.

There was a note on the fridge.

Dinner is in the brown casserole. Just heat in microwave. Look after Vivaldi for me. I love you – and please don't worry.

Reassurance wasn't enough when the emptiness of the house crowded in on him. He made a dash for the phone when it rang. It was Cecily Gifford to say Betony's father had arrived safely home.

'How is Betony?' Cecily said, her voice guarded, as if afraid of being overheard.

'Looking forward to having the baby.'

'Yes, she would be.' There was a pause. 'Are you coping all right?'

He didn't know quite what to say. 'You don't have to worry. I do love her.'

Her voice warmed. 'It was nice to talk to you. Ask Betony to ring me when she comes in.'

'It might not be for a few days.'

'Ah, I see. I suppose she's gone to the retreat.'

He muttered something non-committal. At least he knew where she wasn't, now.

The following day brought an unexpected, and entirely horrifying phone call. 'It's my mother,' Sylvia screamed hysterically down the phone. 'She's dead. They think she committed suicide and I can't handle it. I need you desperately, Noel.'

Torn between wanting to be around for Betony's return and what was clearly his duty, he rang Daphne again to explain the situation. Afterwards, he called Joyce and Daniel into his office. 'I'll need you to cover for me for a few days,' he said to Daniel. 'Can you manage it?'

He looked doubtful. 'It's possible, if I work until midnight.'

White-faced, Joyce whispered. 'Poor Dorothy. I'll rearrange your appointments for the rest of the week. You mustn't worry, Noel. We'll hold the fort.'

'Thanks, you two.' He hesitated a moment before saying, 'Mrs Nichols has gone away for a few days and I can't contact her. If she rings, explain the situation to her and tell her I'll be back after the funeral.'

'Please give my condolences to Sylvia,' Joyce said. Her mouth puckered as if she'd sucked on a lemon. 'Let me know when the funeral takes place.'

'Will do.' He shrugged into his coat and gave her something to do before she burst into tears. 'Book me a hotel whilst I have a word with Daniel. You shouldn't have any trouble at this time of year.'

'I can't have you working round the clock,' he said when she scurried off. 'We talked about employing a part-timer. Go through the applicants for the partnership, interview those who haven't been situated and offer one of them a position. You'll find my comments on the application forms, but I'll leave the choice up to you.'

'Sure,' Daniel said easily. 'Is there anything else you want me to do?'

'Do you know where Betony's gone?'

'Yes. You don't have to worry about her. She'll be back.'

The fact she'd confided in Daniel instead of him, hurt. He swallowed it, relief edging across his face. 'I won't ask you for any more, but don't call her with this, she has enough on her plate.'

Their eyes met.

'You're quite a guy, Noel,' Daniel said, then his voice assumed its usual laconic tone. 'Now, shove off. Somebody has to do some work around here.'

The inquest returned a verdict of death by suicide.

Dorothy Throsby had given no reason for her final act, and no letter of intent had been found at the house. Sylvia told the court her mother had been vague lately, and depressed at discovering her deceased husband had a son by his former mistress – both of whom were harassing her for a portion of her father's estate.

Dorothy's lawyer had given testimony to say she'd been to see him on the day of her death to update her will. She'd seemed her usual self. The letter he'd received the following day contained instructions for her funeral. After failing to raise her by telephone he'd alerted the police. He requested that the house remain sealed until the new will was read.

Sylvia's eyes glittered at that. Why had her mother updated her will? Then she thought, perhaps she'd left a little something to her brother – but hopefully, not too much.

The body was cremated. Sylvia wore a loose black coat with a fur collar that fluffed around her neck. The little veiled hat on her head had cost a fortune, but was quite fetching.

Her uncle was there, as was his wife. Arthur wore a black tie and armband. His face was grey and pinched. His wife wore the same grey coat she'd been wearing for years. Everything about her was grey.

A decent number of people had attended, she saw with satisfaction, including Joyce. Standing next to Noel, she cried all the way through. Her face was blotchy when she excused herself from the funeral tea. 'I have to catch the train back to London.'

Sylvia took a step back when she attempted to kiss her on the cheek. 'Thank you for coming, so kind.'

Flustered, Joyce murmured. 'Such a dreadful thing to have happened to such a fine lady. I'm so sorry, Sylvia, dear.'

Anyone would think she'd been close to her mother, Sylvia thought, watching Noel assist her into a taxi. All she'd done was send birthday and Christmas presents, and visit her occasionally. Joyce needn't think she'd be welcome in her house after she'd sided with Noel.

As she received the muttered condolences she thought about Noel. He seemed like a stranger, not a man she'd been married to for eight years. Seeing him through fresh eyes, she caught herself admiring his strength. He'd arranged everything with calm assurance, and had dealt with officialdom with patience.

His manner had remained detached throughout. He certainly hadn't encouraged any familiarity. In fact, he'd told her to pull herself together when she'd become annoyed with her uncle. Arthur blamed her for the suicide. As if it was her fault that her mother had succumbed to depression.

The next morning dawned miserable and grey. The beneficiaries gathered at the lawyer's office. Sylvia's glance darted about as she tried to gauge what each was worth.

Her mother's cleaning lady looked out of place and self-conscious. She'd be worth a hundred quid at most.

Then there was Noel, who'd collected Arthur from the country. He wouldn't get anything for a start. Her mother had never considered Noel a good enough husband for her. And of course, he hadn't been. They were never compatible, she knew that now.

Uncle Arthur would probably get the ghastly set of hunting prints he'd been nagging about for years. They'd belonged to his father, and he was welcome to them.

'If you would all like to pay attention. This is the reading of the last will and testament of Dorothy Jean Throsby. We will start with the main beneficiary . . . .'

Her expectant smile faded when his words sank in. Once claims against the estate were settled, her mother had left practically everything to her second cousin, Joyce Clark, whom she described as an honest and hard-working woman deserving of her charity.

'The conniving little schemer,' she shrieked. 'No wonder she's not here. She's too frightened to show her face.'

The lawyer gazed disapprovingly over his spectacles at her. 'Miss Clark is unaware of the bequest at this time. Your mother requested she not be told until after the will was read.' He nodded at Noel. 'Mrs Throsby wants you to inform Miss Clark of her bequest, and advise her in its proper disbursement, if that is her wish.'

'I'm sure Joyce is perfectly capable of handling it,' Noel said, a faint smile playing around his lips. 'But I'll be pleased to inform her of her good fortune.'

Sylvia stared at him. The bastard was enjoying this.

'*To my brother, Arthur and his wife, I leave fifty thousand pounds from my personal trust account, and the hunting prints.*'

Sucking in an outraged breath, Sylvia glared at them.

'*To Noel Dearborn, one hundred thousand pounds, as compensation for having the misfortune of being married to my daughter, Sylvia.*'

'What!' Bewildered, she stared at the lawyer. 'My mother would never have said such a horrid thing about me. She detested Noel. She considered him beneath us.'

175

For the first time since his sister's death, Arthur smiled. 'Something must have changed her mind.'

'*To Mrs Robbins, a true and faithful servant of many years standing, ten thousand pounds.*'

Mrs Robbins turned bright red. 'That's right generous of her.'

'*To my daughter, Sylvia Dearborn. I leave all of my jewellery, which is more than she deserves. She is to be accompanied to my home by Noel Dearborn and my brother Arthur, to receive my jewellery box personally into her hands. It is my wish that she never sets foot over the doorstep again.*'

Sylvia began to feel sick.

'*To my unborn grandchild, I leave the remainder of my personal funds in trust. This fund is to be administered by my lawyer until the said grandchild reaches a majority of twenty-one years.*'

'The malicious bitch,' she muttered, her face flushing with fury.

'*If the said grandchild dies before maturity, the funds shall be distributed to the charitable organizations named in the will.*'

The lawyer glanced over his glasses at everyone. 'That is all.'

Rising to her feet, Sylvia directed a scathing glance at him. 'I intend to contest this. My mother was in a depressed state of mind.'

'That's your right, Mrs Dearborn. However, I should inform you Mrs Throsby left a letter in my keeping. She directs it's to be read out in court should you choose to contest.'

Why hadn't she kept her mouth shut about Alex? Fuming with embarrassment she flounced outside. She should have remembered her mother's vindictive streak, and couldn't risk anything coming to light about her activities. It would attract the attention of the press and Clive had told her they must keep a low profile.

At least she'd got the jewellery. There were some valuable pieces passed down through the family which she could sell. She also had the house key in her bag. She could slip back to the house later . . . .

The child inside her moved. Her hands pushed at it. It was worth at least two hundred thousand or more – money which should have been hers. She wished she'd aborted the bastard now.

When they arrived at the house, Noel opened the safe, blocking the door with his body. He turned to place the jewellery box in her hands, then locked it again.

Fool! Did he imagine she didn't know the combination? She examined every piece whilst Arthur talked about his sister, and Noel made suitable and sympathetic comments in reply. Hypocrite! He'd refused to let her mother move in with them. Everything was intact, including her mother's engagement ring and wedding band.

Noel went into the hall to help Arthur take down the hunting prints. She succumbed to temptation, slipping a pair of Dresden figurines into her bag.

Then there was the Lalique bowl. She didn't see why Joyce should have that. She managed to jam it down the front of her pants. The cold glass over her belly was uncomfortable, but at least it didn't show.

A pair of silver salad servers slid easily into one pocket, a silver cream jug into the other. She was just wondering if she could fit the matching sugar bowl into her bag when Noel came back. His eyes went to the sugar bowl in her hands, then flicked up to hers.

'Put it back where you got it from.'

'I was only looking at it.' She replaced it on the shelf in exactly the same position as she'd found it.

He crossed the room in two strides and gazed at the silver collection, suspicion on his face. 'And the rest.'

She turned towards the door. 'I don't know what you're talking about.'

'There are dust-free marks.'

'So?' She shrugged and began to walk away.

His hand closed around her arm and his eyes bored into hers. 'Put everything back or I'll turn you upside down and shake you until you rattle.'

'Oh, stop making such a fuss.' She replaced the salad server and cream jug then glared at him. 'Satisfied?'

'Not entirely. Empty your handbag.'

She clutched it against her. 'I will not.'

Pulling it from her arm he upended it on to the couch.

She shrugged when he pounced on the figurines. 'Careful with those, they're worth quite a bit.'

'I'll remember to tell Joyce. Is there anything else, or do I have to strip you naked?'

Amusement in her eyes she opened her arms. 'Go ahead, if that will turn you on.'

'Nothing about you turns me on,' he said curtly.

'Ah yes, I forgot,' she mocked. 'You have Betony Nichols to warm your bed.'

He stared at her, his dark eyes unreadable.

'My, you *are* a dark horse. To think I actually felt sorry for you for killing her child. I didn't realize you were comforting her by screwing her.'

'Every word from your mouth cheapens you a little bit more,' he said, with barely concealed rage.

'You're to become a father, I hear,' she said. 'Are you sure it's yours?'

His glance went to her stomach and his lip curled. 'I'm sure. Which is more than the father of yours can say. Is that what killed your mother? Did you mention the word incest to her?'

'You don't know what you're saying,' she whispered, her mouth suddenly going dry.

'You have something hidden inside your pants,' he said coldly.

She'd never known him to be quite so ruthless. Turning her back on him she withdrew the bowl from her clothing, turned and hurled it at him.

He caught it, replacing it carefully on the table. 'Now, pick up your things and get out.'

Tears filled her eyes. 'You don't understand, Noel.'

'It's time for you to leave.'

Arthur watched from the doorway, his face a study of disdain. The resemblance between him and her mother had never been more marked. A pity she hadn't made more effort with him. He had no heirs.

'It was mother's fault,' she sneered. 'If she hadn't—'

'Get out,' Noel snarled. 'And if you've got a key to this place, forget it. The locksmith will be here to change the locks any minute.'

'Enjoy your bloody compensation money,' she flung at him. 'I never want to see you again.'

'Ditto,' he said, his expression implacable.

Pushing past them both, she stalked out of the front door, got into the car and squealed off down the road, vowing to get back at him for the way he'd treated her today.

Noel told Joyce to take her annual holidays whilst she sorted her inheritance out.

'Arthur said if you need any help, to give him a call.'

He'd enjoyed her astonishment and pleasure at being named the main beneficiary. He brought her up to date on the legal aspects. 'You'll have to wait until the court case to see what the final figure works out at. The lawyer thinks Alex Green will be entitled to something. The house was registered in Dorothy's name though, and bought with an inheritance from her parents, so it's not subject to claim.'

'It's a big house,' Joyce said. 'Do you think anyone would object if I sold it? It will be vandalized if it's left empty.'

'It's your house, Joyce. Do whatever you think fit.' He handed her the inventory of contents. 'If anything's missing, let the lawyer know. Sylvia tried to steal some things before I changed the locks.'

Joyce looked shocked. 'If she wants anything she's welcome to it. She just has to ask.'

'If Dorothy wanted Sylvia to have anything she'd have bequeathed it to her. There are reasons she didn't, reasons I won't go in to. There's no need for you to feel guilty about accepting the inheritance.'

She looked flustered for a moment, unable to believe what had happened. 'This has come as a shock. I must think about it.'

'Of course you must. Now, off you go, otherwise your holiday will be over before you leave the office.'

There was a flurry of last-minute instructions, to him, to Daniel, and especially to the receptionist, who just managed to stop herself from rolling her eyes until Joyce disappeared through the door.

There was a general feeling of relief when she departed.

On Friday, Noel wondered if Betony would be home for Christmas as he emerged from his office building into the street.

He convinced himself she would be. Hadn't she been looking forward to going to Nottingham with him?

The shops and streets sparkled with lights and decorations and the air had a cold snap to it. Buoyed by thoughts of Betony's imminent return, he bought a pine tree and Christmas decorations to welcome her home.

Two weeks until Christmas, he thought, manoeuvring it through the front door in a shower of pine needles. The doormat was littered with envelopes containing Christmas cards. He set the tree up in the window, then spent the entire evening decorating it with fairy lights, coloured balls and tinsel. He set a delicate spun glass angel on top, a coloured light shoved up her skirt.

An angel to guide her home, he mused.

He'd bought Betony a striped, ginger cat with a mouth-splitting grin. Around its china neck he clasped a slim gold identity bracelet with, 'I love you,' inscribed on it.

He wrapped it, setting the parcel underneath the tree. Next to it, he placed a fluffy white rabbit he'd bought for the baby.

He'd be a father in just under six weeks. Men were supposed to be stoic and proud about impending fatherhood, but he was racked with excitement and worry. She'd missed the last class at the maternity clinic. He'd gone alone, sitting at the back and watching the other couples go through the breathing techniques so he could show her what she'd missed. After that, they'd watched a video of a baby being born.

It had seemed slightly unreal that a woman and her infant could undergo such a gruelling experience, and they could be so perfectly beautiful together afterwards. The expression in the mother's eyes had been so full of wonder and love when she'd set eyes on her child, he'd totally choked up.

He understood then what Betony had lost when Ben had been taken from her. He experienced her grief and grieved with her. Men weren't supposed to cry, but when he got home from the clinic, he cried for Ben and for Betony, and he cried for his own part in the tragedy. He'd never be able to lose his guilt.

Gazing at the angel, he closed his eyes and wished she'd come home so he could look after her.

The next morning he cleaned the house, then took the washing to the launderette round the corner, leaving it with the attendant to be picked up later. For an extra charge she'd iron it, saving him the bother. After he'd shopped, he dumped the bags on the kitchen bench and went through to light the gas fire in the sitting room.

It was still alight. He must have forgotten to turn it off. The room smelled of pine resin, like a forest. A forest of one. He gave the tree a glance, wondering if it felt as lonely as he did. There was something different about it. For a moment he stared at it, puzzled. An extra parcel was set underneath it.

'Betony,' he breathed, something wonderful thudding into his diaphragm. A smile spread across his face. He took the stairs three at a time and stood at the bedroom door, drinking the sight of her in.

She stood with her back to the window, her hair bathed in light. Her smile was tentative, uncertain. 'I watched you come up the street.'

He felt like crying again. 'God, you'll never know how much I've missed you.'

She held out her arms to him. 'Come here, you mutt. You didn't worry about me, did you?'

'Of course not,' he said gruffly. 'You told me not to, and I always do as I'm told.'

'You lie so beautifully,' and she enfolded him in a never-ending hug.

A lump threatened to choke him as he breathed in her familiar perfume. 'I've missed you like hell. Wherever you went, it was too far away.'

'I went to a retreat in Wales. One of my sisters took me there once.'

Cecily had said something about a retreat when she'd phoned. He held her at arms length, gazing into her eyes. 'And you couldn't tell me?'

She shook her head. 'I'd become reliant on prescription drugs. I didn't realize until I stopped taking them.' Her hand caressed his face. 'I was ashamed, and all muddled up inside. I needed peace and quiet to meditate.'

'Did it help?'

'For the moment. I know you and our child are the most precious things in my life. Chances are, I'll suffer withdrawal symptoms and mood swings for some time to come.'

'We'll learn to cope with them.'

'I was hoping you'd say that. I very much need you to trust and support me if things start to go haywire. I'm frightened I might do something to lose you.'

'Not a chance.'

'Promise.'

He tipped up her face and kissed her with all the tenderness he could muster. Tears glittered on her lashes. Gently he took one on his finger. 'You'd better believe it.'

'No more avoiding certain subjects on my part, OK? I've taken too much, and given nothing back.'

'Stop flagellating yourself. You've given me more than you'll ever know.'

She sucked in a deep, shuddering breath. 'Before I burst into a flood of tears, thanks for the Christmas tree. Can I open my present?'

He laughed, finding pleasure in her childish curiosity. 'Certainly not. You can wait until Christmas. In the meantime, you can come and help me unpack the shopping.'

She was laughing through her tears by the time they got downstairs. The awkwardness between them had fled, leaving only the pleasure of intimacy.

'Did anything out of the ordinary happen when I was away?'

His voice sobered. 'Yes, but we can discuss it tomorrow if you like. I don't want to spoil your homecoming.'

She pulled him round to face her. 'When I said no more avoidance, I meant it. If it's something to do with Sylvia, I don't mind. OK?'

He told her about Dorothy's death over dinner. 'She left me something in her will. I thought I'd invest it until it's time to move to a bigger house. What do you think?'

'A good idea.' Her eyes went all dreamy. 'We might have another baby to cater for in a couple of years or so.'

'Hey,' he whispered in her ear. 'This sounds like a long-term plan.'

'Three would be a nice figure to aim for.'

'I always did like odd numbers.'

17th day of March 1798

I have been without food and water for three days. Sebastian intends to starve me to death. In my weakened state I saw a vision. The devil sent a messenger to me in the guise of a woman. Her name was as red as blood and her head wreathed in flames.

The woman revealed to me an image of an infant, who emerged from torment and sorrow. There was an angel at the infant's head, but the red one did not see her because her eyes were blinded by her own power.

'Everything is coming together as Isabella wrote,' Rose said with a smile.

Clive frowned. 'What about the angel?'

'What's one angel worth when lined up against the combined forces of darkness? We are thirteen now. I've contacted Fiorenzo.'

'Cecily won't like it.'

Shivering as a draught drew smoke back down the chimney, Rose pulled her cardigan tightly over her chest. 'Then we won't tell her.'

In the hall outside, Cecily's mouth tightened.

CHAPTER SEVENTEEN

B etony couldn't remember having a nicer Christmas.

The Dearborns' house had been full of visiting relatives, and neighbours who popped in and out. She lost count of the names.

Noel's parents treated her as one of the family. There was a present for her under the tree – a white, cable knit sweater Noel's mother had made herself, a match for Noel's. Even the baby had a present – a hand-made shawl in a delicate lace design.

Tears pricked her eyes. 'It's the nicest present I've ever been given.'

'You said that about my present,' Noel laughed and, advancing on her with a bunch of mistletoe, kissed her thoroughly and said for all to hear, 'I love you.'

'A toast.' His father slid his arm around his wife's waist and held up his glass. 'To Betony, who has brought us much happiness this Christmas, and to our grandchild. May he or she be born healthy, and have a happy life.'

A simple philosophy. The baby kicked her with such vigorous force she knew it couldn't be anything but healthy. As for happy? How could their child be anything else with a family like this to love it.

New Year's Eve came and went, celebrated with a dinner party at Daphne's flat. They left shortly after midnight.

She was nearly asleep against Noel's shoulder when they arrived home. He turned on the electric blanket, then brought her a glass of warm milk, standing over her whilst she drank it.

'Go to sleep,' he said, kissing her on the forehead. 'I'll be up later.'

She'd been finding it increasingly difficult to find a comfortable position, but tonight she fell asleep quickly and slept soundly all night. It was a pattern that continued for two weeks. Even the baby was less restless, its jabs becoming gentle heaves against her stomach.

Full of a new-found energy, she gradually cleaned the house from top to bottom and went for long walks when the weather was fine.

She'd arrived home one day when the phone rang. It was Rose. 'Daddy wants to know when you're coming to see him.'

Her smile faded and a dragging pain gathered in the pit of her stomach. She hadn't given him much thought, apart from sending Rose some money to buy him something for Christmas. 'I don't know.'

'He's got a bad heart. He isn't going to last much longer.'

The censure in her voice made Betony feel guilty. 'After the baby's born. I can't come now.'

'He was hoping to see you at Christmas.'

'We'd made other plans.' Suddenly tired, she sank on to the chair. 'I'll come after the baby's born. I promise.'

Rose's voice brightened. 'And you'll stay for a while?'

She took a deep breath. Noel had been right, she'd have to go back, some-day. With the new baby in her arms, coming to terms with Ben's death wouldn't be quite so difficult. 'Yes, all right. I'll visit for a couple of weeks. Perhaps Noel will be able to come too.'

Her sister's voice took on a frosty edge. 'You'll have us to look after you. We're so much looking forward to seeing the baby. After what Noel did to Ben—'

'It wasn't his fault, but if you're not going to be civil to him . . . .'

'I hadn't considered being rude. I just thought it might be embarrassing if he runs into Sylvia. Such a dear girl. Daddy's quite taken with her, we all are.'

Hurt flickered in her heart. 'Goodbye, Rose,' she said hastily, give my love to Ces . . . and to father, of course.' If love was repaid by love she didn't owe her father anything, and Rose was beginning to make her feel like an outsider.

The thought of Sylvia Dearborn queening it over her family and home to the exclusion of Noel was unacceptable to her. Perhaps it was time to stand up and be counted. Once she'd had the baby she'd do something about it, but right now she was too exhausted to even think straight.

She must have overdone the walking, her back and legs were beginning to ache. Dropping the receiver on to its rest she dragged herself wearily upstairs, pulled on a nightgown and crawled under the blankets. Within minutes, she was asleep.

Two hours later pain drove her awake. Christ! The bed was wet. As the obvi-ous cause hit her she was seized by a contraction that almost made her scream. Sweat beaded her face when the relentless pressure registered. She seemed to be in the final stages of labour.

Dragging her robe round her shoulders she clutched the wall for support, trying to make it downstairs before the next contraction hit her. She failed.

Crouched on the stairs, she waited for the pain to subside then felt carefully between her legs. She could feel the baby's head. How could this have happened? She wasn't due for three weeks.

She made it to the phone, punching in Noel's office number just as the next contraction came. 'Quick,' she gasped to the receptionist, 'Tell Noel to come home, it's urgent.'

She groaned as the contraction swallowed her up and fell to her hands and knees beside the hall table. Contractions squeezed at her in a never-ending succession. She bit into her lip as her body slowly stretched to accommodate the baby's head, feeling as if she were being ripped apart. There was a pause when she managed to bunch the fallen robe between her legs. One contraction later and the baby slithered out between her thighs, quickly followed by the afterbirth.

She was shaking all over and didn't know whether to laugh or cry when the baby whimpered. Her glance slid over the perfect little body, checking all was intact. Tenderly, she wrapped it in the robe and gathered it against her breast as it began to bawl in earnest. Tears poured down her cheeks. 'My darling, darling baby. I love you.'

She was still there, cuddling her infant when Noel burst through the door a few minutes later. His face paled. 'Oh my God! I'll call for an ambulance.'

'There's no need. I've just called one.' She was still trembling all over from cold and shock. 'Can you fetch me a blanket.'

He ran upstairs at the double, nearly falling down them on the way back down in his haste. He draped the blanket round her. Eyes drawn to the crying baby snuggled against her breast, a tender smile drifted across his face. 'What is it?'

'I don't know?' she lied, knowing how much he'd wanted to share the birth with her. 'I thought I'd wait for you so we can discover together.'

His eyes were soft and anxious against hers. 'Will you do the honours, or shall I?'

'You. I did all the hard work.'

Carefully, he uncovered the relevant body part, grinned widely, then covered it again.

'Well?'

He sank to the floor and gathered them both into his arms. 'We won't be calling the noisy little critter Lavender, that's for sure.'

'Stephen, after your father.'

'He has two grandfathers.'

She ignored it. 'Stephen Noel,' she said firmly, laughing when the baby suddenly stopped crying and opened his eyes. 'See, he approves.'

'He's got your hands. Perhaps he'll be a pianist. God, they're so tiny and perfect.'

'His eyes and hair are just like yours. He'll probably be able to count to ten by this time next week.'

Noel laughed. 'He certainly knows what's good for him.'

The baby's mouth was trying to nuzzle her breast, creating all sorts of warm and wonderful feelings in her.

'Typical male,' she whispered, unable to tear her eyes away from him. He was so small, and so sweet and helpless.

They were still admiring their miracle when the ambulance drew up outside.

It was all very cloak and dagger. Fiona pulled her raincoat up around her ears as she hurried into the Fleet Street pub. Her thrill of excitement died when she saw the ordinary-looking man with a red carnation in his buttonhole. She'd expected someone more intellectul-looking.

'Gerald Bender?'

'The same,' he said in a bored voice. He indicated the chair and called to the woman behind the bar. 'Same again, Sharon, and . . .' he gave her a cursory glance, 'a sweet sherry.'

'How did you guess?'

He grinned. 'Second sight.'

'I suppose that's why your editor gave you this job. It took a long time for your newspaper to respond.'

'They've had a dearth of vicar and scout-master scandals, lately.'

'How appalling. It's quite dreadful what people get up to sometimes.'

'Absolutely.' He leaned forward. 'Why don't you turn your collar down, it's dripping rain into your drink.'

She gazed furtively around the bar. 'Somebody might recognize me.'

'Such as whom?'

When she whispered two well-known names his eyes suddenly sharpened. 'You have proof?'

She gazed around her again and lowered her voice to a whisper. 'I happen to know something big is in the offing very soon.'

'You don't have to worry, you know. This place caters strictly for reporters and barristers. Westminster types have a members' bar.'

She turned down her collar and beamed him a smile. 'I was being cautious. I didn't want us to be overheard. This is an exclusive.'

Gerald Bender, freelance since his arse had been kicked out the door a couple of months before, smiled and ordered her another sherry. Thank God he'd kept her letter. The names she'd dropped could be his ticket back in.

The A to Z of Pregnancy and Parenting hadn't mentioned post-natal depression, Noel thought. 'What did the doctor say?'

'It's normal. I should take a little holiday.'

'Why don't you take your sister up on her offer?'

'I should, I suppose. I did say I'd go down after the birth.'

He smiled at the small, squirming bundle in his arms. 'Cecily rang when you were out. She said she's longing to see Stevie, and if you go down by train she'll pick you up at the station.'

'Are you trying to get rid of us?'

Whatever he said would be the wrong thing, so he didn't answer.

She pushed her hair back from her eyes with a weary gesture. 'I'm sorry, that was unfair. I just wish you'd come with me.'

'With both Daniel and Joyce off work with the flu, I can't. Why don't you go down. I'll come as soon as the situation improves.'

She smiled. 'Would you, Noel?'

'Sure,' he said easily. 'I'll have to meet your family sooner or later.'

'What about Sylvia?'

'In exactly four weeks we'll be legally divorced. I'm not going to spend the rest of my life avoiding her.' He crossed to where she sat and kissed her cheek. 'You do believe I love you, don't you?'

A smile lifted the weariness from her eyes. 'I don't know why. If I was you, I'd drown me in the bath.'

He looked down at his son. 'That's not a bad idea, is it Stevie?'

Warmth flooded his sleeve and he laughed. 'He's peed on my arm in protest. I'll change him before you feed him.'

She rose from the couch. 'I'll give Cecily a ring and let her know I'm coming. The morning train will do. I don't feel up to driving all that way at the moment.'

The next morning Noel stood at the barrier at Waterloo station and watched her climb on to the train with their son in her arms.

She stared at him from the door for a few moments, then smiled and blew him a kiss.

A shiver ran through him as the train pulled out. It had just occurred to him, she'd be at Little Abbot for the anniversary of Ben's death.

Four bloody weeks! Sylvia loathed her bloated body. She should have got rid of the brat when she had the opportunity.

Hating the child she carried had become a daily event. She hated the way it hooked itself under her ribs, hated her aching back and her swelling breasts, and hated Clive.

There was one bright spot on the horizon. Joyce had promised her a third of the estate once it was settled. Alex would get the other third if his lawyers were agreeable to a settlement. How fortunate Joyce had a conscience to be worked on.

The week after next was the seance. She had no idea how she'd manage to get through it when she looked and felt like a whale. She should have taken Cecily up on her offer to help abort it.

She didn't want the damn thing anyway, she thought sulkily. Babies were such a nuisance. Anne had always smelled of baby sick when hers were young. Then there were smelly nappies to change and bottles to sterilize. She had no intention of losing her figure by feeding it herself like some wild animal.

If only it would arrive early and put her out of her misery. Her eyes flew open. Betony Nichols' baby had survived an early birth. If Cecily had something to cause a miscarriage, the same remedy would start contractions. William George could deliver it. He would be down for the seance along with Cecily's former husband.

Fiorenzo's presence was to be kept a secret, in case Cecily made trouble. He, Clive and William were to prepare her. She was to meditate, rest and learn a secret catechism to give her the power and strength needed for the rites.

Her eyes narrowed as she tried to remember the bottle Cecily had picked up when she suggested the abortion. There were so many of them in that case of hers, and the case was usually kept in the little room off the kitchen where she made up her preparations. She also kept her recipe book there!

Pulling on her boots, Sylvia headed for the car.

After two years' absence, Betony was shocked at the sight of Little Abbot.

'I'd forgotten how shabby the place is.'

Cecily smiled lovingly at her. 'I've put you and Stephen together in your old room. I thought you'd prefer that. I've lit the fire so it will be warm for him.'

A woman came out of the house as they drew up in front of the door. She was petite, her small mouth making her seem doll-like. The faint shadows under her eyes gave her a fragile air, and were due, no doubt, to the advanced state of her pregnancy. Betony knew exactly who she was as she slid Cecily a glance. 'Sylvia Dearborn, I presume.'

Cecily's breath hissed in her throat. 'What's she doing here? I told her to stay away today. I advise you not to have anything to do with her.'

Sylvia stared at the car with undisguised curiosity. She was waiting to be introduced, the half-mocking smile on her face an indication she knew they were at a disadvantage. It would be childish to walk past her, Betony told herself. This was her house. If she didn't want her to visit whilst she was here she'd make her feelings clear to Rose.

She was unprepared when Sylvia greeted her with a friendly smile. 'I'm Sylvia Dearborn. I'm so glad we have a chance to meet now. It does away with any awkwardness.' Her glance went to the baby. 'How absolutely adorable. He looks just like Noel.'

'Yes, he does,' she murmured, hugging Stevie protectively against her.

Sylvia's glance went past her, to Cecily. 'Alex said to tell you he's gone out for a while.'

'You've been to the cottage?'

Sylvia smiled. 'Is there any reason why I shouldn't? I had something important to discuss with him.'

'Where's Rose?'

'With Richard. We've just had coffee together. Your father's a trifle vague today. I'll ask William George to take a look at him at the weekend.'

The temperature dropped several degrees. 'I hardly think that's your decision to make.'

Sylvia's eyes glinted and she adjusted a blue scarf around her ears against the wind. 'Oh, it wasn't my decision. Rose asked me to. Nice to meet you, Betony. Drop in any time. I'm always at home and I'm sure we have plenty in common to discuss.'

'I doubt it.'

Sylvia's eyes flicked at the baby. 'You'd better take him inside where it's warm. He might catch a cold. They have a habit of turning nasty at this time of year, and you wouldn't want to lose another child.'

The colour drained from her cheeks.

'Malicious bitch!' Cecily muttered when she drove away.

Betony took a deep breath to steady herself. Her laugh sounded high-pitched, almost hysterical. 'I've never known you let anyone get the better of you, Ces.'

'She hasn't, yet. You might as well know there's practically open warfare between us.' She stopped inside the front door, her smile wide. 'Still, that's between her and me. I'm so glad you're home, Betony. You look so much happier than when you left. You must tell me all about Noel when we've got some time alone. I'd love to meet him.'

'And you must tell me about Alex. I've heard rumours.'

'There's always rumours in Abbotsford.' She dismissed them with a shrug and strode towards the stairs, a case clasped in each strong hand. 'Nothing for you to worry about, dear.'

189

Cecily hadn't changed, she quickly realized.

But when Betony met Rose again, she sensed a difference she couldn't put her finger on. On the surface Rose seemed the same, straightforward and slightly eccentric. Underlying that though, was now a secretive slyness and an air of excitement. Perhaps she'd always been like that, and she'd only just noticed. Absence seemed to have put a different perspective on everything.

Her father was a different matter all together.

He was shorter than she remembered, and stooped. He shuffled with an old man's gait. His lips were blue-tinged, his eyes faded, his hair white and wispy. His voice was surprisingly resonant, commanding attention.

She felt no special affinity towards him, no sense of duty. Through her stranger's eyes she knew she'd never be able to like him. Sensing the dislike was returned, she felt uneasy in his company and avoided him.

The house seemed to close in on her. Everything became as it was before and she slipped deeper into depression. It was easier to adopt the ways of the past than fight them. The quarrels between her two sisters followed the same old pattern, only this time their father took part. First taking Cecily's side, then that of Rose. To Betony's relief, he practically ignored her after the first meeting, though sometimes his eyes flickered over her, cold and mean.

'You've grown to be like your mother,' he said once, and she didn't answer, because she'd never known her mother either.

Mostly, she stayed in her room, staring out over the bare winter landscape and looking after her son. She'd tried out the piano. Shoved into a room that never saw a fire, damp had ruined it.

Stevie slept in Ben's cot, in the hollow Ben's body had made. Sometimes she heard Ben's voice calling her in the night, but when she opened the bedroom door the corridor was empty. Stevie could have been Ben, except Ben was lying in a colder bed in the churchyard of the next village. She could just see the snub Norman tower in the distance, shrouded in mist. She shivered.

At night she tossed and turned. It was bitterly cold. Stevie grew irritable, his mouth sucking desperately at her breast until he fell asleep, exhausted with the effort. He'd wake two hours later, his cry strident for more. She began to resent his constant demands.

She woke one morning to discover her milk had gone. In panic, she ran to find Cecily. Rose was in the kitchen eating bacon and eggs. 'Where's Ces? I need milk for the baby.' Upstairs, she could hear Stevie crying, a thin, keening wail. She should have known what the problem was, she thought guiltily.

Rose turned, her face curiously blank, her eyes vague. Egg dripped from her fork and on to her jumper. 'Katherine is calling for you, Isabella.'

Goose bumps prickled at Betony's spine. 'Where's Ces,' she screamed.

'Goodness!' Two spots of colour appeared in Rose's cheeks and she became animated. 'I was miles away, dear. What did you say?'

'I was looking for Ces. I need her to drive me to the shop to get some milk and a feeding bottle for Stevie.'

'She's taken the dogs out. She might be at the cottage, she goes there sometimes for a cup of coffee on the way home.'

Stevie's cries had become a howl. 'Look out for Stevie while I go and see.'

'Of course, dear.'

Halfway across the lawn she realized she was still in her pyjamas and bare feet. The frost-rimed grass was as sharp as glass shards and cut at her feet. She didn't care. Everything was panicky and unreal. She knew it, but didn't seem to be able to do anything about it. Her chest began to hurt as she ran, her breath steaming from her nostrils in spurts. She shouldn't have come here. Damn Noel for making her, damn him to hell!

Stevie was starving. She'd failed him, like she'd failed Ben.

'Ces,' she screamed.

In the distance dogs began to bark. Smoke spiralled from the cottage chimney, rising into the air. Everything was sharp-etched against the sky, a terrible stillness hung in the air. The forest beyond seemed brooding and watchful. She wanted to scream and never stop. Her fists pounded at the cottage door.

'What the hell's going on?'

She fell through the door into a pair of strong arms. They closed round her and she found herself gazing into a pair of strange, green eyes. Her head began to spin.

She came to in an armchair. Cecily looked worried as she gazed at her. 'Are you all right?'

It took her a moment to gather herself together. 'I need milk for Stevie. He's hungry and I can't feed him.' She glanced at the man, who was standing silently by the sink. 'I'm sorry. I felt panicked. You must be Alex.'

His mouth eased into a smile. 'Tell me what you need. I'll go and get it.'

She gazed helplessly at Cecily, her mind a blank.

'Buy two feeding bottles and a tin of infant formula for now,' she said crisply.

Cecily waited until Alex had gone, then fetched a blanket to drape round her. A pair of rubber boots were slid on to her frozen feet. 'Let's get you back to the house before someone notices you've gone.'

'Rose knows. She's keeping an eye on Stevie.' Cecily's eyes sharpened. 'How did she seem to you?'

'She called me Isabella. What's wrong with her, Ces?'

'Nothing, dear. I'm sure everything will be all right.' But when Ces hurried her back to the house she began to worry.

Stevie was screaming at the top of his lungs. They could hear him from the garden.

Betony began to run, some unnamed dread clutching at her innards. Cecily overtook her on the stairs. Stevie was lying uncovered on the bed. Rose was staring down at him. 'Dear little Katherine,' she crooned. 'You must tell Rose where you're buried.'

'Rose!' Cecily shouted.

She looked up and smiled. 'He wouldn't stop crying. I was going to change his nappy. He's not as handsome as Ben, is he? Quite bad-tempered in fact.'

Betony pushed her aside and snatched him against her chest. 'Hush, my darling. I won't let anyone hurt you.'

'I wonder if Ben minds having his killer's son for a brother?' Rose said. 'What were you thinking of, Betony? Ben's spirit still lives in this house. You must have heard him calling. He's alone, and frightened to contact you now.'

'Get out,' Cecily hissed at her.

Of course she'd heard Ben, and the vision of him being lonely and afraid was so real, it was too much for her. She began to cry as though she'd never stop.

Cecily's hand touched her shoulder. 'You're too sensible to take what Rose says to heart. What's troubling you, Betony.'

'The doctor said it's post-natal depression and I'll get over it,' she choked out between sobs.

'Oh, is that all. Get into bed and rest, dear. I'll see to the baby first.' She picked up Stevie, wrapped him in his shawl and began to caress his head with her finger. His screams gradually became sobs then he fell asleep, sucking on his thumb.

Gently, Cecily placed him in her arms. 'Don't worry, I'll look after you both. I'll give you something to help you feel better. Once the baby's on the bottle he'll be less fractious and you can rest. We'll have you back to normal in no time at all.'

Ces was so capable. Feeling helpless and inadequate, Betony surrendered herself into her care.

Sylvia shuddered as she swallowed a tablespoon of the concoction she'd made. It tasted foul. She gagged a couple of times before she finally got it down.

Fiorenzo and William George were due to arrive tomorrow. Everything was planned. Tomorrow the baby would be born, and with a bit of luck, it would be born dead.

She was convinced now that the child had been fathered by Alex. She shuddered. It would probably be an idiot. Her brother had forced himself on her, like Sebastian had forced himself on poor Isabella.

But she wasn't Isabella. Nothing would induce her to love the brat. She hated it without even seeing it.

The following week she'd bring Sebastian to account before the circle, and Isabella would be avenged.

She began to laugh. And so would she be avenged. Rose would see to that!

CHAPTER EIGHTEEN

Fiona's stable loft was a good vantage point.

Disgraced journalist, Gerald Bender, had occupied it for two days. The restless, farting horses underneath took some getting used to and, the rural mice seemed to have no fear of mankind, emerging at mealtimes to compete for the crumbs he dropped.

His bed was a bale of scratchy hay with a sleeping bag on top, but the loft was warmed by an oil heater, which kept the bitter, February temperature at bay.

He'd slept in worst places and, at least this came with a plentiful supply of food. So far he hadn't seen much to inspire him through the brass telescope at the window. A few comings and goings at the manor. Dogs being walked.

If nothing else, he could write an exposé of country voyeurs. Fiona's ingenuity by spying on her neighbours had surprised him. There was even a hand-drawn map of the village with each householder named.

He swung the telescope towards Clive Harrington's house when a movement caught his eye. A car was pulling into the drive. Three men got out. One was Clive Harrington, whom he knew by sight. With him was a tall man in a cashmere overcoat, and a short, dapper man who stamped his feet against the cold and waved his arms around a lot. Taking cases from the boot of the car they proceeded to the front door and went inside.

A few minutes later, Fiona and horse emerged from under a tree at the side of the house. She stuck out like a sore thumb in her red anorak. The equestrian pair cantered along the lane and into the stable below. A few minutes later her feet clattered on the wooden ladder and her head emerged through the hole in the floor. 'What luck! Did you see them arrive?'

He nodded. 'Who were the two men with Harrington?'

'The tall man is William George. He's a doctor with a practice in Harley Street. The other one had an accent. I'm not sure, but I think he's the former husband of Cecily Gifford.'

'Can you remember his name?'

'Funzelli, or something. He's a sculptor. In fact, one of his statues is on display at the council offices.' Her mouth pursed and her voice dropped an octave. 'It's a nude figure of Cecily Gifford.'

Cecily Gifford had walked dogs past the stable the day before. He grinned. What a woman! All curves, and her legs went on forever. He'd wished he hadn't hocked his camera when she'd glanced up at the stable loft, tossing her hair and looking like the original gypsy queen. She'd gone into the phone box on the corner, which had struck him as odd. The conversation hadn't lasted long.

'Have you found me a camera yet?'

Her beaming smile revealed expensive crown work when she shoved a box across the floor. 'I borrowed one from Mr Phillips. He used to be a bird-watcher, now he's got Parkinson's disease and doesn't use it any more.'

Probably a poncey little instamatic. He smiled when he unwrapped the ancient, single-lens reflex Nikon. He'd learned his craft on the same model.

Cecily didn't quite know who to trust. Dereck Wallwark was a possibility.

Alex's interest in the circle had waned now he had the scent of money in his nostrils. He said he was going for a quick settlement and had already signed the papers. He wouldn't hang around long afterwards. Rose had the rest of the circle under control. Whether they liked it or not, they'd do what she wanted. They had too much to lose.

She whistled for the dogs and pulled on her coat. Betony and Stevie were asleep. The girl worried her. She seemed too quiet and withdrawn. The mild dose of valerian she'd given her had relieved her anxiety and helped her sleep. She couldn't stay on it indefinitely, though. Sooner or later she'd have to come to terms with Ben's death.

She'd spoken to Noel Dearborn about her just the day before. He'd said he was just recovering from the flu, but would try and get down at the week-end.

She wished Betony wasn't here for the damned rites. Not that she'd be attending. The sky was overcast. Snow powdered the coats of the dogs. Her back prickled as she walked down the lane. She'd had the same feeling for the past few days, that someone was watching her. It could be the Bunnings woman. Yesterday, she'd caught a glimpse of someone in the stable loft.

Interfering bitch! She grinned. It would give her a shock if she caught her at it, and let her know her interest in the comings and goings at Little Abbot might bounce back at her. Instead of taking her usual route, she cut up to the main road and circumnavigated the village. Leaving the dogs tied to a tree, she came into the stable yard from behind.

The horses stamped and blew when she entered the stable building. The ladder creaked slightly whilst she crept her way up it. She gazed round in disappointment. It was empty, except for a sleeping bag and a rucksack.

There was a telescope at the window. Placing her eye against it she swung it towards Abbot's Field and caught Fiona in the act of dismounting. She laughed when the women crept through the reeds towards the cottage with her arse in the air. She'd be disappointed. Alex was at the house doing some work in the cellar.

A wallet and notepad on an upturned orange box caught her eye. She flipped open the wallet. Not much money, but a press card. Gerald Bender.

'Coffee?' someone said from behind her.

Guiltily, she spun round, to be confronted by a hollow-faced man carrying two steaming mugs. His eyes were blue and astute. 'I put sugar in, you struck me as the type who took it.'

'I don't.'

He indicated the orange box and grinned. 'Have a seat.'

'Have you been spying on Little Abbot?'

'Yes, and you in particular, Cecily. You have a hell of a walk on you.'

She automatically took the coffee, watching him warily as she sipped at it.

'You don't seem the type to be mixed up in what's going on up there,' he said.

'What *is* going on?'

'You know damned well. This black magic stuff.'

'Magic!' She nearly choked on the coffee.

He flipped open the notebook and reeled off a list of names. 'Do you want to tell me about it?'

'It's a group of stupid people getting their kicks by playing at being witches.'

He raised a cynical eyebrow. 'Do you call trying to prove a legend, play-acting.'

She stared at him, her blood running cold. 'What are you talking about?' But she knew what he was talking about. Isabella and Katherine! God, why hadn't she cottoned on to what Rose was up to before? Why? Her face blanched when she thought of Betony and Stevie, so innocent and vulnerable. The whole bloody circle would be there at the weekend – and it was the anniversary of Ben's death.

Fiona Bunnings was in for a shock if she'd called in a newspaper reporter, for her husband was involved in it up to his neck. She remembered Rose talking to Stevie, calling him Katherine. Alex was working in the cellar. He must be opening up the chamber.

'Oh, God,' she whispered, feeling sick. 'I think Rose intends to sacrifice!'

Gerald took the cup from her shaking hands. 'You're the person on the inside. Help me to put a stop it.'

'Yoo-hoo!' Fiona's head appeared through the hatch. Her smile was sickly when she looked from one to the other, her voice became a falsetto. 'Oh, it's you Miss Gifford!'

Grabbing her by the shoulders, Cecily dragged her through the hatch and thrust her on to the bale of hay. Her eyes were fierce. 'You interfering old fool. If you don't tell me what you know and where you got your information from I'll shake the bloody eyeballs from your head.'

Gerald's eyes filled with admiration. 'What a woman,' he said reverently when Fiona started to talk.

She shot him a look to kill. 'Print one word of what's going on and I'll have your balls for breakfast.'

Within half an hour Daphne received a phone call from a thoroughly frightened Fiona Bunnings.

'You idiot,' she yelled. 'Betony's down there and she's not well. Put that tabloid snoop on the line. I want a word with him.'

'Um . . . actually, Cecily Gifford would like to talk to you.'

Five minutes later they'd devised a rough plan, and a few seconds after that, Gerald Bender got his second bollocking for the day.

'You must see, dear. Having a relationship with the man who killed Ben is ridiculous.'

'An eye for an eye,' you said, tears filling her eyes. 'All I wanted was a child to replace Ben. I never thought it would go this far.'

'You mustn't let it go any further. We can't have him coming down here. He might say you're mentally unfit, and take Stevie away.'

'He wouldn't, would he? Not Noel. He couldn't!'

'He might.' Rose patted her hand. 'It runs in the family, this weakness. Your mother committed suicide, you know. It was hushed up, of course. But you're old enough to know the truth. Father never got over it.'

'I didn't know,' she said, trying to think through the buzzing in her head. The thought of losing Stevie filled her with horror. 'What should I do, Rose?'

Rose thrust a pen in her hand and set a notepad on the table. 'Write to him, dear. Make a clean break. I'll post it for you.'

Noel would be devastated to lose his son. Her hand hovered over the paper.

Rose picked Stevie up from his cot. He began to whimper. 'His soul is Ben's. You can see it in his eyes.' Her hand splayed across Stevie's forehead and her eyes glazed over. 'Ben's so sad. He doesn't want you to associate with his killer. Noel Dearborn has served his purpose. You must cast him aside.'

Betony held out her arms for him. 'Stevie's hungry. He needs his bottle.'

'When you've finished the letter I'll have his bottle ready. And you must call him Ben. That's what he wants.'

Dear Noel. No! She couldn't call him that now she didn't love him. *Mr Dearborn* . . . . A few minutes later she handed the letter to Rose and impatiently held out her arms.

'Give Ben to me,' she said firmly.

'Rose kissed her cheek and gave a conspiratorial smile. Go back to bed before Ces gets back. I'll bring the bottle up to you.'

It was nice to have Ben snuggled against her again. 'You promise?'

'Of course. And don't tell Ces about our little secret. She wouldn't understand about Ben.'

. . . don't come down to Little Abbot. I realize now that I never loved you. An eye for an eye, remember? You gave me Ben back and that was all I wanted.

Yours sincerely,

Betony Nichols.

Noel found the letter on the door mat when he finally dragged himself out of bed after his bout of flu. Weak and shaky, he sat in the chair Betony had bought him and stared unseeingly at Vivaldi. How could she do this to him? How could she?

He gazed at the letter again. The writing was almost illegible, as if she'd been under stress. Had her condition deteriorated? He snatched up the receiver and dialled her number. Nothing, not even a dial tone. Then he remembered he'd pulled out the plug whilst he'd battled his way through chills and fever for two days. As soon as he plugged it in it began to ring.

'Where the hell have you been,' Daphne shouted. 'Don't go out, I'm coming over.'

Sylvia swallowed another tablespoon of the mixture. Nothing, not even a twinge so far. Grimacing, she placed the bottle on the shelf and made herself a cup of tea.

The murmur of voices came from the sitting room. Fiorenzo was holding court. He'd wanted to sketch her in the nude. It was too cold to run about naked even with the central heating going full blast. She looked a fright anyway.

Madonna, he'd called her. Stupid prat! She couldn't understand what Cecily had ever seen in him, unless he was good in bed. Even that held no attractions now. She felt like a frump with her fat stomach and swollen tits. Pregnancy sucked. She shouldn't have gone through with it.

The seance was in two days. She knew all the secret rites. She had the power now. Clive was treating her with the respect she deserved. If she hadn't been pregnant she would have enjoyed the whole thing. Her glance went to the bottle. Perhaps she hadn't taken enough. If she took it all at once . . . . Reaching out for it, she twisted off the top.

If the bottle hadn't been knocked over, Cecily wouldn't have known it had been tampered with. There were traces of powder on the neck and the liquid was cloudy.

She frowned. Betony's condition should have alerted her. The girl was too passive, and was staring out of the window with a dull expression, as if she wasn't absorbing what she saw. Rose was visiting Sylvia and Clive. Fiorenzo and William George were there as well. At least they were all in once place and out of the way. Rose's bedroom was strewn with clothes, the bed unmade. In the bedside drawer she found a bottle containing sedatives. It had Betony's name on it and the use-by date had long since passed.

Taking the capsules into the kitchen she carefully emptied them out, replacing the contents with caster sugar before returning them to Rose's bedroom.

The phone was ringing when she started back downstairs. Just as she reached the angle of the first landing the receiver was picked up.

'Who? Ah, Mister Dearborn. No, Betony doesn't want to speak to you. Don't bother us again.'

She flew down the rest of the stairs, but was too late. 'Why did you say that? She might have wanted to speak to him.'

The slap came so quickly it caught her unawares. She rubbed the reddening patch on her face as her father roared, 'She'll do what I tell her.'

He was still in his pyjamas and dressing gown. His eye sockets sagged and his breath was stale. She wondered if he'd been drinking. 'Where's my breakfast, girl?'

She'd forgotten his nasty streak and how she'd lived in fear of him as a small child. When he married Julia Dubeney, and they'd come to live in this house it had started again. First with Julia as his victim, then Betony. Julia had fallen from her bedroom window and broken her neck. Rose had been with her at the time. She'd said Julia had slipped, but could Rose have pushed her?

Only Rose had missed their father after he'd gone. She'd never borne the brunt of his temper and had done everything in her power to please him, as she did now.

Cecily didn't dare oppose him at the moment. She had to tread carefully. Forced to swallow her ire, she murmured 'Go into the sitting room where it's warm.'

'Where's Rose? At least she has respect for her father.'

'She's gone to see Sylvia.'

'Ah yes, the rites. Sylvia should do well. She's very receptive to suggestion.' He nodded to himself. 'Soon we'll have it all. The Dubeneys will be no more.'

Cecily's blood ran cold as he shuffled off in a pair of worn carpet slippers, grumbling under his breath. *Damn him – damn them all!* Somehow, she had to get Betony and Stevie out of here before the weekend.

18th Day of March 1798

The flame-haired woman came again. She took me to the secret place. There were others assembled. On the altar was the infant in which Katherine is to be reborn. Her face is waxen.

When the angel took my hand, calm flooded through me. I understood then, she acts in my interest. The chamber erupted into light and smoke, and there were terrible screams of anguish and anger as the vision faded.

Sebastian came. He offered me sustenance if I would reveal Katherine's resting place. I need no sustenance, for I'm filled with the strength of my resolve. He left his knife on the table when he left.

'Who is this angel she mentions?' Fiorenzo said imperiously.

'Sylvia of course.' Rose beamed at everyone. 'I knew it as soon as I saw her. She's the only one who can contact Isabella.'

'Ah, the angel of darkness,' Fiorenzo said.

From her chair, Sylvia smiled regally at them all. She wished she had the power to make them all disappear. She had a headache and felt sick. There had been a bright spot this week. Clive had given her a bracelet of rubies strung on a gold chain when she'd perfected the rites.

Fiorenzo was talking again. His teeth flashed with gold fillings, and he waved his arms around as he enthused about his talent. He dropped famous names all over the place. Everyone listened to him, except her. He was an egotistical bore.

She needed a rest. Rising to her feet she raised a hand and gave a smile designed to arouse sympathy. 'You won't mind if I excuse myself. I have an awful headache.'

Immediately, Clive was by her side, his hand under her elbow. 'I'll take you upstairs.' He tucked the quilt tenderly around her and kissed her cheek. 'You've done really well, Sylvia. I'm pleased with you. When it's all over I'll send you away for a little holiday. I have influential friends who would be glad to entertain you.'

A holiday was exactly what she needed, but not with Clive's friends. She had plans of her own.

Betony was feeling a bit more human. Stevie had been fed, and was settled down for the night.

She'd dreamed he was Ben. She'd dreamed she'd written to Noel saying it was over between them. It had seemed real, but it must have been a nightmare. She missed Noel. He'd been suffering from the flu last time she'd rung him. He'd said he'd be down here with them as soon as he recovered.

Longing to hear his voice, she glanced at her watch. It was past two, yet the urge to hear his voice was overwhelming. She pulled on her robe and crept downstairs to the hall. The door to the sitting room was ajar. A candle burned. By its flickering light she saw the dark shape of a man wearing a monk's habit. Rose was there and they were talking together.

She stifled a gasp as the man's eyes seemed to bore straight into hers, glinting like glass in the candlelight. He seemed familiar, but she couldn't think where she'd seen him. She fled back to her room, and locking the door behind her moved to the window and gazed out over the village.

It was all so peaceful. A sprinkling of lights in the houses, the snow drifting from the sky. Her eyes widened when she heard a distant, long drawn-out scream. It wasn't repeated. A fox killing its prey perhaps?

She shivered as she switched out the light and, slipping into bed, snuggled the hot water bottle against her stomach. She closed her mind against what she'd seen. It was none of her business. Instead, she thought of Noel, lying in the bed they'd chosen together. Was he thinking of her, missing her as much as she missed him?

Her thoughts reached out to him, telling him how much she loved him. After a while she could almost feel his presence near her. Comforted, she fell asleep.

*

Sylvia had never felt such torturous pain.

'Do something,' she begged.

William gave her a glum look. 'The baby's in the normal position. I'm not a gynaecologist. You'll have to go into hospital if the pain becomes too severe.'

Clive took him by the shoulders and shook him. 'She can't. We need her.'

'If anything goes wrong I'll be ruined. I can't take the responsibility.'

Another contraction racked her. Moaning, she tensed herself against it. Sweat flooded her body as she writhed in agony. She'd been in labour for several hours, and hadn't expected giving birth to be so hard. 'How much longer will this take?'

'First child. It could be another twelve hours or so.'

Christ! She couldn't stand it.

'You have a small pelvis, but the baby's tiny so you should be able to give birth naturally.' He strapped a blood pressure cuff around her upper arm and pumped. 'Mmmm, a bit up, but that's to be expected.'

She felt as if she were being torn apart. 'Can't you give me something for the pain?' she whined.

'I only carry a limited supply of drugs in my bag. It's better we save them until the pain gets really bad.'

'It's almost unbearable now.'

William's smile had a touch of superiority about it. 'It will get worse as the contractions get closer. Childbirth is a natural process, my dear. Women are built for it.'

'Save me the lecture until *you* have to give birth,' she snarled.

William murmured one of the platitudes he kept for difficult patients. 'Take a warm bath, relax and let nature take its course. Before too long you'll have a sweet little baby to love and the pain will be forgotten.'

'Love,' she shrieked. 'You can take it away after it's born. I don't even want to see the brat.'

Clive hovered over her after William had left. 'Is there anything I can do?'

'Yes. Go and ask Cecily if she's got something for pain in her bag of tricks.' Her eyes widened when agony rippled across her abdomen. 'Tell her I took something from her bag to start the labour off. I don't know what it was. I think I took too much. I'm scared. I don't want to die.'

Her stomach suddenly heaved and she headed for the bathroom.

Stupid bitch, Clive thought. He didn't want her to die either. It would ruin his career.

*

Betony had insisted on visiting Ben's grave. Cecily decided to walk though the lanes to the graveyard with her. Although the day was cold, the snow was just a sprinkling on the ground and the sun made everything sparkle.

Noel Dearborn had arranged to be there. Cecily had met him on her early walk when she'd deviated to the stable. She'd taken to him straight away, finding his sincere concern for Betony refreshing.

She hadn't told Betony yet. She'd do so on the way over. Stevie was rugged up against the cold in his pushchair, only his face and a wisp of dark hair visible under his knitted helmet. An outing would do him no harm. The phone rang in the sitting room just as they were about to leave.

'Ces,' Rose shouted out. 'It's Clive. Sylvia's in labour. She said she took something from your case to start her off. She's in terrible agony. Will you help her?'

'I was just going out with Betony.'

'I'll go with her to visit Ben's grave.'

'No!' The word shot from her mouth before she could stop it. She couldn't risk Rose running into Noel.

'Nonsense, Ces. You can't keep Betony all to yourself.'

Something unexpected happened. Betony drew herself up and bestowed a strangely disgusted look on Cecily. 'I'm not anyone's possession, and I'd prefer to go by myself.'

'I can't allow you to go alone.'

'Allow? I'll decide what I can or can't do in my own home.' Taking hold of the pushchair she manoeuvred it down the steps without another word and strode off down the drive.

'Well!' Colour mounted to Rose's cheeks. 'She's being quite the little madam this morning.'

'How very odd.' Inside, Cecily applauded Betony's new independence. The girl had more guts than she'd given her credit for.

'Perhaps William George could prescribe something to calm her down. That stuff you give her doesn't seem to work.'

Cecily gazed straight into her eyes. 'On the contrary. It's worked wonderfully.'

Rose's eyes wandered shiftily to a picture on the wall. 'You *will* look after Sylvia. Clive said she's quite desperate.'

'She deserves to be.' Stomping through to the kitchen she glanced along the range of numbered bottles. Each seemed as full as before. She held them up to the light, checking the density of the liquids.

'Mistletoe,' she muttered. 'She's topped the bottle up with water.' There hadn't been enough liquid in the bottle to harm her permanently, but it would certainly make her uncomfortable. She was tempted to let Sylvia suffer, but there was the baby to think of. It was already under a handicap having Sylvia for a mother.

She smiled to herself, wondering if they'd hide Fiorenzo away in a cupboard for the duration of her visit. She hoped so, because eventually she intended to flush the slimy little rat out and make him squirm.

Selecting several bottles, she stuffed them in her pockets, pulled her scarf up round her ears and set out to rescue Sylvia from her own stupidity.

CHAPTER NINETEEN

Noel smiled when he saw Betony coming up the path. Dressed in a bulky, navy duffel coat and thick boots that hid her calves, she still looked elegant. Lengths of hair flowed from under a blue knitted hat and tumbled over her shoulders. He stood in the shelter of the church porch. He'd arrived too early in his eagerness to see her, and was frozen. Warmth flooded him now, just at the sight of her.

She turned along the path leading to her son's grave. It was situated at the far end of the graveyard under the spreading branches of a tree, and next to his father. Noel had been there before her, placing a couple of snowdrops on top of Ben's gravestone, and offering a silent apology to them both.

She stood staring at the grave for a long time. God knew what was going through her mind. He wanted to join her, to draw her into his arms and shield her from whatever she was going through. But she had to face it alone and he had to allow her the privacy to do so. Her loss was etched in one simple statement on the gravestone.

Ben, taken from his loving mother by accident.

He'd been the accident, and the cause of that loss.

She unbuttoned her coat and drew out a yellow teddy bear. He closed his eyes when she stooped to place it on the grave. Ben's bear, the one he'd been carrying that day? It had to be.

When she straightened, the snowdrops caught her eye. She picked them up and stared at them, then at the ground and the path with its tell-tale set of footprints in the snow leading to the porch. There was a stillness about her. Her hand came up to shade her eyes and she stared at the porch.

He stepped out of the shadows.

'Noel?' Her mouth formed the word, the sound escaped him.

He started towards her, then lengthened his stride when she smiled, folding her against him when he reached her. Hugging her tight, he was close to tears. 'I came to say sorry.'

'Don't ... don't,' she murmured, gazing up at him. 'It's not your fault. It's mine.'

'How can it be yours? It was me who was driving the car.'

She laid a finger over his lips. 'Simon was drunk that day. We had a blazing row.'

He held his breath, waiting for her to continue.

'I told him I wanted a divorce.' The breath she took was a raw, trembling shudder. 'His rage was frightening, so I slipped a sleeping pill into his drink to calm him down. I expected him to fall asleep, but he didn't.'

'You needn't go on,' he said quietly. 'I can guess the rest.'

'No you can't, Noel, and I have to tell you.' Her voice strengthened. 'He took Ben from his cot, dressed him and said he was taking him away from me.'

'Hell,' he growled.

'Cecily heard the row and hid his car keys. He knocked her unconscious before leaving. He screamed out he was going up to the road to catch a bus.'

'Oh God.' He held her against him, rocking her back and forth. 'You've been living with this all this time?'

'The pill must have kicked in a few minutes later,' she said dully. 'It was *my* fault Ben died. *My fault!* Don't you see, Noel. The anger I directed towards you was easier than living with my own guilt.' She began to cry, a soft despairing sound that tore him into little pieces.

'Don't be too hard on yourself,' he murmured against her hair. 'Simon had a hand in it too.'

'But he's dead now, and he took Ben with him. There was only you and me left to blame. Now there's only myself.'

'Is that going to bring Ben back?'

She glanced at the grave. 'Nothing can do that.'

'Then let's build on what we have. We owe it to Stevie to make the best of life. It's not fair to expect him to take second place to a memory.'

She gazed down at the teddy bear. 'His name's Snooky.'

'If I were Ben, I think I'd like my little brother to look after him.'

Smiling through her tears she bent to scoop it up and handed it to him. 'I guess he would, at that.'

He dropped a kiss on her nose. 'If you're finished here I'll take you back to the village. There's something going on you need to know about.'

He expected her to protest when he mentioned the seance. 'There's a newspaper reporter sniffing around. Cecily is trying to keep a lid on it, but I want you and Stevie out of there if the seance goes ahead.'

She looked amused. 'I'll tell Rose to cancel it.'

'Do you think she'll listen to you?'

'You'll be pleased to hear I've decided to take Daniel's advice and sell the place. I'm going to tell them today.'

'Shall I come with you for support?'

'No, it's time I made a stand.' Leaning into his body she kissed him. 'Where are you staying?'

'In Fiona Bunnings' stable loft. We all are.'

'All?'

'Daphne, Daniel, Jeff Sullivan and Gerald Bender.'

She looked totally bemused. 'Who's Gerald Bender?'

'The reporter. Cecily wants us to keep an eye on him in case he takes too much of an interest in Little Abbot.'

She grinned. 'I didn't realize Ces had such a vivid imagination.'

'She made an indelible impression on me.'

'Really, Noel. I'm surprised at you. I didn't imagine you'd call out the mounties over such a trivial matter.'

His smile was self-effacing in the face of her wry amusement. 'It may be trivial to you, but I'm not taking any chances.'

'That's why I love you.' The kiss she gave him made his toes curl. 'Pick me up tomorrow evening. I'll be ready and waiting.'

Sparkling with a new found self-assurance, she strode off towards the house with his sleeping son. When she blew him a kiss and disappeared from his sight, he looked down to find the teddy bear still clasped in his hand.

He smiled and slipped it inside his coat, feeling like a bit of an idiot for over-reacting.

Of all the stupid and dangerous things to do. Cecily kept her thoughts to herself as she worked on Sylvia. The woman was frightened out of her wits.

Of Fiorenzo there had been no sign, but the smell of cigars lingered in the air. Neither Clive nor William smoked. Fiorenzo could wait. The whole damn pack of wolves could wait.

Twelve drops of lavender oil joined the bergamot and neroli in the carrier oil. She poured the slightly warmed mixture on to her palms and began her massage. Sylvia was trembling all over, every muscle tense.

'This should help you relax,' she murmured. 'It will only make the birth harder if you fight it.'

Every bone of Sylvia's spine stood out in sharp relief, her ribs etched a cage against her skin. She was painfully thin, her abdomen tight and hard, like a ball. 'Has your water broken?'

'I don't think so.' Fright appeared in her eyes. 'Should it have?'

'Not necessarily. Nature takes its own course.'

'I won't have to go into hospital, will I? The seance is important.'

'What's so important about it? Rose has been trying to raise Isabella for years.'

Sylvia's eyes glittered. 'But I'll be the one to do it.' She groaned when another contraction twisted into her stomach, and drew her knees up.

Cupping her hands Cecily placed them over her nose and mouth. 'Take a deep breath in, then let it out slowly. One . . . two . . . three . . . good . . . relax, that's great.'

'Promise you won't leave me. William doesn't understand how bad the pain is.'

'I won't leave you.' She resumed the massage. If she kept Sylvia calm, the birth would go smoothly, she told herself.

Cecily worked on Sylvia for two hours, until she fell into an exhausted sleep. Exhausted herself, she gazed down at her, wondering if she'd have the stamina to see the ordeal through.

By three o'clock the next morning Sylvia was almost uncontrollable in her pain. Cecily woke William up. He checked her blood pressure and gave her a painkiller with a complete lack of compassion. 'It shouldn't be long now.'

Another hour and it was over. The baby was a girl, and small. A wisp of dark hair was plastered on top of her head. She was pale, and limp.

'Stillborn,' William pronounced, glancing at his watch.

For the first time in several hours, Sylvia smiled.

William drew her aside. 'Get Alex out of bed to dig a hole and bury it.'

'I'll do it.'

'Aren't you going to stay and clean me up?' Sylvia whined.

'You know where the bathroom is.' Wrapping the baby in a towel, Cecily left. The poor little soul deserved better than to be unloved and unwanted. She'd name her, then bury her in the cemetery with Ben. Tucking the baby against the warmth of her body she strode rapidly away from the house.

Halfway up the lane, something moved against her ribs. She gazed down at the small head visible between her breasts. The baby's mouth opened and it gave a thin wail. Altering direction, she headed for the cottage.

Alex wasn't there, but he'd left her a farewell note.

Betony stood at her window, disliking what she was about to do. She was going to tell her family of her decision, and give them three months notice to vacate.

She put it off until eleven, when it was their habit to take coffee together in the sitting room. Her father acknowledged her presence with a grunt and an intimidating stare. It didn't work. She'd discovered a well of strength she hadn't known she possessed.

Cecily smiled at her in encouragement.

She took a deep breath. 'There's something I have to say to you. I've decided to sell Little Abbot. It's upkeep is beyond my means.'

Her father's hands began to shake. 'This house belonged to my wife. You have no right to throw me on to the street.'

'You won't be thrown out on the street. I'll give you enough time to find somewhere to rent. Three months to be exact.'

'You can't,' Rose snapped. 'Ben's spirit roams this place, and Katherine's bones haven't been found.'

'Ben's spirit lives in my heart. And as for Katherine's bones I don't give a damn about them. Your interest in the occult has become unhealthy, Rose. Any activity related to it will cease while I own this house.'

Rose gave her a baleful glance. 'If it hadn't been for me you'd have ended up in an orphanage.'

Cecily smiled. 'She most certainly would not.'

'Trust you to take her side.'

'It's not a question of sides, it's a question of what's right. Betony shouldn't be obliged to give us a home after all these years.'

Rose shot to her feet, her face enraged. 'You can do what you like, Ces. She'll have to evict me to get me out.'

'If it comes to that, I will,' she said calmly. 'My accountant says I'll be bankrupt in five years if I hang on to it.'

'Your accountant being Noel Dearborn, I suppose. We all know he's got a vested interest in your bank account.'

Blood rose to her face. 'Noel's got nothing to do with it, and don't you talk to me about vested interests. For years you've been using this place for your own ends and now it's going to stop.'

'And what about your father? Don't you owe him something?'

'Ah yes . . . .' She turned a scathing look on him. 'If there wasn't a photograph in the hall I wouldn't know what he looks like.'

'Shut your mouth, missie. You're my daughter, and you'll show me some respect.'

'Respect has to be earned, and you've been bleeding me dry for years. Now you'll have to learn to live on your pension like everyone else.'

Three pairs of eyes stared at her. Two were full of hate. She shivered, and strode from the room. She hadn't expected it to develop into a slanging match.

She felt her usual twinge of guilt. But God, it felt good to have the upper hand for once.

She went through to the kitchen, put Stevie's bottles in the sterilizer and sat down with a cup of coffee to think.

Cecily slid into the seat opposite her and smiled. 'You've got nothing to feel guilty about, you know.'

Betony's eyes softened. 'I knew you'd understand, Ces. I'm sure the three of you will find something suitable to rent.'

'I have no intention of living with Rose and father.' Her eyes became dreamy. 'I'm going to find my own little place in Wales, where I can do what I like. I was offered a good price for the shop the other day, and have decided to sell it. You don't have to worry about me.'

'What about Alex. Will he go with you?'

She gave a strange, sad smile. 'Alex has gone. We wouldn't have been compatible, anyway. He's too young, and not the type one can rely on.' Her eyes were troubled. 'Now, I must tell you the truth of what's going on, and you must leave when Noel comes. Nothing will stop Rose, now.'

It was almost unbelievable, Betony thought. Rose must be insane – the circle must be insane to think they could raise the dead through sacrifice. A shudder ran down her spine as she threw clothes haphazardly into her suitcases. Did evil influences roam the house? It had a record of death and unhappiness.

She grinned at the way her thoughts were running. She'd never once felt a ghostly presence in all the time she'd lived here, just been frightened witless by Rose's stories. Then again, a ghost might be an asset when selling. Even the cellar chamber Cecily had told her about could be an asset. Some people liked the macabre. With the Dubeney family gone and an infusion of money, eventually it could become a happy, comfortable family home.

Curiosity ate at her. She should go down and inspect it if she was going to put the house on the market. Stevie had just had his bottle and was sound asleep, his cheeks glowing with contentment. How like Noel he was. She kissed his sweet, rosy cheek, glad he didn't look like Ben.

Beyond the vacant wine racks was a rough archway in the wall. Brick rubble was stacked to one side. It must have been bricked up and recently opened. Light cast from one bare globe failed to illuminate inside the archway. There were candles and matches on the table. Everything was covered in a fine film of plaster dust.

Something snapped in the silence.

'Hello?' she said nervously. 'Is anyone here?' A large black spider scuttled out of the rubble. She shuddered and backed away. There was a noise that sounded like a chuckle. The lights went out, plunging her into darkness.

Betony tried not to panic, though the suffocating darkness brought with it an acute sense of her own hearing. Every little crack and rattle seemed significant and sinister. Someone was in here with her. Above the blood roaring in her ears she heard a soft, sibilant whisper of breath.

Edging carefully in the direction of the cellar stairs, she encountered something warm. As she opened her mouth to scream, someone reached around her from behind and effectively muffled her.

Sylvia regarded the birth as a bad dream. She'd put it behind her, vowing never to become pregnant again. By late afternoon, she felt rested enough to get up.

After going through the rites with Clive again, she went back upstairs to prepare. The bleeding was going to be a problem, but she didn't mention it to William. Nothing was going to be allowed to stand in the way of her triumph tonight.

Her eyes began to shine as she readied herself for the seance.

Fiona Bunnings was in her kitchen making dainty chicken and asparagus sandwiches when Judy Cross came in.

Judy's eyes went curiously to Fiona's best Wedgewood tea service spread on the dresser. 'What on earth's going on. Are you having a party?'

And Fiona, brimming with excitement and self-importance, couldn't keep the news to herself any longer as she announced triumphantly, 'I'm expecting Daphne Harrington and Betony Nichols for supper.'

His head turned and he smiled at her, his eyes full of madness. 'Nothing will stop the sacrifice now. The house vibrates with the power of Mamon.' Foam gathered around his mouth as he lurched across the floor.

Betony strained to loosen her bonds as he bent over Stevie's cot, a silent scream ripping her insides apart.

It happened so quickly she didn't have time to experience relief. Richard Gifford dropped to the floor, gurgling and clutching his chest. A few seconds later the gurgling stopped. His dead eyes glittered in the light.

Cecily appeared a few seconds later, her face ashen as she loosened her bonds. 'Are you all right?'

Betony fought to control her hysteria. 'They were going to sacrifice Stevie. Father just fell to the floor and died.'

'Karma,' Cecily said calmly. 'It was bound to catch up with him sometime.' Lifting Stevie from the cot, Cecily bundled him into her arms. 'Get a grip on yourself, Betony. Noel's waiting to take you to safety.'

The wind rose quite suddenly and howled around the house with wild abandon. Windows rattled, curtains billowed into rooms and candle flames flickered.

Noel kissed her and covered Stevie's head with the shawl. 'Daphne's waiting with the car?'

Betony reluctantly nodded. 'I wish you'd come with me. Why don't you just leave them to it?'

'Because I can't leave Cecily to manage alone after what she told me. We'll meet up later.'

Still, she hesitated.

'Don't worry. Everything will be all right, I promise. Just get our son to safety.'

If Noel said everything would be all right, she knew it would be. Her fingers lightly caressed his cheek. 'Be careful.'

'Trust me.' For a heartbeat their glances joined.

She gave a faint smile when she saw the sharp sense of purpose in his eyes. Trust was not an issue, there was something more at stake. Noel needed to prove himself.

She swallowed her fear and nodded, knowing the next hour or so would be the longest of her life.

CHAPTER TWENTY

19th Day of March 1798

> *I have been thinking of the vision all day. My destiny is to die by my own hand, and I know the time has come to act. How I long to be with her again, two souls joined in eternity until God takes her home. I do not fear the blade. The cold steel has touched Katherine's warm heart, and will stroke against mine like a true friend.*
>
> *But first I must hide this journal from Sebastian's sight, for I cannot allow him the knowledge of Katherine's resting place. To those who may discover this journal, it's my wish that she be buried in consecrated ground with the remains of her loving mother.*
>
> *With my blood I curse Sebastian Dubeney, and condemn him to everlasting purgatory. I curse the House of Dubeney and all who bear the blood, until Katherine's remains shall be buried in consecrated ground.*

Sylvia fought back tears as an unaccustomed sympathy for Isabella filled her thoughts. It was more than a coincidence that she too had borne her brother a daughter, then lost the child to death. She and Isabella were alike in many ways. To go against her wishes and use her child's bones for the power it would give them, seemed like an act of sacrilege.

She cast her doubts aside as she surveyed the people gathered in the chamber. The men wore black, cowled robes. All the women were dressed in purple, the exceptions being herself and Rose, both in white.

Rose looked dramatic with her red hair spread in ripples around her shoulders. Her mouth pursed with annoyance as she gazed towards the door. 'Alex must come before we can start or we won't have enough power.' Her glance fell on Cecily, who was handing round the drinks. 'I'll do that. Go and find Alex.'

Cecily strolled off, her purple gown outlining every curve of her magnificent body.

Sylvia wondered where she'd buried the baby. Goodness, how weepy she felt. Her head ached and she was hot, as if she was starting a fever. She wished it was all over. The chamber was small and stuffy with everyone crammed in. The men looked silly. She couldn't tell one from the other.

Cecily returned with another cowled monk. Good. Once this was over she'd leave and never come back. She wanted nothing more to do with any of them. Not Rose, certainly not Clive. Her glance strayed to Dereck. He was a possibility.

On the other hand, once she got the conscience money from Joyce, she could buy herself a house and go into business as a mystic. People were fools when it came to that sort of thing. She downed her drink in one gulp and headed for her seat, which was placed opposite Rose's in the centre of the circle.

The circle contained a pentagon, in which the names of Sebastian, Isabella and Katherine had been drawn. The altar was an oblong stone covered by a black cloth. At its base was a hollow where Katherine's bones would be laid, once they'd got them. On the top was a candleholder, a small dagger and a bowl.

Those were for the master's use. Her head began to swim when she gazed at the light flickering on the bowl. She didn't want to think about how Noel would feel. The baby would feel nothing, he'd be drugged.

A gust of wind found its way to the cellar and one of the candles guttered out. The stench of hot wax nearly made her gag. Rose leaned forward and gazed into her eyes. They were as black as sin in this light, with flickering specks where the light danced on their surface. Sylvia saw madness in them and shuddered. This was no longer a game.

'We will begin the incantations.'

Her head began to spin. Feeling nauseated, she suddenly couldn't remember a word of them. 'I can't, Rose. I feel ill.'

'You must,' Rose screamed.

Somehow, she found the words, pushing them out by rote and not really understanding them. Perspiration covered her face and trickled between her shoulder blades.

Upstairs, the wind made a thin shrieking sound. Slates clattered from the roof. A tree branch snapped off and shattered a bedroom window, sending a pair of dusty velvet curtains billowing. The weight of them pulled the ancient fittings from one end of the wall and the rod canted sideways. The curtains slowly slipped down the rod towards an electric fire.

'Now,' Rose whispered to her when the incantations were over. 'Rest and meditate. Bring the spirit of Isabella and Sebastian forth. Cecily, fetch the sacrifice. Alex. Go with her and inform the master we're ready for him.'

Until this moment, the reality of what she was involved in hadn't really dawned on Sylvia. Now, she was horrified. The circle had joined hands and were chanting something to help her meditate. She bent her head, closed her eyes and desperately wished it would end. They couldn't sacrifice Noel's baby. She didn't want to get her revenge like this. It was murder. She began to sob.

Rose's fingers taloned into her shoulders. 'Stop it, you little fool. You'll spoil everything.'

'I feel ill. I'm bleeding,' she whined. 'The drink wasn't properly prepared. I can't concentrate.'

'Shut up and meditate, or I'll tell the master to sacrifice you instead.'

Someone came to stand beside her. Clive, she thought.

'Get back into the circle,' Rose hissed at him. 'She's just scared. She'll get over it in a minute. I'll help her. Sylvia, look into my eyes. I'll give you my strength.'

Nothing would give her strength, but she looked anyway, deep into the eyes of Rose. The insanity in their depths repulsed and scared her. She wanted to look away and she wanted to scream, but she did neither. She pretended to slip into a meditative state. It was easier than fighting her.

A small sigh went round the room when Cecily and Alex came back. Cecily was carrying a wrapped bundle in her arms. She laid it on the altar and went back to her position by the door.

A murmur went up when a man entered the chamber and made his way to the altar. '*The master!*'

He stood quite still.

'Bring Isabella,' Rose murmured.

'Isabella won't come if you're going to sacrifice a child,' Sylvia dared to say. 'Besides, it's a boy. Isabella said it would be a girl.'

'This is the only infant available. It will have to do.'

'I thought a pig was to be sacrificed,' the actress said.

Nobody took any notice of her, they were watching the power struggle between Rose and Sylvia.

'Do you think Isabella wants a baby sacrificed after what happened to her own,' Sylvia argued. 'You can't do this without me, and I won't be party to it. Cecily, take the child back to its mother.'

'We need to know where Katherine's bones are,' Rose shrieked. 'Command Isabella to come to us. Let her decide.'

Cecily smiled. 'Katherine's bones are with her mother. Fiorenzo and I found them years ago and buried them where Isabella wanted.'

'You liar,' Rose hissed.

'Ask him,' Cecily mocked.

Fiorenzo pushed the cowl from his head and spread his arms in an expansive gesture. His teeth gleamed in a sickly smile. 'Is true. You didn't know?'

'Of course she didn't know, you greasy little runt. She wouldn't have let you within a yard of her knicker elastic if you'd told her. If you don't want your tonsils kicked, get the hell out of here and don't come back.'

His hands curved an arc through the air as he backed out of the chamber. 'I did it for you, *Cara*.'

Sylvia appealed to the rest of the circle for support. 'Tell her it's wrong.'

All the men, except three, one of which was Alex, pushed back their cowls.

'I want nothing to do with this,' Gregory Lord said pompously.

'Nor me,' Clive said. 'I draw the line at murder.'

Rose glared at him. 'It was your sodding idea in the first place.'

Sylvia gazed at Alex. 'It could have been our child being sacrificed if she hadn't died.'

'It would have been. Your child was a girl.'

'You murderous bitch!' Sylvia struggled to her feet and advanced on Rose, her legs almost buckling under her. 'All this time you've played us off one against the other. You knew Alex was my brother. I bet it was you who wrote those anonymous letters to my mother.'

'It was Alex,' Cecily said quietly. 'Now he's got his blood money, he's gone. He left a note saying he's sorry about your mother. He didn't expect her to kill herself.'

Sylvia's head began to pound. Dampness spread between her thighs. 'I'm bleeding,' she said to no one in particular.

'Kill the child anyway,' Rose commanded the master. 'She isn't the only one who can bring Isabella. It will give me the power I need.'

A murmur of unease ran through the room.

The actress pointed at one of the three remaining cowled men. 'If that's not Alex, who is he?'

Noel removed his cowl with a flourish. 'Noel Dearborn, accountant, at your service.'

The other two followed his lead.

'Daniel Jacobs standing in for Dereck Wallwark.'

'Jeff Sullivan for Richard Gifford.'

They looked at each other and grinned, then gave sweeping bows. 'The seance is over.'

'No it's not.' The master picked up the knife and slashed downward. There was a collective gasp when blood sprayed across the room.

Pandemonium broke out. Both women and men screamed. Rose lunged at Sylvia. The vicious blow she received knocked her to the floor. She stayed there,

THE GRACE OF DAY

her head buzzing and blood seeping through her dress on to the floor.

The master pulled back his hood. Light glinted from his glasses. Good God, she'd never have guessed! When she started to laugh, blood spurted, but she couldn't control herself. Rose rushed over to the altar and snatched the sacrifice up by its arm. A lump of liver slipped from under its wrapping.

'A doll,' she snarled, throwing it forcefully at Cecily. Snatching up the knife she lunged at Noel, her eyes deranged. 'This is for Ben.'

He twisted the knife easily from her grasp and pushed her aside. 'Where's my father?' she spat at him.

'Dead,' Cecily said. 'All this was too much for him.'

Rose rushed away, her eyes frantic.

Noel came to kneel at her side. His eyes held the same concern he'd reserve for an injured dog, but nothing more. 'Are you all right, Sylvia?'

'I'm bleeding,' she whispered. 'I need to go to hospital.'

William George headed for the door. Before he reached it, Cecily clamped a hand around his wrist. 'You're a doctor. Help her?'

'She's haemorrhaging. Call an ambulance.'

Daniel shouldered him aside. 'I'll go and ring for one.'

'Can anyone smell smoke?' someone shouted above the din.

There was a stampede towards the door. William got there first, knocking people aside in his haste to get out.

Noel removed his monk's habit and wrapped it round Sylvia's trembling body. 'Put your arms around my neck. I'll get you out of here.'

'I'm scared.' she whispered, fearful of the smell of her own blood, fearful of the darkness edging into her consciousness. A tear slid down her face. 'I lost my baby, Noel.' He nodded dispassionately. 'Perhaps you'll have another, one day.'

She shuddered. 'Never again. I hated her. I wouldn't have made a good mother.'

'I know.'

The pity growing in Cecily's heart disappeared like a magician's rabbit into a hat when she heard Sylvia's words. Taking one last look around, she followed Noel and his burden out. It was time to let Gerald Bender out of the store cupboard. She didn't want him to fry, she rather liked him.

The whole village turned out to watch the burning of Little Abbot. Fuelled by the strong wind, flames and sparks cracked into the sky with volcanic fury. Soon, the whole building was gutted. Explosions sent sparks flying like tracer bullets, setting fire to Clive Harrington's house.

Fiona caught her husband sneaking in the back door. His monk's robe was singed, his face streaked and dirty with blood and smoke.

'I'll give you Masonic Lodge!' she screamed, and cracked him across the skull with her Wedgewood teapot. Daphne gazed at Betony and began to laugh when he yelped and scurried off upstairs with Fiona after him.

The bodies of Rose and her father were never found. The fire had been too fierce for anything to survive.

At the next meeting of the Village Betterment Committee, Judy Cross swore she saw Rose Gifford at one of the upstairs windows, her head wreathed in flames.

Another woman reported seeing a woman standing on the lawn with a baby in her arms. Everyone saw chanting monks stream from the house to disappear into darkness.

Fiona said it was all nonsense.

None of them commented on the fact that Fiona's husband wasn't around. Still, if she didn't miss him, why should they?

A story of the fire appeared in the press. The photographs accompanying it were dramatic, and won Gerald Bender an award. It also put him in Cecily Gifford's good books.

The story won him his job back. After a while, he realized the job wasn't as good as he'd imagined it was with its day-to-day grind. He grew bored and dissatisfied, tired of playing the cynical reporter.

He began to dream of the future. He didn't have a novel in him, but perhaps a book on the alternative lifestyle would be popular, he thought.

He wrote to Cecily regularly for advice, and in time, gave up smoking and drinking. He saved his money, and waited.

Nothing was ever mentioned about the inner circle. Yet within three months of the fire, both the cabinet minister and Clive resigned their posts, and William George retired with his wife to his villa in Spain.

A year later, Gregory Lord wrote a best-selling novel. He donated the proceeds to charity. It was made into a film starring the ageing actress, and bombed at the box office. At the beginning of winter, bulldozers moved into Abbotsford. A discreet sign was erected on the cleared site. *Dereck Wallwark Homes of Distinction*.

Mrs Wallwark managed his social life, redecorated his house to her own taste, entertained her friends with tarot card readings and generally made life hell for her mother-in-law, who lived with them.

Dereck couldn't get enough of her, or her cooking, and soon assumed the corpulent look executives on the endangered species list get.

Spring brought new life. The snow melted on the Welsh Hills and the garden surrounding the cottage came to life.

Cecily pulled the weeds from the garden bed. She smiled as her daughter toddled towards her, the dogs trailing behind her. Katherine was small for her age, but healthy. Her eyes sparkled green in the sunshine, her dark hair curled in wisps about her delicate face.

Cecily swung her up in her arms and kissed her, making her chortle with laughter. Spring surged through Cecily's body. The sheer joy of being alive was like a raging river inside her. She'd been too long without a mate. She thought of the letter she'd received from Gerald that morning, and smiled.

'I think it's about time we found you a daddy,' she whispered to the child.

At the end of March, Noel was gazing down at the street below when he saw a woman with a child head for the entrance of the building. A smile spread across his face.

Two minutes later he drew Betony and Stevie into his arms and whispered, 'Well?'

Her smokey violet eyes met his, full of laughter. 'I guess we'll have to start looking for a bigger house now.'

'I love you, Mrs Dearborn.'

Stevie wriggled to be put down. He headed towards Noel's desk and climbed on the chair. He giggled as a row of figures danced on the screen and banged his palm on the keyboard in excitement.

Samuel Levy's chain of jewellery shops suddenly went bankrupt.